The Cottages on Silver Beach

Center Point
Large Print

Also by RaeAnne Thayne and available from Center Point Large Print:

Redemption Bay
Snowfall on Haven Point
Serenity Harbor
Sugar Pine Trail

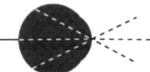

**This Large Print Book carries the
Seal of Approval of N.A.V.H.**

The Cottages on Silver Beach

A Haven Point Novel

RaeAnne Thayne

CENTER POINT LARGE PRINT
THORNDIKE, MAINE

This Center Point Large Print edition
is published in the year 2018 by arrangement with
Harlequin Books S.A.

The text of this Large Print edition is unabridged.
In other aspects, this book may vary
from the original edition.
Printed in the United States of America
on permanent paper.
Set in 16-point Times New Roman type.

ISBN: 978-1-68324-958-0

Library of Congress Cataloging-in-Publication Data

Names: Thayne, RaeAnne, author.
Title: The cottages on Silver Beach / RaeAnne Thayne.
Description: Center point large print edition. | Thorndike, Maine :
    Center Point Large Print, 2018.
Identifiers: LCCN 2018032546 | ISBN 9781683249580
    (hardcover : alk. paper)
Subjects: LCSH: Large type books.
Classification: LCC PS3570.H363 C68 2018 | DDC 813/.54—dc23
LC record available at https://lccn.loc.gov/2018032546

Whenever I try to write the acknowledgments for any of my books, I am overwhelmed, thinking of all the people who help bring my stories to life. As always, I am deeply indebted to my editor, the wonderful Gail Chasan (and her assistant Megan Broderick); to my agent, the indomitable Karen Solem; to Sarah Burningham and her hardworking team at Little Bird Publicity, for tirelessly helping spread the word about my books; and to everyone at Harlequin—from the art department for their stunning covers to the marketing team to everyone in editorial and sales (and anyone else I have neglected to mention!). My two assistants, Judie Bouldry and Carrie Stevenson, make everything in my world so much easier and I would be completely lost without my dear friend Jill Shalvis, who sends me encouragement and virtual cookies when the words seem clogged.

Finally, I must thank my hero of a husband and our three children, who have somehow managed to put up with my deadline brain nearly sixty times now. I love you dearly.

Chapter One

SOMEONE WAS TRYING to bust into the cottage next door.

Only minutes earlier, Megan Hamilton had been minding her own business, sitting on her front porch, gazing out at the stars and enjoying the peculiar quiet sweetness of a late-May evening on Lake Haven. She had earned this moment of peace after working all day at the inn's front desk then spending the last four hours at her computer, editing photographs from Joe and Lucy White's fiftieth anniversary party the weekend before.

Her neck was sore, her shoulders tight, and she simply wanted to savor the purity of the evening with her dog at her feet.

Unfortunately, her moment of Zen had lasted only sixty seconds before her little ancient pug, Cyrus, sat up, gazed out into the darkness and gave one small harrumphing noise before settling back down again to watch as a vehicle pulled up to the cottage next door.

Cyrus had become used to the comings and goings of their guests in the two years since he and Megan moved into the cottage after the inn's renovations were finished. She would venture to say her pudgy little dog seemed to actually enjoy the parade of strangers who invariably stopped to greet him.

The man next door wasn't aware of her presence, though, or that of her little pug. He was too busy trying to work the finicky lock—not an easy feat as the task typically took two hands and one of his appeared to be attached to an arm tucked into a sling.

She should probably go help him. He was obviously struggling one-handed, unable to turn the key and twist the knob at the same time.

Beyond common courtesy, there was another compelling reason she should probably get off her porch swing and assist him. He was a guest of the inn, which meant he was yet one more responsibility on her shoulders. She knew the foibles of that door handle well, since she owned the door, the porch, the house and the land that it sat on, here at Silver Beach on Lake Haven, part of the extensive grounds of the Inn at Haven Point.

She didn't want to help him. She wanted to stay right here hidden in shadows, trying to pretend he wasn't there. Maybe this was all a bad dream and she wouldn't be stuck with him for the next three weeks. Megan closed her eyes, wishing she could open them again and find the whole thing was a figment of her imagination.

Unfortunately, it was all entirely too real. Elliot Bailey. Living next door.

She didn't want him here. Stupid online bookings If he had called in person about renting a cottage next to hers—one of five small, charming two-bedroom vacation rentals along the lakeshore—she might have been able to concoct some excuse.

With her imagination, surely she could have come up with something good. All the cottages were being painted. A plumbing issue meant none of them had water. The entire place had to be fumigated for tarantulas.

If she had spoken with him in person, she may have been able to concoct *some* excuse that would keep Elliot Bailey away. But he had used the inn's online reservation system and paid in full before she even realized who was moving in next door. Now she was stuck with him for three entire weeks.

She would have to make the best of it.

As he tried the door again, guilt poked at her. Even if she didn't want him here, she couldn't sit here when one of her guests needed help. It was rude, selfish and irresponsible. "Stay," she murmured to Cyrus, then stood up and made her way down the porch steps of Primrose Cottage and back up those of Cedarwood.

"May I help?"

At her words, Elliot whirled around, the fingers of his right hand flexing inside his sling as if reaching for a weapon. She could only hope he didn't have one. Maybe she should have thought of that before sneaking up on him.

Elliot was a decorated FBI agent and always exuded an air of cold danger, as if ready to strike at any moment. It was as much a part of him as his blue eyes.

His brother had shared the same eyes, but the similarities between them ended there. Wyatt's blue eyes had been warm, alive, brimming with personality. Elliot's were serious and solemn and always seemed to look at her as if she were some kind of alien life form that had landed in his world.

Her heart gave a familiar pinch at the thought of Wyatt and the fledgling dreams that had been taken away from her on a snowy road so long ago.

"Megan," he said, his voice as stiff and formal as if he were greeting J. Edgar Hoover himself. "I didn't see you."

"It's a dark evening and I'm easy to miss. I didn't mean to startle you."

In the yellow glow of the porch light, his features appeared lean and alert, like a hungry mountain lion. She could feel her muscles tense in response, a helpless doe caught unawares in an alpine meadow.

She adored the rest of the Bailey family. All of them, even linebacker-big Marshall. Why was Elliot the only one who made her so blasted nervous?

"May I help you?" she asked again. "This lock can be sticky. Usually it takes two hands, one to twist the key and the other to pull the door toward you."

"That could be an issue for the next three weeks." His voice seemed flat and she had the vague, somewhat disconcerting impression that he was tired. Elliot always seemed so invincible but now lines bracketed his mouth and his hair was uncharacteristically rumpled. It seemed so odd to see him as anything other than perfectly controlled.

Of course he was tired. The man had just driven in from Denver. Anybody would be exhausted after an eight-hour drive—especially when he was healing from an obvious injury and probably in pain.

What happened to his arm? She wanted to ask, but couldn't quite find the courage. It wasn't her business anyway. Elliot was a guest of her inn and deserved all the hospitality she offered to any guest—including whatever privacy he needed and help accessing the cottage he had paid in advance to rent.

"There is a trick," she told him. "If you pull the door slightly toward you first, then turn the key, you should be able to manage with one hand. If you have trouble again, you can find me or one of the staff to help you. I live next door."

The sound he made might have been a laugh or a scoff. She couldn't tell.

"Of course you live next door. I should have known."

She frowned. What did that mean? With all the renovations to the inn after a devastating fire, she couldn't afford to pay for an overnight manager. It had seemed easier to move into one of the cottages so she could be close enough to step in if the front desk clerks had a problem in the middle of the night.

That was the only reason she was here. Elliot didn't need to respond to that information as if she was some loser who hadn't been able to fly far from the nest.

"We need someone on-site full-time to handle emergencies," she said stiffly. "Such as guests who can't open their doors by themselves."

"I am certainly not about to bother you or your staff every time I need to go in and out of my own rental unit. I'll figure something out."

His voice sounded tight, annoyed, and she tried to attribute it to travel weariness instead of that subtle disapproval she always seemed to feel emanating from him.

"I can help you this time at least." She inserted his key, exerted only a slight amount of pull on the door and heard the lock disengage. She pushed the door open and flipped on a light inside the cheery little two-bedroom cottage, with its small combined living-dining room and kitchen table set in front of the big windows overlooking the lake.

"Thank you for your help," he said, sounding a little less censorious.

"Anytime." She smiled, her well-practiced, smooth innkeeper smile. After a decade of running the twenty-room Inn at Haven Point on her own, she had become quite adept at exuding hospitality she was far from feeling.

"May I help you with your bags?"

He gave her a long, steady look that conveyed clearly what he thought of that offer. "I'm good. Thank you."

What else could she do but shrug? Stubborn man. Let him struggle. "Good night, then. If you need anything, you know where to find me."

"Yes. I do. Next door, apparently."

"That's right. Good night," she said again, then returned to her front porch, where she and Cyrus settled in to watch him pull a few things out of his vehicle and carry them inside.

She could have saved him a few trips up and down those steps by lending a hand, but clearly he wanted to cling to his own stubbornness instead.

As usual, it was obvious he wanted nothing to do with her. Elliot tended to treat her as if she were a riddle he had no desire to solve.

Over the years, she had developed pretty good

strategies for avoiding him at social gatherings, though it was a struggle. She had once been almost engaged to his younger brother. That alone would tend to link her to the Bailey family, but it wasn't the only tie between them. She counted his sisters, Wynona Bailey Emmett and Katrina Bailey Callahan, among her closest friends.

In fact, because of her connection to his sisters, she knew he was likely in town at least in part to attend a big after-the-fact reception to celebrate Katrina's wedding to Bowie Callahan, which had been a small destination event in Colombia several months earlier.

Megan had known Elliot for years. Though only five or six years older, somehow he had always seemed ancient to her, even when she was a girl—as if he belonged to some earlier generation. He seemed so serious all the time, like some sort of stuffy uncle who couldn't be bothered with youthful shenanigans.

Hey, you kids. Get off my lawn.

He had probably never actually said those words, but she could clearly imagine them coming out of that incongruously sexy mouth.

He did love his family. She couldn't argue that. He watched out for his sisters and was close to his brother Marshall, the sheriff of Lake Haven County. He cherished his mother and made the long trip from Denver to Haven Point for every important Bailey event, several times a year.

14

Which also begged the question: Why had he chosen to rent a cottage on the inn property instead of staying with one of his family members?

His mother and stepfather lived not far away and so did Marshall, Wynona and Katrina with their respective spouses. While Marshall's house was filled to the brim with kids, Cade and Wyn had plenty of room and Bowie and Katrina had a vast house at Serenity Harbor that would fit the entire Haven Point High School football team, with room left over for the coaching staff and a few cheerleaders.

Instead, Elliot had chosen to book this small, solitary rental unit at the inn for three entire weeks. Did his reasons have anything to do with that sling he was sporting? How had he been hurt? Did it have anything to do with his work for the FBI?

The answers to those questions were none of her business, Megan reminded herself. He was a guest at her inn, which meant she had an obligation to respect his privacy.

Elliot came back to the vehicle for one more bag, something that looked the size of a laptop, which gave her something else to consider. He had booked the cottage for three weeks. Maybe he had taken a leave of absence from his job at the FBI to work on another book.

She pulled Cyrus onto her lap and rubbed behind his ears as she considered the cottage next door and the enigmatic man currently inhabiting it. That was another component to the mystery of Elliot Bailey. Whoever would have guessed that the stiff, humorless, focused FBI agent could pen gripping true-crime books in his spare time? She would never admit it to Elliot, but she found it utterly fascinating how his writing managed to convey pathos and drama and even some lighter moments.

True crime was definitely not her groove at all but she had read his last bestseller in five hours, without so much as stopping to take a bathroom break—and had slept with her closet light on for weeks.

That still didn't mean she wanted him living next door. At this point, she couldn't do anything to change that. The only thing she could do was treat him with the same courtesy and respect she would any other guest at the inn.

No matter how difficult that might prove.

WHAT THE HELL was he doing here?

Elliot dragged his duffel to the larger of the cottage's two bedrooms, where a folding wood-framed luggage stand had been set out, ready for guests.

The cottage was tastefully decorated in what he termed Western chic—bold mission furniture, wood plank ceiling, colorful rugs on the floor. A river rock fireplace dominated the living room, probably perfect for those chilly evenings along the lakeshore.

Cedarwood Cottage seemed comfortable and welcoming, a good place for him to huddle over his laptop and pound out the last few chapters of the book that was overdue to his editor.

Even so, he could already tell this was a mistake.

Why the hell hadn't he simply told his mother and Katrina he wouldn't be able to make it to the reception? He had flown to Cartagena for the wedding three months earlier, after all. Surely that showed enough personal commitment on his part to his baby sister's nuptials.

They would have protested a bit but would have understood—and in the end, it wouldn't have much mattered whether he made it home for the event or not. The reception wasn't about him; it was about Bowie and Katrina and the life they were building with Bowie's younger brother Milo and Kat's adopted daughter, Gabriella.

For his part, Elliot was quite sure he would have been better off if he had stayed holed up in his condo in Denver to finish the book, no matter how awkward things had become for him there. If he closed the blinds, ignored the doorbell and just hunkered down, he could have typed one-handed or even dictated the changes he needed to make. The whole thing would have been done in a week.

The manuscript wasn't the problem.

Elliot frowned, his head pounding in rhythm to each throbbing ache of his shoulder.

He was the problem—and he couldn't escape the mess he had created, no matter how far away from Denver he drove.

He struggled to unzip the duffel one-handed, then finally gave up and stuck his right arm out of the sling to help. His shoulder ached even more in response, not happy with being subjected to eight hours of driving only days post-surgery.

How was he going to explain the shoulder injury to his mother? He couldn't tell her he was recovering from a gunshot wound, not given his family's history.

Charlene had lost a son and husband in the line of duty and had seen both a daughter and her other son injured on the job.

Nor could he tell his brother Marshall or his brother-in-law Cade about all the trouble he found himself in. He was the model FBI agent, with the unblemished record.

Until now.

Moving into the cottage was an easy job that took him all of five minutes, transferring the packing cubes from his duffel into drawers, setting his toiletries in the bathroom, hanging the few dress shirts he had brought along. When he was done, he wandered back into the combined living room/kitchen.

The front wall was made almost entirely of windows, perfect for looking out and enjoying the spectacular view of Lake Haven during one of its most beautiful seasons, late spring, before the tourist horde descended.

On impulse, Elliot opened the door and walked out onto the wide front porch. The night was chilly but the mingled scents of pine and cedar and lake intoxicated him. He drew fresh mountain air deep into his lungs.

This.

If he needed to look for a reason why he had been compelled to come home during his suspension and the investigation into his actions, he only had to think about what this view would look like in the morning, with the sun creeping over the mountains.

Lake Haven called to him like nowhere else on earth—not only the stunning blue waters or the mountains that jutted out of them in jagged peaks, but the calm, rhythmic lapping of the water against the shore, the ever-changing sky, the cry of wood ducks pedaling in for a landing.

He had spent his entire professional life digging into the worst aspects of the human condition, investigating cruelty and injustice and people with no moral conscience whatsoever. No matter what sort of muck he waded through, he had figured out early in his career at the FBI that he could keep that ugliness from touching the core of him with thoughts of Haven Point and the people he loved who called this place home.

He didn't visit as often as he would like. Between his job at the Denver field office and the six true-crime books he had written, he didn't have much free time.

That all might be about to change. He might have more free time than he knew what to do with.

His shoulder throbbed again and he adjusted the sling, gazing out at the stars that had begun to sparkle above the lake.

After hitting rock bottom professionally, with his entire future at the FBI in doubt, where else would he come but home?

He sighed and turned to go back inside. As he did, he spotted the lights still gleaming at the cottage next door, with its blue trim and the porch swing facing the water.

The swing was empty now. She wasn't there.

Megan Hamilton. Auburn hair, green eyes, a smile that always seemed soft and genuine to everyone else but him.

He drew in a breath, aware of a sharp little twinge of hunger deep in his gut.

When he booked the cottage, he hadn't really thought things through. He should have remembered that Megan and the Inn at Haven Point were a package deal. She owned the inn along with these picturesque little guest cottages on Silver Beach.

In his defense, he had no idea she actually *lived* in one herself, though. If he had ever heard that little fact, he had forgotten it. Should he have remembered, he would have looked a little harder for a short-term rental property, rather than picking the most convenient lakeshore unit he had found in his web search.

Usually, Elliot did his best to avoid her. Megan always left him . . . unsettled. It had been that way for ages, since long before he learned she and his younger brother had started dating.

He could still remember his shock when he came home for some event or other and saw her and Wyatt together. As in, together, together. Holding hands, sneaking the occasional kiss, giving each other secret smiles. Elliot had felt as if Wyatt had peppered him with buckshot.

He had tried to be happy for his younger brother, one of the most generous, helpful, loving people he'd ever known. Wyatt had been a genuinely good person and deserved to be happy with someone special.

Elliot had felt small and selfish for wishing that someone hadn't been Megan Hamilton.

Watching their glowing happiness together had been tough. He mostly had managed to stay away for the four or five months they had been dating, though he tried to convince himself it hadn't been on purpose. Work had been demanding and he had been busy carving out his place in the Bureau. He had also started the research that would become his first book, looking into a long-forgotten Montana case from a century earlier where a man had wooed, then married, then killed three spinster schoolteachers from New England for their life insurance money before finally being apprehended by a savvy local sheriff and the sister of one of the dead women.

The few times Elliot returned home during the time Megan had been dating his brother, he had been forced to endure family gatherings knowing she would be there, upsetting his equilibrium and stealing any peace he usually found here.

He couldn't let her do it to him this time.

Her porch light switched off a moment later and Elliot finally breathed a sigh of relief.

He would only be here three weeks. Twenty-one days. Despite the proximity of his cabin to hers, he likely wouldn't even see her much, other than at Katrina's reception.

She would be busy with the inn, with her photography, with her wide circle of friends, while he should be focused on finishing his manuscript and allowing his shoulder to heal— not to mention figuring out whether he would still have a career at the end of that time.

Chapter Two

LATE-SPRING MORNINGS on Lake Haven were the very definition of heaven on earth.

Megan stood outside the three-story inn inhaling the most perfect combination of scents she could imagine. Freshly turned earth, lilac shrubs and silver-green lavender plants, still several weeks away from blooming but still sending out their luscious aroma from the greenery alone.

If she could bottle that scent, she would make a fortune.

Late spring or not, the early hours before the sun climbed the top of the mountains were still cool. She wore her favorite sweatshirt as she worked on the flower beds around the entrance to the inn. Even in July and August, visitors invariably needed sweaters and jackets in the mornings and evenings, especially at this altitude. Still, the possibility of warmer days was just around the corner.

She had about a million and one things to do this morning but couldn't resist standing here a little longer so she could embrace this particular moment that would never come again.

Lately, Megan had tried to make a conscious effort to focus on living in the moment, savoring the joy of the now instead of worrying about that to-do list or about the latest crisis among her staff or guests or about the photography exhibit that consumed every waking moment.

To that end, she lifted her face to the sunshine, trying to focus on the warmth on her skin, the music of birds greeting the day in the treetops around the inn, the fragile perfection of a May morning on the shores of a stunning mountain lake.

"You look like you're either trying to pass a kidney stone or solve the world's problems. Which is it?"

Megan tried not to sigh as the familiar voice intruded into her moment.

"Good morning, Verla," she greeted the longtime head housekeeper at the inn, who had been with them for years.

Verla McCracken was in her early seventies but refused to retire. During the year the inn shut its doors to rebuild after a disastrous fire, Verla had busied herself traveling the region and visiting with her grandchildren, but had begged for her job back the moment the inn was ready to reopen.

She was thin and wiry and could probably bench press a camel.

"Beautiful day, isn't it?" Megan said conversationally, turning back to the weeding.

"Sure is. The kind of day that makes me want to jump into the lake in my skivvies."

She did *not* need that image in her head. Before she could scrub it clean, Verla went on.

"I saw a car parked at Cedarwood Cottage. Our favorite author must have turned up in the night. Should I add the cottage to the cleaning schedule?" Verla asked eagerly.

Though Megan didn't think she and the other woman had all that many things in common, they both, oddly, found Elliot's books fascinating. Unlike Megan, Verla had been thrilled that Elliot had decided to make the Silver Beach cottage his temporary home for a few weeks.

Almost against her will, Megan looked past the line of pine and spruce toward Elliot's place. He wasn't anywhere in sight, and she couldn't immediately ascertain whether that feeling in her chest was relief or disappointment.

"I don't know. His rental contract only calls for twice-weekly housekeeping service, but I can ask if he would like that expanded to daily service."

"Have you talked to him yet?"

Megan tried not to think about that strange, awkward interaction in the moonlight—or about the bizarre, heated dreams that had kept her tossing and turning all night.

She needed a social life.

"Briefly. He came in last night just before I went to bed."

"He still as hot as ever?"

Ew. Verla was old enough to be Elliot's *grand-mother*.

"I can't say I really noticed," she lied. "He's a guest here. That's all that matters."

Verla snorted, clearly not impressed by Megan's somewhat pious response.

As if on cue, Elliot chose that particular moment to come jogging into view along the pathway around the lake. He wore shorts and an FBI T-shirt that clearly showed the man had serious muscles and was, indeed, as hot as ever. He ran with an odd, stiff sort of gait and it took her a moment to realize the cause was likely because his shoulder was still in a sling and he was bracing it somewhat as he moved.

What had he done to hurt himself? She found it surprising that neither of his normally chatty sisters had mentioned anything about an injury. They usually delighted in telling the group about whatever Elliot was doing—his latest book award or FBI commendation. None of the Baileys had said anything about an injury.

She had to wonder again why he had chosen to pay the rental fee to stay here rather than with his mother or one of his siblings.

"Hey, Elliot." Verla waved at him eagerly. He paused, turning toward them. Then he trotted in their direction.

"That is one fine-looking man," Verla murmured as he approached them.

On closer inspection, Megan could see pain lines bracketing his mouth, and his right hand below the sling was clenched into a fist. None of that took away from the impact of him, lean and hard and dangerous.

"Nice morning for a run," she said, though she wouldn't know. She hated running. She didn't mind walking or hiking or riding her bike but would rather scrub all the inn's toilets than throw on running shoes.

Okay, that might be a slight exaggeration. Anything was better than scrubbing the hotel toilets.

"It's beautiful," Elliot agreed, though he said this with all the enthusiasm of a man selecting among brands of dental floss. "I'm having a little trouble with the desk lamp in the second bedroom. I tried swapping out light bulbs with the bedside lamp and that didn't do the trick. The cord appeared a little frayed, which leads me to the assumption that the malfunction is somehow related to that."

Why couldn't he just say the lamp had a bad cord? "Right. I forgot about that. A previous guest brought it to my attention and I meant to switch it out before renting the cottage again but the matter completely slipped my mind. I'll be sure to send another one over today." She would take the one off her own desk if she had to, but hopefully it wouldn't come to that.

"Thank you," he said, as formally as if they were discussing international trade treaties among countries. "At your earliest convenience would be fine. I'm not in a big rush, though I do see myself working there when possible. I just wanted you to know. Any frayed cord could pose a fire hazard."

Thank you, Safety Patrol Leader.

She forced a smile, trying not to be snarky. "I appreciate the notice and will take care of it this morning."

He nodded and turned toward the direction of Cedarwood Cottage but Verla waylaid him.

"Hey, Elliot. You might not remember me. Verla McCracken. You played baseball with my son Cort."

He shifted and gazed down at her diminutive form, then offered Verla a smile much warmer than anything he had yet to bestow on Megan.

"Oh, yes. I remember. You always brought the best treats after games for Cort to share with the rest of us. My favorites were your sweet rolls with the maple frosting. I've had dreams about your sweet rolls."

She laughed, looking pleased and completely charmed. "I'll be sure to make you some while you're back in town."

"I would never refuse your sweet rolls, Ms. McCracken. How is Cort these days?"

"Good. He works for the car dealership in

Shelter Springs. You need a new Toyota, he can hook you up."

His teeth gleamed in the sunlight as he smiled again. "I'll keep that in mind."

"He's got three of the cutest kids in the world. A boy and two girls. Oldest is six and the youngest is only a few months. Want to see a picture?"

Before he could answer, Verla whipped out her phone and scrolled through until she found a picture Megan had taken of her grandchildren, all sitting together on a bench with the oldest girl holding the youngest girl and a little towheaded, grinning boy in the middle.

Megan had to admit, they were pretty darn cute.

"Beautiful," Elliot replied dutifully.

"I'm sure he'd love to see you while you're in town. His wife is a big fan of your books. Megan and me are, too."

His gaze shifted to Megan, brows lifted slightly. "Is that right?"

"Oh, yes. She got me hooked on them and I passed them along to Marie. That's my daughter-in-law. You've got a way of telling a story that just hooks a person in."

"Uh, thanks," he said.

Verla launched into a review of his latest book. Elliot listened, nodding in all the right places, though he looked uncomfortable, and Megan had the distinct impression his attention wasn't wholly focused on the other woman's words.

She was trying to figure out a way to step in and distract Verla when a familiar pickup turned in to the parking lot and pulled up next to them.

Megan swore under her breath, wanting to kick herself. She'd never told her brother Elliot was renting a cottage at the inn. She had meant to the moment she realized who had made the reservation, but somehow she could never quite bring herself to raise the subject, knowing it would lead to an uncomfortable discussion.

She should have. She should have called him right away. If she had, she might have avoided what was bound to be an awkward confrontation now.

Elliot spotted the pickup truck almost as soon as she did. He tensed slightly, a reaction she had a feeling he would have had regardless of who was driving, until he could establish there was no threat.

He didn't know her brother was driving. He couldn't, she realized, her mind quickly racing for the best way to avert a scene between two men who had become outright hostile to each other after Elizabeth disappeared.

The moment Luke parked the pickup, Cassie jumped out and rushed over to her, full of energy and excitement and life.

"Aunt Meg, guess who gets to be the starting pitcher at tonight's game?"

As always, her heart overflowed with love for

this girl. She couldn't imagine ever loving a child of her own womb as much as she did her niece and nephew.

"Um, Miranda."

"As if! She's too busy making sure she doesn't break a nail. No! It's me. Last night at practice, Coach Hunter says I did such a good job as the relief pitcher that she's willing to take a chance. Are you coming to watch?"

"Of course. You know I wouldn't miss it."

She loved small-town ball games. It was one of her favorite aspects of living in Haven Point.

"What about you, Bridger?" she asked her nephew as he and Luke approached them. "Are you playing tonight, too?"

"Sore subject," Luke said, with a warning look.

Because of the angle of the shrubs, he couldn't see Elliot yet, she realized. If only she could keep the two men apart.

"It's not fair." Her nephew pouted. "I'm ready. My arm doesn't even hurt much anymore. The cast has been off for two weeks."

Bridger had broken his arm a few months earlier in a bad tumble while spring skiing at the end of the season. He wasn't handling being benched very well.

"Coach said you can play in two more weeks."

"By then, it will be too late. We're losing every game and won't have any chance of playing in the league championship."

31

"But if you let your arm finish healing all the way, the doctor said you won't need surgery on it," she reminded him.

"I guess."

"Thanks for letting them hang out here this morning, especially on such short notice," Luke said. "I know it's Saturday and you have plenty of things to do for your photography exhibit."

He appeared distracted—nothing new for him—and still hadn't yet noticed Elliot. Wouldn't it be wonderful if he didn't even see the other man and simply climbed back into his pickup and drove away?

"No problem. I'll put them to work." Through her nerves, she managed to muster an evil grin. "We've got weeds to pull."

"Sorry. I wish I could help," her nephew said, putting on an apologetic expression that didn't fool her for a minute. "If I can't play baseball, I guess the doctor wouldn't like me pulling weeds either."

"Does that mean I have to do all of it by myself?" Cassie's eyes widened and her shoulders slumped dramatically.

Megan patted her niece's shoulder. "We'll work together. Don't worry."

"Guess I'd better get going. Those rooms won't clean themselves," Verla finally said. Luke glanced in her direction and she knew the moment he spotted Elliot. Shock flickered in his eyes, replaced by an angry hardness that he quickly concealed.

"Elliot. I hadn't heard you were in town."

"I only checked in last night."

There it was. Meg closed her eyes briefly then opened them to find her brother gazing between the two of them in shock.

"You're staying *here? At the inn?*"

"Yes. In one of the cottages. Right next door to Megan, actually."

Luke's expression darkened further and tension seemed to broil off the two men, thick and heavy like the August sky above the lake just before a thunderstorm.

"Hi. I'm Cassie Hamilton and this is my brother, Bridger. I'm nine and he's seven and a half. He always gets mad if I forget the half."

To her surprise, Elliot's features softened a little as he looked at the girl. "Hi. I'm Elliot. And the half is very important."

"That's what Bridger says. He says we're only eighteen months apart, not two years, and I don't have to be so bossy all the time."

"That's probably true. But sometimes you have to take charge, when it's the right thing to do."

"That's what I always say. Like if he was just about to sit on a big spider, I would have to be bossy and tell him not to."

"Somebody has to make the hard decisions and say what needs to be said. But it doesn't always make you the most popular person, I'm afraid," Elliot said.

"Hey, I hurt my arm, too. I was skiing and I fell. What did you do?" Bridger asked.

Elliot glanced down at his sling as if he'd forgotten all about it. "Long story. It was a work thing. Nothing as fun as skiing. But it's fine, really. Sorry about your baseball game. You'll be playing again before you know it."

Bridger seemed to take comfort in that and Elliot gave a general wave to the group. "I should go. Bridger, Cassie, it was nice to meet you."

A moment later, he took off in the direction of Cedarwood Cottage, leaving a tense awkwardness behind him.

The children didn't seem to notice anything. "Can we go make waffles in the breakfast room before we start weeding?" Bridger asked his father.

"If it's okay with Megan."

"Please, Aunt Meg? Can we? We only had cereal at home," the boy said, looking disgusted at the apparent dearth of culinary options available to him that morning.

"It's fine," she said. "We're only half-full, so there should be plenty of breakfast left."

"I'm heading that way," Verla said. "Here. You can help me push the cart."

The kids jumped in willingly and headed for the door, chattering to the housekeeper about school getting out in only a few more weeks and what they planned to do with their summer vacation.

The moment they were out of earshot, she braced herself as Luke turned on her, his features tight. "Elliot Bailey? Seriously, Meggie?"

"What should I have done? He booked online before I knew what was happening. Even if I *had* known, I couldn't legally refuse to rent to him simply because I don't like the man."

"This isn't about whether Elliot could win a popularity contest with the Haven Point Helping Hands." Luke glowered and Megan could feel her tension level ratchet up. When he was angry, Luke looked entirely too much like their father. Which made her tend to slip back into old childhood patterns and fight the urge to run and hide from what used to be hard fists and cruel words.

Luke wasn't their father, she reminded herself. He might look like Paul Hamilton on the outside, but he was a very different man. No matter how angry he was, Luke never lost control of his emotions.

"It's done now and I can't cancel his reservation without reason. It's only a few weeks. I don't see the harm in allowing him to rent the cottage for a few weeks."

"I can give you one really big one. The man would like to see me in prison . . . or worse."

Would this nightmare ever end for their family?

She cursed her selfish sister-in-law, who had left behind so much devastation.

"He's here to see his family, I'm sure. Katrina's reception is next week and that's probably what brought him home. He's not going to go digging up the past."

As far as she knew, anyway.

"If he's so keen on seeing his family, why isn't he staying with one of them?"

She would like to hear the answer to that herself. "I don't know. You could ask him."

Luke made a face at that suggestion and she knew he wouldn't do any such thing. He and Elliot hadn't had a civil conversation in seven years.

"It's only a few weeks," she said again. "He'll be gone before we all know it and then life can get back to normal. You'll see."

Luke didn't look convinced and she couldn't blame him. For her brother, life hadn't been normal in seven years. He had lived under a dark cloud of suspicion and doubt.

He looked through the gap in the trees, where the roof of Cedarwood Cottage was only just visible. "I don't like him being here at all, Meg, and especially not next door to you. I don't like it one bit. If he gives you any trouble, you let me know."

She forced a smile. What would Luke do? Take him on? If he thought she was in any sort of danger, he wouldn't hesitate. But while that might make her brother feel better, he would end up in jail for assaulting an FBI agent.

No, she would just have to make sure the two men didn't come into contact much during Elliot's stay at the inn. Considering that Luke was a silent partner at the inn—and hadn't wanted even the 25 percent share her grandmother insisted on leaving her step-grandson—that shouldn't be impossible. The only time he came around was to drop off the kids or do some handyman job for her.

"He's not going to give me any trouble. This is Elliot Bailey you're talking about. What's he going to do? Bore me to death reciting all the recent FBI policy directives?"

Luke didn't look convinced. He gazed over at the cottages again, shook his head as if to clear away a headache, then climbed into his pickup truck.

"I should be done at the job site before lunch-time. I'll get the kids then. Thanks again."

"You're welcome," Megan said.

Luke looked like he wanted to say something else, but he finally waved, put the pickup in gear and drove away.

She watched after him for a moment, until his taillights turned onto the main road, trying to push away the sense of impending disaster.

Chapter Three

"THAT'S IT, CASSIE. You're doing great. Focus on your sweet spot."

Megan grinned through the chain-link fence at her niece on the pitcher's mound, and Cassie shifted her steely-eyed attention from the pigtailed batter at the plate to send Megan a quick flash of smile. The slanted lavender light from the dying sun hit the girl perfectly, turning her face golden in the reflection. Almost without thinking, Megan lifted her camera between links of the fence, focused and clicked away.

The evening somehow managed to improve on the perfection of the morning. The air was soft and warm and lovely with the scents of freshly cut grass, popcorn and cotton candy from the Lions' Club booth a few hundred yards away.

Behind Megan, families of the girls cheered them on with enthusiasm.

She snapped several more of Cassie then turned her 70-200 zoom lens to the batter for the opposing team, Rosie Sparks, whose parents went to school with Megan. She was a power hitter— if such a thing could exist in a softball league of nine- and ten-year-old girls—and she stared down Cassie, her face screwed up with concentration as the count rose to two strikes and one ball.

"One more, baby," Luke called from the bleachers. "You got this. Just bring it home now."

Megan shifted her lens to her brother, unable to resist. His features were intense and focused, without the shadows that usually haunted him, and she snapped away to capture Luke in a rare, unguarded moment.

Her brother rarely showed emotion. Some of that control had been ingrained in them from childhood but much came out of the past difficult seven years.

She photographed him for a few more moments, then amused herself by taking candids of some of the others in the stand, though she purposely avoided capturing the image of at least one person in the crowd—the man sitting on the top row of the bleachers, wearing a white dress shirt and jeans so precisely creased they might as well have been ironed.

Trust Elliot Bailey to harsh the mellow of a beautiful spring evening.

She knew why he was here. His brother's stepdaughter was on Cassie's team and all the Baileys were there in force. Charlene and Mike sat just below him, along with the rest of the Bailey clan.

It warmed her, the way they stepped up to support each other. There wasn't a softball game, dance recital, soccer match or spelling bee the family would consider missing.

She wouldn't have expected Elliot to join them all, but here he sat, part of his family, yet somehow always remote in his own way.

She shifted back to the action in time to see Cassie deliver a perfect pitch, right in the strike zone. Behind the plate, the ump thumbed over his shoulder to indicate Rosie was out, and the crowd erupted in cheers.

The Baileys and the rest of the crowd leaped to their feet, cheering wildly—okay, maybe a little more enthusiastically than a softball game between preteen girls really warranted, but Megan wasn't about to argue.

"Good game," Luke called to Cassie. "Way to go, Pitch."

"Yay Cass!" Bridger called out, and his sister turned to both of them and beamed.

"Hamilton has a good arm, and she's fast."

Behind her, Bobby Sparks spoke loud enough to be heard by many of the people in the stands. It was his daughter Rosie who had just struck out. "She must get that from her dad. He was always fast. Look at how he's been running from a murder charge for all these years—and getting away with it, too."

The reference quieted the crowd around them with an almost collective hush and she caught several furtive looks at Luke, whose features looked etched in granite. She gave a hurried glance toward Bridger and saw with

40

relief he wasn't paying any attention to the adult conversation but was busy chattering with Elliot's nephew by marriage, Marshall's stepson Will.

"Cut it out, Bobby." Wyn Emmett glared at the man, who flushed.

This was the sort of thing her brother lived with all the time, finding himself the center of whispers and veiled—and not-so-veiled—accusations. It broke her heart every single time. Since the day Elizabeth disappeared seven years ago, Luke had faced this. Despite the fact that no charges had ever been filed against him, Luke had been tried and convicted in the court of public opinion.

Not everyone in Haven Point felt that way. Many, like Wyn, had been supportive. But enough small-minded people remained in the area, especially in the other towns that surrounded Lake Haven, to make things harder than they had to be for Luke and the children.

Paul Hamilton cast a long shadow on this community. Sometimes she didn't know if Luke was being punished for his own perceived sins or because he looked like their bully of a father.

Megan couldn't understand why her brother didn't simply pick up and move away from the rumors and innuendo. His life would be so much easier. His construction business had struggled

41

the last few years. Funny, but people could be a bit wary about employing a suspected murderer to build their homes.

Every time she asked him why he stayed, Luke only said this was his home and his children's home and he wouldn't let small-minded people push him out of it.

Because he stayed, she stayed. As simple as that. He needed her help with Cassie and Bridger and she didn't know how she could walk away either.

"You're coming to help us with the project tomorrow, aren't you?" Katrina Callahan asked as everyone began gathering up their belongings and started clearing out the bleachers to make room for the next game. Kat held hands with a little girl who had the distinctive features of someone with Down syndrome—her daughter, Gabriella, who grinned at Megan.

"Oh, I forgot about the project," she exclaimed. "What time?"

"We're hoping to finish scraping the paint in the morning so we can start priming the place in the afternoon."

Since the previous Christmas, the service organization they both belonged to had taken on the cause of an older woman in the nearby town of Shelter Springs, helping spruce up her house and yard. Before Christmas, Janet Wells had taken custody of her three grandchildren after their mother had been arrested on drug-related charges. The cobbled-together family was struggling with even the most basic care.

Megan had helped do a few other things at the house and greatly respected the woman for what she was doing. It was, unfortunately, a too-common situation, grandparents raising grandchildren.

Or in her own case, aunts helping to raise nieces and nephews.

"I would love to help but I'll have to see how the day goes," she said to Kat.

"I hope you can make it."

"I can't make any promises. I've got a million things to do tomorrow, between the inn and the art exhibit in a few weeks."

Wynona Emmett, wife of the Haven Point police chief, joined them in time to hear that. "I can't believe your gallery exhibit is all the way in Colorado! We have galleries here. Why couldn't you have it somewhere closer to home?"

Maybe because nobody here had invited her to do a showing.

"It's crazy that you have to leave the state entirely to exhibit a photography collection that focuses on Haven Point," Katrina added.

"I guess it doesn't really matter where it is," Wyn went on. "I'm just so excited someone besides us is finally recognizing how amazing you are."

"Thank you," Megan said, warmth seeping through her at her friends' confidence, which she was far from sharing.

What would she do without the Haven Point Helping Hands? They had carried her through some dark and difficult times.

"Don't worry about tomorrow at Janet's place," Wyn insisted. "We should have plenty of volunteers. You should focus on the preparation you need to do for your gallery showing, doing whatever it takes to knock their socks off."

"I'll see how things go. I might be able to make it over in the afternoon to work on the painting," she said, just as the girls finished giving their cheer and headed out into the bleachers to greet their families.

Cassie came straight toward her, beaming a thousand-watt smile. "Did you see me, Auntie Meg?"

"I watched the whole thing. Great game, kiddo."

"Coach said I can pitch again next week."

She set her camera aside to hug her. "Perfect! I can't wait."

"Did you get any pictures of me?"

"You know it, honey. We can look through them later while we're having pizza."

"Yay! Pizza!" Bridger exclaimed as he and Luke walked down the steps of the bleachers toward them.

"Are you sure you have time?" her brother asked. "I heard you tell Wyn and Kat how busy you are."

"Don't worry. I always have time for pizza."

"We'll meet you at Serranos, then. I'm not crazy about the crowd here." Luke didn't look in the direction of Elliot but she knew exactly what he meant.

The two men once had been close friends, but all that changed after Elizabeth vanished, when Elliot came down firmly on the side of those who thought Luke had been involved.

Elliot wasn't the only friend Luke had lost following his wife's disappearance, but it was probably the relationship he missed most. Not that her brother would talk about things like relationships or hurt feelings, but she could tell.

Having Elliot here had to be painful for Luke. Oh, she wished the man had never come home.

"GREAT TO HAVE you join us for dinner, though I'm a little surprised."

At his brother's words, Elliot raised an eyebrow. "What's so surprising about gathering with my family to celebrate a mighty victory?"

Chloe, seated across the long expanse of table from him, preened at his words, and he gave her a little smile. She was a cute kid, he had to admit. So was her brother Will. The two of them had enriched all their lives.

Two years ago, he hadn't had any nieces or nephews. Now he counted five. Milo, Gabriella, Christopher, Will and Chloe. Three-year-old Gabi, the child Katrina had adopted from Colombia earlier that year, was the youngest.

All of the children had been absorbed into the Bailey clan through rather unorthodox ways, but now he couldn't imagine their family without them.

"Nothing, really," Marshall said. "Only that you seemed in a big hurry to leave after the softball game, for a moment there. I'm glad you changed your mind, especially since I'm sure you've got work to do on your book."

"There's nowhere else I'd rather be," he claimed. It wasn't precisely the truth, but close enough.

"Whatever your reason, I'm so glad you're here." Marshall's wife, Andie, beamed at Elliot. "My children don't see enough of their favorite uncle."

"Hey, what about me?" Cade Emmett protested.

"Or me," Bowie Callahan said with a mock glower.

Andie smiled diplomatically at Wyn's and Katrina's respective husbands. "Their *other* favorite uncle."

Over the past eighteen months, he had come to care deeply for Andie. She had been wonderful for Marshall, had softened his hard edges and brought laughter and joy into his world.

"My point is, I'm glad you could join us," Andie said.

"So am I."

"How long are you staying?" Katrina asked from her spot at the other end of the table.

"I've got the rental cottage for three weeks. Long enough for your wedding reception and a couple extra weeks to finish my manuscript."

After that, he had no idea what he might be doing. That was nothing he was ready to share with his family yet. Nobody here in Haven Point knew about the shooting and he intended to keep it that way.

Yes, that was right. He had lied to his family.

He had told them he had bone spurs removed, though technically that wasn't completely a lie since the surgeon had reported he had decided to take out a couple of small ones he'd seen while he was in there.

Elliot just hadn't mentioned the bullet the guy had also removed—nor did he plan to.

"We're so glad you can spend some time with us, darling." Charlene smiled at him, but it didn't quite push away the worry in her eyes. She had a fairly well-developed lie detector, especially after raising five children. Despite what he told her, he had a feeling his mother sensed something else was going on.

She wouldn't hear it from him, though.

"You know I wouldn't miss Kat's big party," he said.

His youngest sister looked up from helping Milo and Gabi color on the white paper tablecloth with the crayons Barbara Serrano had provided before they sat down. "Excuse me—did I imagine a phone conversation a month ago where you specifically apologized and told me you wouldn't be able to make it?"

"Things change." He shifted. "I'm here, right?"

"And we're all so glad," his mother soothed. "I'm not glad you needed surgery on your shoulder but it was so nice of the FBI to give you time off for your sister's reception."

"Wasn't it?" he murmured. *Nice* hadn't been part of that conversation. He had been ordered off the job while his shoulder healed and his actions were reviewed.

"We should order before Elliot changes his mind and decides he's had enough of us all," Katrina said, and he reminded himself to hug her later.

They were debating how many pies and what toppings when Wynona suddenly looked up.

"Oh, there's Megan and her niece and nephew." Wynona beamed and waved vigorously. "Hey, Hamilton family!"

His heart gave a ridiculous sharp kick and he couldn't resist looking up. Megan was walking with Luke and his children. He knew he shouldn't notice how bright and lovely she looked, with her auburn hair pulled back into a ponytail and her cheeks a little flushed from the cool of the evening.

She smiled at the Baileys, though it became more like a grimace when her gaze landed on him before she quickly pasted her features back into a smile.

Had anyone else noticed? he wondered.

"Hey, everyone," she said. "Great game, Miss Chloe. You rocked shortstop this week."

His stepniece grinned. "Thanks! Cassie was the star of the game, though."

"Great pitching, Cassie," Elliot's mother agreed.

"You should join us for the celebratory pizza!" Katrina gestured to a table next to theirs. "We can pull up some chairs."

He could see instantly that idea didn't appeal much to Luke. The other man gave the table a curt nod. "We wouldn't want to intrude. Matter of fact, kids, maybe we should order our pizza to go. It's been a busy day and I know we're all beat."

The kids looked as if they wanted to protest but finally nodded.

"You can at least wait here and visit while she brings it out to you, then," Elliot's mother insisted.

Luke clearly didn't like that idea but he was

apparently just as helpless against Charlene's sheer force of will as the rest of them.

"I'll go talk to Barbara," he said to Megan and the children. "Go ahead and sit if you want."

"There's room here by Chloe and Will," Andie said.

The children sat down and were soon talking to their friends, and Megan sat down and did the same with Elliot's sisters. He knew he didn't imagine the way she carefully avoided looking in his direction.

As for Luke, he stood near the hostess table talking to Barbara Serrano and didn't even come back after making their to-go pizza order.

The man wanted nothing to do with him. Elliot sipped at his beer, trying not to look at either Hamilton sibling while he pretended to be engrossed in the conversation Marshall and Cade were having about a local auto burglary investigation.

After fifteen minutes or so, a server came out from the kitchen with a large pizza box and a bag that probably contained side items like garlic bread and salad. She carried them over to Luke, who thanked her, still unsmiling, then carried the order over to their table.

"Kids, here's our food. Let's go."

Cassie and Bridger grumbled a little but slid their chairs back from the table obediently.

Luke turned to his sister. "You're welcome to

stay. I can leave you a few slices of our pizza or you can get something else."

She hesitated for only a moment, glancing around the table until her gaze landed on Elliot.

"No. I have plenty of things to do at home tonight. I'd better run. Good night, everyone."

"Yeah. Night," Luke echoed.

The family left with Megan leading the way out of the restaurant, holding hands with her niece on one side and her nephew on the other.

The moment the door closed behind them, Elliot finally felt as if his lungs could expand again.

Charlene heaved a big sigh, watching after the Hamiltons. "Those poor children. My heart aches for them, growing up without a mother."

"They seem fairly well-adjusted," Andie said. "They have lovely manners and seem to be doing well in school and have many friends."

"I think they're doing great," Katrina agreed. "I'm just sad for Luke, always living under the cloud of suspicion."

"Maybe there's a reason for those suspicions," Marsh said solemnly.

"Oh, come now," Charlene said. "Surely you don't think he had anything to do with Elizabeth's disappearance."

When Marsh didn't answer, their mother turned on Elliot. "Tell him, Elliot. Lucas was one of your best friends. I can't even begin to count the number of times he stayed at our house. You know he couldn't have hurt his wife."

Elliot's mother had been the wife of the Haven Point police chief for decades. She had to know the world was not always a safe and beautiful place. Husbands beat their wives, mothers hurt their children, strangers attacked strangers.

Sure, compared to most places, Haven Point was a fairly safe community, but it wasn't perfect.

"It's been quite a few years since I had a sleepover in the backyard with Luke Hamilton," Elliot said quietly.

"But you know who he is inside."

He didn't. Not anymore. His friend had become a stranger since Elliot left town after high school. Most of that was Elliot's fault. He hadn't kept up with old friendships as well as he should have, too busy building his career and carving out his new life. But when he *had* come home and contacted Luke to grab a beer or something, the other man inevitably seemed to have other plans.

People drifted apart. It wasn't uncommon, especially when geography and time intervened.

Elizabeth had been his friend, too. They had even been partners on the debate team the year he had been a senior and she had been a junior. They had both been officers in Honors Club and she had been funny and smart, the female lead in almost all the school plays and one of the prettiest girls in town.

"You heard what Bobby Sparks said after the game. That's a tough cloud for a man to live under, all these years later," Charlene said. "It must be so hard, not knowing what happened to her. There's nothing worse for a family. I wish one of the departments that have handled the case could have been able to discover something— *anything*—that might have helped find her."

"I can't even begin to tell you the hours that have been devoted to the case, both by the police department and now the sheriff's department. It's still very much an open investigation," Marshall said.

"With little progress, apparently," Charlene said tartly.

"You know as well as anyone that there can be a lot going on behind the scenes that the public never knows about," Marshall said.

"Meanwhile, Luke Hamilton has to live his life under a cloud of suspicion," Charlene said.

The server brought their pizza just then, which effectively ended the conversation. Marshall should consider himself lucky Charlene was distracted by the children, Elliot thought. Their mother could be relentless.

Later while the women were busy talking about details for Katrina's upcoming reception, Elliot turned to his brother.

"What *is* the status of the investigation into Elizabeth's disappearance?" he asked.

Marsh looked down the table at the women, busy chattering away with each other, before answering. "Cold as that lake out there in January," he admitted, frustration shading his voice. "Not much has happened for years. Every six months or so I'll send my investigators through the files to do a fresh read, but all we have are dead ends. We get a few leads here and there, a tip called in that goes nowhere and the occasional crank call, but that's about it."

"You must have a theory."

Marshall's mouth tightened. "Depends on the day. I've gone back and forth. We have no eyewitnesses who saw or heard from Elizabeth Sinclair Hamilton past about eight p.m. the night she vanished. According to Luke, she went to bed early. He took a phone call from a subcontractor—we have the phone records that place him at home—close to ten, then says he fell asleep on the sofa before the evening news. When he woke up, it was five a.m., the baby was crying, and his wife was gone. Her car was still there, so if she left on her own, she walked— something she apparently liked to do. They had been fighting the night before, so he says he thought she went somewhere to cool down or maybe teach him a lesson about how hard it was to be home with a couple of little kids all day."

"Seriously?" Elliot couldn't dispute that the burden of caring for a couple of tiny children might be tough on a relationship, but he had a hard time picturing Elizabeth being so petty.

Marshall shrugged. "Doesn't make much sense to me either. But that's Lucas's explanation for why he didn't call police until almost dark. The thing is, his alibi is solid all day, between the nanny who showed early and the crew and subcontractors who were with him all day."

His brother paused. "There were rumors about trouble in the marriage before she disappeared but no actual facts to back that up."

"Any domestic disturbance calls?"

"One," Marshall acknowledged. "About a week before she disappeared, the neighbors went overseas for a month and had a couple of college students house-sitting for them. The house sitters called 911, said they heard shouting and crying coming from Luke and Elizabeth's place and a woman in distress. Dad went to the house to check things out, talked to both of them, but didn't end up making any arrests. He reported it as a misunderstanding."

Elliot didn't want to think his father might have downplayed an actual domestic disturbance report simply because Lucas had been a friend of the Bailey family. He couldn't be completely sure, though, especially in his father's last few years on the job.

"There were others who came forward after she disappeared and reported she seemed increasingly

55

unhappy in the previous days," Marshall went on. "There are also . . . certain indications she might have wanted to hurt herself. That's one theory, anyway. Apparently she was suffering severe postpartum depression and was being medicated."

He had heard those rumors, too, but couldn't easily credit it. The girl he had known in high school had been mercurial, certainly, but he wouldn't have ever thought her capable of self-harm. It was entirely possible he didn't have the whole picture, however.

"Would you mind if I look over the files while I'm in town? Not that I don't think your detectives are competent but maybe some fresh eyes could offer a new perspective."

Marshall gave him a closer look and Elliot tried to keep his features expressionless. "Why would you want to do that? Don't you have enough on your plate, trying to finish a book?"

More than enough, he had to admit. He would be working late every night to finish the revisions of his manuscript. But Elizabeth's disappearance had haunted him for years and he hated unanswered questions.

"She was a friend. I'd like to find out what happened to her. More than likely, I won't see anything your people haven't already considered, but it wouldn't hurt to look."

"Sure. Why would I mind if the Bulldog takes a look?"

He frowned at the nickname his siblings still sometimes called him. At least that one was better than the other one he knew Megan and some of her friends had called him. He'd overheard them talking at Marshall's wedding.

Mr. Roboto.

Yeah, he knew exactly what she thought of him.

"You're welcome to take a look," Marsh said. "Come over to the office tomorrow and you can see everything we have."

"Thanks."

He didn't know if he would discover anything new, but the prospect of digging into an investigation filled him with anticipation. He would much rather focus on an intriguing case that had bothered him for years than the woman who lived next door to him, the woman he could never have—or the mess he had left behind in Denver.

"YOU NEED TO go home. Right now."

Megan took in the pinched features of her head housekeeper. Verla looked as if she would fall over at any moment. The only spots of color on her otherwise pale features were the bright blue of her eye shadow and a bright splotch of rouge on each cheek.

"I'm okay." Verla mustered a smile. "I'm almost done."

"No. You're done now. The last thing I need is for you to end up in the hospital. Go home, climb into bed, turn on some trash TV and stay there until you feel better."

She didn't miss the relief on the other woman's features, though Verla did try to hide it. "We're short-handed," the housekeeper protested. "Everybody else has left for the day and I don't have anyone to clean the cabins, which are due for housekeeping services today. Cedarwood is actually overdue since Elliot put up a do-not-disturb sign all week."

"I'll take care of it. Only two of them are occupied right now, so it shouldn't take me more than an hour."

She didn't want to think about who was staying in one of those cabins.

Elliot had been there for a week, and though she had seen him coming and going, she had somehow managed to avoid being face-to-face with him since the night of the girls' softball game.

"I'm so sorry." If anything, Verla's voice sounded weaker than it had at the front end of their conversation.

She pushed away thoughts of her unwanted guest. "You have nothing to apologize for, honey. You didn't ask to get the flu. Now, go home and rest and don't worry about anything for the next several days. I can organize the housekeeping crew and make sure they step up to take care of the workload. I prescribe sleep, chicken noodle soup and daytime television. In that order."

"Yes, Dr. Hamilton."

"Do you think you're okay to drive home? I can have someone on the staff take you."

Verla rolled her eyes. "It's three blocks. I think I'll be fine."

Megan didn't doubt it. Verla was agile and strong as a mountain goat, tough enough that even with the flu, she could probably parkour all the way home.

"Take as long as you need. I'm not heading to Colorado for another week, and even if you're still sick when it's time for me to go, the rest of the staff can fill in."

"I hate to leave you in the lurch, but I don't think I'd be much good to anyone until I kick this."

Megan ushered her out the door with all the assurances she could muster. As soon as she closed the office door behind Verla, her smile slipped away. Drat. She didn't want to do this. Why did Verla's remaining workload have to include the cottages?

One would be relatively easy. The occupants of Hummingbird Cottage were a couple in their sixties, both retired schoolteachers, who were spending the week bird-watching and hiking around the area. They were quiet and pleasant, both tidy as could be.

The other one, however, was the cottage next to hers, Cedarwood Cottage. Elliot Bailey's temporary home.

She could probably skip it for another day or two but that seemed cowardly, especially considering he had been there a week and the cottage hadn't been cleaned by her staff in that time.

He seemed to be keeping busy, doing his level best to avoid everyone. He went jogging around the lake every morning and sometimes again at night, his arm still in a sling and held tight to his body. She had also seen the occasional take-out delivery and he had come back once with a few bags of groceries.

Not that she was watching him or anything.

At night while she was glued to her computer, editing photos, she would look over and see lights still on at the cottage next door. Sometimes the curtains moved when she looked over, as if she had just missed him standing there, looking in this direction.

In a way, she found it rather comforting to know that she was not alone in her after-midnight creative endeavors. It formed an odd connection between them. She and Elliot were both makers, toiling away in the dark hours when most others were sleeping.

She rolled her eyes at herself. Her attraction to him made no sense whatsoever. Except for their apparent shared affinity for working after hours, the two of them were complete opposites. She considered herself creative, impulsive, drawn to color and light and energy.

He was a tight-assed stick-in-the-mud.

Mr. Roboto. That was the nickname she and her friends used to call him.

It wasn't kind and it probably wasn't a fair assessment. While he might seem serious and focused on the outside, the books he wrote offered a different perspective. They were full of insight into the human character, deft turns of phrase, even clever humor that always took her by surprise.

She wasn't going to think about him anymore, she told herself. He had already occupied entirely too much of her time on a day she had so much to do. She loaded up the inn's housekeeping cart with cleaning supplies and clean linens, then headed for the rental cottages.

The schoolteachers were gone for the day. At the inn's complimentary breakfast—which Elliot had yet to enjoy—they told her they were driving to Stanley for the day in search of red-naped sapsuckers. Whatever the heck those were.

As Hummingbird Cottage was currently vacant, she decided to start there. It made sense, she told herself. She wasn't simply delaying an unpleasant task.

This would be her workout for the day. She always worked up a sweat scrubbing floors, changing sheets, wiping out bathtubs. It wasn't the most exciting job in the world, but she loved making the rooms and cottages of the

Inn at Haven Point sparkle for their guests.

She didn't mind the physical labor. As long as she had headphones and a good audiobook to hold her attention, she could clean for hours. She turned on the latest thriller by one of her favorite authors, grabbed her cleaning tools and headed into the cottage.

Unfortunately, she was a little too efficient. She was still listening to the first chapter by the time she finished straightening up after the orderly bird-watchers.

One down, one to go.

She walked out of their cottage, leaving behind the lemony smell of the cleaning spray they used.

Elliot's vehicle was there, parked behind the cottage. Seeing it made her insides tremble with nerves. She didn't want to face the man but had no idea how to get out of the task now.

With luck, maybe he would refuse house-keeping services. Sometimes when people rented the cottages for longer than a few days, they preferred not to be bothered and wanted to clean up after themselves.

As much as she dreaded talking to him again, she had to ask.

She walked up the porch, inhaling the sweet blooms of the lilac trees along the porch as she went. This was secretly her favorite of the five cottages. The view was the same as the others, but the flower boxes seemed to bloom more vibrantly and she loved the little pine tree cutouts on the shutters.

She gripped her supplies tightly with one hand and knocked on the door with her other fist.

Only the lap of the water against the shore at Silver Beach and the twittering of the Steller's jays that nested in the big pine tree next to the cottage answered her. After a long moment, she knocked again. "Elliot? It's Megan. I'm here to clean your place."

She still heard no response and stood there, torn by indecision for several moments. She *wanted* to trot down those porch stairs and head back to the main building, leaving him to deal with his own mess.

She couldn't do that. Verla said he had been there a week without housekeeping services. That may be the way he preferred it, but she needed to hear it from him.

The inn had a reputation for immaculately cleaned rental properties, one she and Verla protected with vigor. She wasn't about to let him give them a less-than-perfect review in that department.

She tried one more time then convinced herself that he must be taking a run or perhaps he had walked up to one of the restaurants in town for brunch with someone in his family. After knocking hard a third time with no answer, she finally used her passkey to open the door.

She hadn't been in the cottage since Elliot took up his temporary residence a week earlier. It shouldn't have surprised her how quickly he seemed to have made it his own. A jacket had been draped over the back of the sofa, a tin of cashews sat next to the sofa and a pair of binoculars rested on the window seat overlooking the lake. Maybe Elliot had more in common with the bird-watching schoolteachers than she might have guessed.

Beyond that, the entire surface of the kitchen table was covered in papers, along with a sleek dark gray laptop.

What fascinating case was he writing about this time? She had a wild temptation to leaf through the papers but quickly turned her attention to cleaning the place, not comfortable invading his space more than she already was.

The cottage really didn't need much beyond what the housekeeping staff liked to call a spit and polish.

She quickly straightened up the bathroom, hung fresh towels, remade his bed and ran the vacuum around, muscles tensed as she waited for him to show up.

After she had wiped the last countertop and dumped the last wastebasket, she finally couldn't help herself. She eased over to the table and glanced down at the manila folder on top of the stack of papers. Just a peek, she told herself. She was dying to know what his next book would be about so she could tell Verla.

With the sound of her heartbeat loud in her ears, she glanced toward the door one last time, then casually opened the folder halfway for a little peek. She caught the words *Haven Point Police Department* along the top and realized these were copies of an official police file.

Was he working on a local case? Her gaze sharpened and she opened the folder all the way. It only took an instant to pick up one clear name.

Elizabeth Sinclair Hamilton.

Her sister-in-law.

Chapter Four

WHAT WAS HE doing with the case files for what was still an open investigation? She dropped the cleaning wipe on the table and leafed through the folders, growing more sick to her stomach with every passing second.

File after file, all marked with the same case number as the cover page. These were all part of the investigation into that terrible time that had changed everything for her family.

Her breathing came fast and hard, and she tasted bitter bile in her throat. The usually pleasing lemony scent of the cleaning supplies suddenly seemed to choke her.

Her instincts were to pick up everything, even his laptop, and throw it all into the lake.

The thought only had a few seconds to register when she suddenly heard the click of a key in the lock. Before she could make her frozen limbs cooperate to drop the files, the door swung open and Elliot stood in the doorway.

"What are you doing?" he asked, his voice as sharp as a new chain saw.

She had been working at the Inn on Haven Point for years, since her grandmother took her in after her mother died. She knew this was an egregious invasion of a guest's privacy. If she had found one of her housekeeping staff snooping through a guest's files, that person would have been fired on the spot.

She knew she was horribly in the wrong but she couldn't focus on that right now. All she could think about was the scope of his betrayal.

Elliot stepped into the room. "Put that down. I had things in a particular order. I hope you haven't rearranged anything."

She stared at him. "Are you freaking kidding me?"

He didn't look at her. "It might seem like a jumble of files to you but I have a system."

"You son of a bitch."

It was the least offensive of the names she wanted to call him but everything else seemed to clog in her throat. She couldn't seem to think straight, her thoughts a wild snarl of anger.

"I don't believe my mother would appreciate you calling her names," he said stiffly.

Now she wanted to throw *him* in the lake, along with all his files.

"How dare you?" Her hands were shaking and the sick feeling in her stomach seemed to be spreading through the rest of her.

He gave her a cool stare. "I'll remind you that I'm not the one who broke into your place and started digging through your belongings."

In another moment, smoke would be coming out of her ears, she was sure of it. "I was cleaning the cottage! Making your bed, changing your toilet paper, dumping your trash. Twice-weekly housekeeping service is provided to the cottages. It was listed in your rental agreement."

"It's not necessary. I don't like my things bothered."

"Again, are you freaking kidding me? This isn't about me reordering a few pieces of paper. This is about you dragging my family through hell again! You're writing a book about Elizabeth's case, aren't you?"

He met her gaze with an impassive look of his own. The man never gave anything away. Did they teach FBI agents how to go all stone-faced at Quantico? He must have aced that class, as he'd been practicing since elementary school.

"No," he finally answered.

She narrowed her gaze. His hair was wet and it took her a moment to realize it was drenched with sweat. He had been running again. He wore long shorts and a Denver Rockies T-shirt that clung to the muscles of his chest. His right arm was still in a sling and she couldn't imagine all that bouncing around could be particularly healing.

He had no right to look so good, damn him. Not when he was a sneaky, underhanded snake.

"You're lying."

"I'm not," he answered firmly. "The book I'm writing concerns a serial killer in Montana who preyed on hitchhikers in the seventies and early eighties."

She frowned. "Then why do you have all of Elizabeth's files? What does a serial killer in Montana have to do with a missing mother in Idaho? Do you think they're connected?"

A little bubble of hope rose in her chest. How terrible, that she could actually want to cling to any possibility that someone else might have been involved in Elizabeth's disappearance, even a serial killer.

She didn't want Elizabeth to be dead. She just wanted to prove Luke had nothing to do with her disappearance.

Elliot quickly squashed that half-formed possibility.

"No," he said bluntly. "James LeRoy Barker was killed in a shoot-out with local police three years before Elizabeth disappeared. He was dead and buried in an unmarked grave outside Great Falls before she ever vanished."

Megan despised herself for the little niggle of disappointment. She truly didn't wish harm on Elizabeth. She, like everyone else in town, only wanted answers.

"If this isn't part of the book you're writing, why do you have those files?" she asked again.

For a long moment, she wasn't sure he was going to answer her. He shifted position almost imperceptibly then finally spoke. "The Lake

Haven County Sheriff's Department took over the investigation after my father was shot. The case has been cold for some time, though the investigation is still active. I asked Marsh if I could take a look at the files while I'm in town."

"Can he do that? Just loan out police files willy-nilly?"

"There was nothing *willy-nilly* about it. I'm a sworn officer of the law, Megan."

His words chilled her. "What are you saying? Is this an official FBI investigation now?"

Again he paused, obviously weighing his words carefully before he would respond. "No. I'm looking out of my own curiosity. This was the one case that haunted my father—and still haunts Marsh and Cade. A young mother of two small children, someone we all knew, disappears without a trace in the dead of night. The investigation is at a standstill. Everyone is frustrated by the lack of progress. Marshall and I decided a pair of fresh eyes looking at the files could only help the investigation."

She drew in a shaky breath. "That's where you're wrong. It would hurt very much."

"I don't agree."

"Of course you don't! You have no idea what things are like here for Luke."

His lips pursed. "He's not in prison, so things can't be that bad."

"He might as well be! Imagine how you would

like being tried and convicted without ever being charged with a single crime. As far as some people around Lake Haven believe, Luke killed his wife and got away with it. He and the children can't go to the grocery store in Shelter Springs without whispers and rumors trailing after them like cats after dead trout. *That's Luke Hamilton, the man who killed his wife. I heard he killed her, chopped her into pieces and threw what was left into the middle of the lake.*"

That was the least offensive of the things she knew Luke and the children had overheard at various times.

"Gossip can be vicious."

"You have no idea. And it's not even behind his back sometimes. People come right up to him and tell him he should be in prison."

To her endless frustration, Luke never hit back. Whenever she was tempted to stand up for him, he would simply shake his head, place a steadying hand on her arm and say the same words.

Let it go. It doesn't matter. We know the truth. I didn't hurt Elizabeth. The answer to where she went has to be out there. Someday we'll find out the truth.

She wasn't as sanguine as he was, facing down the haters with her brother's typical quiet patience. The reminder of all those slings and accusations made her fists clench again.

71

"Luke is just starting to put his life back together again. His business has picked up and Cassie and Bridger are doing better. The other kids at school no longer bring it up every day. Sometimes two or three days can go by without someone mentioning her. They're moving on, Elliot. The last thing any of us needs is for some hotshot big-city FBI agent to waltz in and start stirring up the past again."

"I'm only looking over old reports. That's all."

That wasn't all and both of them knew it. If people found out someone like Elliot—considered a hometown hero by many, the very antithesis of Luke—was combing through Elizabeth's case file, the sludge would come bubbling up to the surface again. All the old accusations and false claims. She couldn't bear it.

"You can do it somewhere else." She faced him down, willing her lips to stop quivering. "Gather your things and get out of my cottage."

He looked startled. "What? Are you serious?"

"Do I look like I'm joking? I take threats to my family very seriously indeed. Get out."

"I paid in advance for two more weeks."

"So I'll refund the balance. Do you honestly think any amount of money you could pay me would be worth letting you put my family through hell again? There are other rental properties in town. Find one of those."

"I don't want another one. I like this one. The bed is comfortable, it has a great view and it's quiet. No one bothers me here."

"Too bad for you. What you like or want stopped being important to me the moment I saw you were digging into Elizabeth's case again."

He leaned a shoulder against the door frame and studied her with an intensity that left her feeling exposed and disquieted. "I must admit, I find your reaction interesting. What are you so afraid I'll find in those files?"

She glared. "Nothing! I just don't want you dragging up the past."

"I would think any loving family who lost someone important to them would want to know the truth about what happened to her."

"Of course I want to know. But I would prefer an unbiased investigator, not someone who already has an ax to grind against my brother."

"I am an unbiased investigator," he said, sounding stung.

"You haven't been unbiased in seven years! Admit it! Luke used to be a friend, but from the moment Elizabeth disappeared, you've been clear about what you think. You made up your mind he was guilty from the very beginning, didn't you?"

"I'm only interested in the facts. There was blood found in their home. Elizabeth's blood."

"That could have been left there days or weeks before she went missing!"

"Or it could have been left by her that night when her husband killed her."

"Except he didn't! I know he didn't and some part of you knows that as well."

"I can't be certain of anything."

Though she knew where he stood from his actions and his attitude since Elizabeth's disappearance, hearing his blunt words still cut through her. "How can you say that? He was your friend. You know him. You know he is not capable of hurting a woman, especially not someone he loved as much as he loved Elizabeth."

"I have a police report here that would say otherwise." He picked up one of the files from the bottom.

Megan knew what it was, what it had to be, and suddenly she wanted to cry. The tears welled up in her throat and she had a hard time swallowing past them.

This was why Luke was the prime suspect in his wife's disappearance. One moment—and one sad, troubled woman.

"Yes, you can see the police were called by the neighbors who reported a domestic disturbance. But as you read the report, you can see no charges were ever filed against my brother. The report was of shouting and crying coming from the house. Not of anyone actually witnessing abuse. Your father wrote on the file *misunderstanding*."

She had seen the report. And more than that, she knew Elizabeth's fragile emotional state leading up to it.

"Women are often afraid to file charges," Elliot said. "The law requires that one of the parties should be removed from the home temporarily during the investigation. Clearly, that didn't happen on the night in question. I'm not sure why, but that's not the point. The disturbance was reported to police, which indicates something happened that night."

"It indicates nothing, only that Elizabeth was mentally unstable before she disappeared. You've got that in your reports, too, don't you? She was on medication for postpartum depression. She wasn't acting like herself. Luke was afraid to leave her alone with the kids, for crying out loud. He paid a babysitter to care for them in the day, worked a full-time job, then came home to take care of them all night."

He continued gazing at her in that stony, emotionless way that made her want to scream, as irrational as Elizabeth in those last months.

She sighed. "I don't know why I'm wasting my breath. Your mind is made up. Nothing I say will convince you that Luke is a victim here, just like his children. He lost his wife, they lost their mother, but Luke hasn't been allowed even a moment to grieve for Elizabeth. The people around Lake Haven are too busy whispering about him and throwing around baseless accusations."

"Not completely baseless."

"Fine. Then wholly circumstantial. If the Haven Point Police Department or the sheriff's office had anything more concrete against him, they would have filed charges years ago. Instead, he's been hung out to dry to face the whispers."

Despite her best efforts to hold them in, a hot tear escaped and slipped down the side of her nose. She swiped at it angrily even as his gaze seemed to sharpen. She wasn't upset that she cried, only that he saw her at it.

"I want to know the truth," Elliot said quietly. "Yes, Luke was my friend. So was Elizabeth. If she's out there somewhere, I want to find her."

"While staying at my inn, eating my breakfast, walking my stretch of beach. And I'm just supposed to stand by and give you a place to sleep while you ruin my brother's life? What kind of woman do you think I am?"

Chapter Five

THAT WAS A question with no easy answer. He had always been fascinated by Megan Hamilton. With each passing day he spent living next to her, he was finding her more irresistible.

There was something so enticing about her, something fresh and bright and genuine. In the mornings when he was running along the lakeshore, he would see her from a distance as she greeted some of the inn guests or walked her grumpy-looking dog and he had the weirdest feeling, warm and soft like he was being bathed with sunshine.

At night, he would look over while he was working and see her lights on next door and he would remember what Verla McCracken had said, that she was a fan of his work. The idea of her reading the words he had written somehow inspired him to work harder.

He had heard other writers talk about their primary reader, the person they pictured while they wrote and imagined reading their words. Now that person in his head was Megan.

This fascination with her had to stop. It was completely ridiculous. He had been telling himself that for years. She was not his type at all. He preferred professional, composed, intellectual women whose agendas closely matched his own. Not sweet-faced photographers who had once been in love with his brother.

It didn't matter that he was drawn to her. The feeling was definitely not mutual. She made no secret of her dislike for him. She thought he was uptight, rigid, unfeeling. Mr. Roboto.

If she only knew.

Added to that, now she was furious with him for digging into Elizabeth's disappearance. He supposed he couldn't really blame her.

She was waiting for a response, he realized, and it took him a moment to remember the question.

"You asked me what kind of woman I think you are. I think you're a caring, compassionate woman who loves her brother and is loyal to him. I respect that, Megan. Believe me."

In his line of work, he often saw the opposite, people willing to stab their best friends in the back if it would protect themselves and their own interests.

"You would do the same, if one of your family members had to face what Lucas has over the last seven years."

"That's probably true," he acknowledged. He would go to the wall for any one of his siblings. "I understand your anger and your urge to defend your brother. I'll leave the cottage if you insist, but I would rather not. I like it here. I'm not sure why, but I've been able to get more done on my manuscript in the last week than I have in months."

It was true. Even before the stupid choices he had made leading up to his injury, his life had felt on hold, somehow. He had been going through the motions at the FBI, doing his job without the passion he had once brought to the work and treating his side hobby of writing the same way.

In the week since he'd come to Haven Point, Elliot felt as if he had returned to center somehow. He had managed to regain a little equilibrium, to find the peace that had been missing in Denver, probably because he had been wearing himself so thin trying to do everything.

"Why should I let you stay?"

"Because you signed a rental agreement? And because I haven't done anything that would provide you grounds to break that agreement?"

She shrugged. "Sue me if you want to. You think I care?"

Come at me, bro. She didn't say the words, but she might as well have.

"If I let you stay, would you promise to leave Elizabeth's case alone? Let Marshall's department handle it?"

He thought of the last few fevered nights of writing and the stacks of finished pages that had come out of them. He needed more of those nights and that same productivity and wanted nothing more than to agree to her demand.

His innate sense of justice and the desire to find the truth wouldn't allow it, however. The community deserved answers. For that matter, so did Elizabeth's children.

"No," he said, with blunt honesty. "I can't promise you anything of the sort."

She made a face. "You're so predictable. That's exactly what I knew you would say."

"Why did you bother to ask the question, then?"

"Idle curiosity, to see if I was right."

She studied him for a long time and he waited, quite certain she was going to show him to the door, literally and figuratively. After a long moment, she sighed. "I can't kick you out. You paid for two more weeks and the paperwork to issue a refund would be a nightmare. Not to mention—you being predictable and all—I could see you being the kind of person who would follow through and take me to court."

He wouldn't, but he let her keep her illusions. "It's a distinct possibility."

"Beyond that, your sisters would probably have something to say about it. It's not worth the trouble."

He doubted Katrina or Wyn would take his side.

The women of Haven Point tended to stick together, even against family at times. Cade and Marshall could attest to that.

He wasn't about to argue, though, especially

if it meant he could stay at the cottage. "You're probably right."

"About many things," she retorted. "First and foremost, I need to say this one more time. Luke did not harm his wife. She was a troubled woman, Elliot. Ask anyone. She was suffering postpartum depression. She struggled with it when she had Cassie and it never really went away when she had Bridger only eighteen months later. She was angry and moody and not the woman we all knew and cared about. None of that was Luke's fault and it's completely unfair that he has had to shoulder suspicion all these years."

Her words rang with a sincerity he couldn't avoid, but he had been an investigator too long, had seen too much, to share the same kind of faith in her brother. While he still found it surprising, he had read in the file numerous reports about how depressed and angry Elizabeth had been before she disappeared.

That didn't clear Luke, not by a long shot. If anything, he might have even more motivation to lose his temper with an unhappy wife, then somehow tried to cover it up.

"If he had nothing to do with her disappearance, wouldn't it be in your family's best interest if I could find some kind of evidence that might prove it?"

"Keep an open mind. That's all I ask. Will you tell me if you find out anything new?"

She deserved nothing less. "Yes," he answered.

By the careful way she studied him, then finally nodded, he assumed she took him at his word. "Thank you. And you promise you're not writing a book about the case?"

"I swear."

She bit her lip and he could tell she was already regretting her decision to allow him to stay.

"I'm sorry I snooped in your papers. I shouldn't have spied on a guest like that. I was hoping to steal a sneak peek at your new book, but that's still no excuse for invading your privacy. It won't happen again."

His face felt suddenly warm but he ignored it, touched that she would apologize despite her anger at what she had found. She was remarkable.

"The book is still in revisions, too rough for anyone else to see. You wouldn't enjoy it at this point. A few more weeks and you can read it."

"Really?"

"Sure. If you want to."

"Thanks." She glanced at her watch. "I should go."

Do you have to?

The question welled up inside him but he sternly shoved it back before he could do something stupid like actually say it.

He reached to pick up the handle of her plastic tote of supplies and she reached down at the same time. His forehead brushed against hers and the tiny, fleeting contact burst through him like rockets exploding in the sky during Lake Haven Days.

For an instant, they gazed at each other and he could almost swear he saw awareness bloom there.

Something clutched at his insides, a fierce, long-buried longing.

No. Impossible. This was Megan. The woman who had once loved his younger brother and still grieved for Wyatt.

"Careful," he said, his voice more abrupt than he intended. "I wouldn't want you to get hurt."

"Thanks," she murmured, her expression now impassive.

He felt awkward and stupid, suddenly aware he was still sweaty from his run and his arm hurt like a mother.

He gestured to the bucket. "For the record, I won't require housekeeping services for the remainder of my stay."

"It's included in the price of the rental. Twice weekly. You've already paid for the service. You might as well take advantage of it."

"Just leave towels and fresh sheets a few times a week. I can make the bed myself and take care of the rest."

She looked as if she wanted to argue, but finally shrugged. "Your choice. I'll instruct my staff. I certainly can't force you to accept housekeeping services, especially when we're shorthanded."

She left before he could answer, leaving him to watch her walk down the steps of the porch into the afternoon sunlight.

SHE SHOULD HAVE thrown him out.

As she returned the cleaning supplies to the housekeeping cart and started pushing it back to the main inn, Megan wanted to kick herself.

She couldn't shake the sense of impending disaster. She didn't want Elliot anywhere near the case file on Elizabeth's disappearance. He was a single-focused investigator, from everything she knew about the man. His siblings called him the Bulldog, for heaven's sake. Something told her Elliot wouldn't rest until he found answers—or twisted the facts to suit his version of the story, anyway.

No, she caught herself. That wasn't fair. Elliot was a man of integrity and honor. He was a decorated FBI agent. He would work tirelessly until he found out what truly happened to Elizabeth. That could only be good for Luke, surely, to finally know the truth.

Still, that apprehension niggled at her. Innocent people went to prison all the time. She watched plenty of television, had seen the documentaries. A mistaken eyewitness here, a botched forensics collection there. It happened. She couldn't let Luke be one more of those wrongly convicted.

Her phone rang just as she pushed the cart into the supply room for the staff to refill the next morning before their rounds.

She glanced at the incoming caller ID. Speak of the devil.

"Hi, Luke," she answered. "I was just talking about you."

A long silence met her thoughtless words. "Oh?"

She should never have brought it up. She certainly couldn't tell him she had been conversing with a certain FBI agent about him—or that Elliot was digging into Elizabeth's disappearance while he was in town.

"It doesn't matter. What's going on?"

Luke hesitated before continuing. "We're trying to finish the trim on this house and I need a few more hours. I hate to leave the job site, especially when we're so close to finishing, but the kids' babysitter can't stay late tonight. Any chance I could have her drop them off at the inn for a couple of hours?"

She thought of all she still had to do before she could head back to her cottage and work on photos again late into the night. That didn't matter. The kids came first. "Of course. I love having them here."

"Thanks. You're a lifesaver."

"I try," she joked.

He took her words seriously. "I don't know

what I would have done without you the last seven years," he said quietly.

"I love them. You know I do."

"They're lucky to have you. So am I," he said gruffly.

"Go Team Hamilton," she said.

He gave a short laugh, just about all she could ever get out of him these days. "Thanks again. I owe you. I should be done about nine."

"Perfect. Just enough time for me to fill them with sugar and get them all jacked up for you so they're awake all night."

"I can always count on you to have my back."

She smiled, said goodbye, then returned her phone to her pocket. He meant his words in jest but both of them knew they were true. She would protect her family no matter what.

Even if the threat happened to come from the entirely too attractive Elliot Bailey.

SHE MANAGED TO avoid Elliot for several more days, until circumstances and the intertwined nature of their lives made that impossible.

"Isn't this a stunning reception?" Charlene Bailey gave a happy sigh Saturday evening. "Probably the most beautiful you've ever photographed, wouldn't you say?"

Megan couldn't help but smile. "Simply breathtaking," she answered. "Katrina makes a lovely bride."

Charlene preened. "I always knew she would be. She was a pretty girl who grew into a beautiful young woman."

It was true. The couple was perfect together. Bowie Callahan was lean and sexy, with longish dark hair and sculpted features, while Katrina had always turned heads. As perfect as they seemed together, the most adorable part of this particular wedding reception was the two children they were raising as their own—Bowie's young half brother Milo and the young girl Katrina had recently adopted in Colombia.

"I wish you could have been at their wedding. Everything was perfect," Charlene said.

"That's what I understand. I'm so sorry I missed it."

The pair had chosen to be married in a last-minute ceremony at a small destination wedding a few months earlier on a private island off Cartagena.

Megan would have moved heaven and earth to be there and had been planning on shooting it for Katrina, but Luke ended up needing an emergency appendectomy the day before she was supposed to leave and she couldn't leave when he needed her.

"The backup photographer you helped us find did a wonderful job of capturing the day."

"Is there anything else in particular you want me to shoot at the reception today? I want to be sure I don't miss anything on your list."

In the last five years of photographing wedding celebrations, she had learned to always ask that question of the mother of the bride. It could save a great deal of heartache later.

"I can't think of anything, except maybe a few more shots of her brothers together over there."

Megan tensed. She didn't even want to talk to Elliot Bailey, let alone photograph the man. "Sure," she answered, with what she hoped was a pleasant smile that hid any sign of nervousness.

Photographing this reception was Megan's gift to Katrina and Bowie. What she might prefer personally in this situation didn't matter. If Katrina or Charlene wanted her to climb to the top of the tallest pine tree and shoot the wedding from above, she would do her best. Instead, the mother of the bride was only asking for some pictures of her handsome sons.

"Any particular pose?"

"No. Just them interacting would be fine. It does a mother's heart proud that her children enjoy each other's company. I love seeing them together, even if they're only comparing notes on cases."

Was Elliot talking to Marshall about Elizabeth? Probably not. She could imagine they had scores of cases they could discuss. Their conversation didn't necessarily need to involve her sister-in-law.

Still, nerves crackled through her stomach. Why did he have to come home and stir everything up again?

"Sure. I'll just shoot the two of them being mad, bad and dangerous to know."

"Exactly." Charlene smiled. "Thank you, my dear." With a vague air-kiss, his mother fluttered away to speak with McKenzie Kilpatrick.

Megan squared her shoulders and picked up her camera bag. She had worked hard to avoid Elliot throughout the wedding celebration but apparently that state of affairs couldn't continue.

Sunlight glinted in the brothers' dark hair as she walked across the impeccably manicured lawn of Bowie Callahan's home on Serenity Harbor.

The two Bailey boys really were good-looking. Seeing them together, she couldn't help thinking about the brother who was missing. Wyatt should have been here.

In the past year, three of the four surviving Bailey children had married. First Wyn, then Marshall, now Katrina. At each ceremony, Megan knew she wasn't the only one who keenly felt Wyatt's absence.

She shifted her camera bag higher on her shoulder, annoyed with herself for letting those sad feelings intrude on what was an otherwise lovely day.

Wyatt was gone. She couldn't change that. She had grieved for him and the dreams they had only been in the beginning stages of building together and it was way past time she moved forward with her life.

She pushed away the little pang in her heart as she approached Wyatt's brothers.

Marsh was the larger of the two—broad shoulders, square jaw, solid strength. That didn't make Elliot appear any less predatory next to him. He was leaner, yes, but every bit as dangerous—the contrast between a shotgun blast or a precisely timed knife thrust.

Was it her imagination or did Elliot tense when she approached? She could read nothing in his gaze but she could swear his shoulders tightened and his head came up as if sniffing for trouble.

"Hello," she said, trying for a casual tone.

"Hey, Meg." Marshall smiled and she thought how much more mellow and friendly he seemed since he had married her friend Andie Montgomery. He had never been precisely *un*friendly, simply too focused on work to pay much mind to her.

Elliot, she noticed, said nothing. He only watched her out of those dark blue eyes that reflected none of his thoughts.

"How's it going?" Marsh asked. "Are you finding the photos you need?"

"Good. It's a beautiful day and Katrina and Bowie seem so happy together. Milo and Gabi just make their happiness sweeter. Chloe and Will are taking good care of them."

"They're great kids," he said, smiling fondly at his stepchildren.

"Agreed. You hit the jackpot there."

"You don't have to tell me."

They lapsed into a rather awkward silence and she picked up her camera and aimed it at the two of them. "Your mom sent me over here with orders to shoot a few pictures of you guys together."

"Do you have to?" These were the first words Elliot had spoken to her that day.

She raised an eyebrow. "Do you want to be the one to tell your mother why I was unable to fulfill her simple request?"

Marshall chuckled. "Sure, Elliot. That can be your job."

"It will only take a moment, I promise," she said.

"Says every photographer, always."

She had to smile. Elliot had a point. She wasn't necessarily a perfectionist, but her photo shoots always took longer than she expected.

"You don't even need to do anything. Just keep talking. She wanted me to photograph candid shots of the two of you together. The Bailey brothers in all their glory."

Marshall rolled his eyes while Elliot gave her a look she couldn't interpret.

He was frustrating that way. Spending so much time behind the camera lens reading and recording people's facial expressions usually gave her some insight into their thoughts. Not Elliot's. That whole stone-faced FBI agent thing again.

"What do you want us to talk about?" Marshall asked, clearly uncomfortable at having her lens trained on him.

"Doesn't matter. Whatever you were talking about before I came over."

The two men exchanged glances and the currents zinging between them made her even more suspicious about the topic of their previous conversation.

"Anything. Baseball. The weather. You can talk about the lovely dress that Samantha Fremont created for Katrina."

The idea of these two masculine law-enforcement officers discussing their sister's wedding dress almost made her smile.

Marshall played along. "There you go. Hey, Elliot, did you notice what Kat was wearing?"

"I think it was a dress or something. It was white or maybe yellow. Did it have lace?"

She sniffed at their teasing, though she still clicked away at her shutter. Charlene would probably love this tongue-in-cheek side of them.

"For your information," she answered, "the gown is gorgeous, an original creation by up-and-coming local designer Samantha Fremont. It was tailor-made for Kat, specifically designed to highlight her shoulders and make her neck look longer and more graceful. Your sister is simply stunning in it."

Both men gave her matching looks of incomprehension and she snapped away. "Sorry," Elliot said, "but to us, Kat will always be the little pigtailed tattletale who hated being left out of anything."

"Good thing she grew out of that," Bowie Callahan drawled as he approached their group. "Though she still doesn't like to be left out of things, particularly her brothers sharing such charming opinions of her. Hey, Megan." He greeted her with a kiss on the cheek. Since he had moved to Haven Point, Bowie had become one of her favorite people. Not only was he gorgeous, rich, successful and talented, Bowie was always so kind to her and all the rest of the Haven Point Helping Hands.

"How's the photo gig going?" he asked.

She shrugged, though she didn't stop aiming her camera, knowing Charlene would love pictures of the groom interacting with the bride's older brothers. "It's fine, I suppose," she teased. "If you're into this kind of thing. Beautiful people, spectacular location, divine food. Too bad there's nothing exciting around here to shoot."

"I could always throw one of these jokers

into the lake. That might liven things up." Cade Emmett, married to their sister Wynona, joined the group. Megan had a strong feeling the police chief of Haven Point was one of the few men in town who just might be able to pull that trick off.

"Do I get to pick which one?" Megan asked.

The others laughed—except Elliot, who continued to gaze at her with that unreadable expression that suddenly sent nerves flopping through her like trout jumping out of the water to catch flies on a lazy summer afternoon.

"No problem," Marshall said, "just as long as you pick Elliot."

"Why me? What did I do?"

"Hold all your cards too close to your vest, for one thing." Cade sipped at his drink. "I for one would like to know the truth about what happened to that shoulder."

"I told you. I was in the wrong place at the wrong time."

Marshall snorted. "Oh. That explains everything. Thanks for offering one more example of the FBI's fine attention to detail."

"Not to mention their continual willingness to share information with us lowly local law-enforcement types," Cade said.

As Megan continued photographing the men, for the first time she saw Elliot's features reveal an expression. Discomfort. He didn't want to talk

94

about his injury, especially not with his brother and brothers-in-law.

Interesting. What had happened? Why was he so quick to evade talking about his injury?

She didn't miss the way he quickly and skillfully turned the subject by asking Bowie about his plans to buy a boat. Before long, all of them were debating the merits of various boat models.

While they talked, she continued shooting, trying to be as unobtrusive as possible. Though Elliot participated in the conversation, smiling at all the right moments, she couldn't seem to escape the odd sensation that he was separate from them, somehow. There was an air of loneliness about him she couldn't have explained.

When she caught her camera lens straying almost exclusively to him, she decided she needed to go find another subject.

"Thanks, guys." She waved to the group as a whole, careful not to let her gaze catch Elliot's, then headed off in search of new prey.

THE PHOTOS FROM this celebration would be truly spectacular, if she did say so herself, she thought two hours later. The late-May evening light had been perfect, with the dying sun reflecting off the lake in shades of violets and coral and casting a perfect pearly light on everyone gathered here for the festivities.

Now it was past dark and the sky above was a glitter of stars. Here and there, globe lights had been spaced across the lawn and several propane patio heaters sent out their artificial warmth against the cool evening.

Megan sank into an empty bench while she scanned through the images on her camera. What she saw filled her with pride. She would still have to spend hours at her computer, touching up the photographs in her post-process routine, but even with the raw images, she knew she had several stunners in the bunch.

She loved the one of Eppie and Hazel laughing so hard, they shook with it.

She had caught Charlene and Mike, married a year and still acting like newlyweds, in a heated embrace that would likely embarrass Charlene's children when they saw it.

She particularly loved several cute ones of Milo and Gabi awkwardly dancing with the bride and groom.

As she scanned through the frames, she discovered she hadn't shot any direct images of the wedding cake, only featuring it in the periphery of other shots. That was an oversight she had to quickly correct. She made her way through the crowd, greeting friends and neighbors as she went.

When she reached the luscious froth of a cake, topped with live flowers she knew had been flown in from Colombia, she found Chloe Montgomery, daughter of her friend Andie Montgomery Bailey, had pulled one of the folding chairs over and sat in front of the cake, vigilantly eyeing the crowd.

"You look like you're keeping watch," Megan said.

"Some of the little kids were playing around over here. I was afraid somebody might knock it over," she said.

"Good for you," Megan said, surreptitiously taking a few pictures of the girl and the cake. Kat would get a kick out of knowing her cake had such a champion. "Would you mind pulling your chair back a few feet, only for a moment? I need to take some pictures of it. Don't worry. I'll be careful."

Chloe appeared to think this over and finally nodded and stood up. "I guess it's okay."

"You can come right back when I'm done," Megan promised.

She shot the cake from various angles. One moment, her viewfinder was filled with flowers and cake and fondant. Then she lifted the lens slightly and somehow there was Elliot Bailey filling the frame again, his features hard and remote as he looked out at the play of lights sparkling on the water.

She lowered her camera, unable to look away.

She was struck by that distant expression. He had so many secrets. They surrounded him, layer after layer. She should not find them so intriguing.

"Are you done taking pictures?" Chloe asked her.

She forced herself to turn her attention away from Elliot. "For now," she answered. "Here. Let me help you move your chair back."

"I got it." Chloe wrestled the folding chair back into place in front of the table.

Megan couldn't help but smile. "Kat will be really happy to know you protected the cake for her."

"It's so pretty. I don't want it ruined."

"You stand strong, then, my dear."

Chloe grinned at her and Megan left her to the job. With this unspoken tension curling around her and Elliot, she was in no hurry to put herself in close proximity to him, yet somehow her path through the crowd inevitably seemed to tug her toward the spot where he sat on a bench overlooking Bowie's wooden boat dock. She couldn't seem to help it, any more than she could stop the water lapping at the pilings.

"What are you doing over here by yourself?" she asked as she sat beside him on the bench. "You're missing all the fun."

"Am I?" He sipped at his drink. "You may not be aware of this, but my family can be a little overwhelming sometimes."

"Good to know," she said dryly. "Thanks for the information. I'll keep it in mind."

In reality, she suspected she had actually spent more time with this family over the past decade than Elliot had, considering he lived a day's drive away.

"I love them. Don't get me wrong," he went on, "but a guy sometimes needs to give his ears a rest."

"They're wonderful. All of them. Take a look at this."

She scrolled through the pictures on her camera until she found the one she wanted, one that showed Charlene and Mike surrounded by all the grandchildren they had recently acquired through marriage—Chloe and her brother Will, Milo and Gabi, even his brother Marshall's teenage son, Christopher. In the frame, everyone was laughing at something Mike had said and the sun caught their faces perfectly, with the ideal catchlight in their eyes.

His hard features seemed to soften as he looked at the image. "Nice. Mom will treasure that. Mind if I take a look at a few others?"

She was a little territorial about her work but couldn't figure out a way to refuse. She handed the camera to him. "Keep in mind, they're all raw photos that I haven't had the chance to work on yet."

She held her breath as he scrolled through

the frames on the camera, his harsh features softening with every picture. "These are great, Megan. You've got a really unique perspective. I love the way you take something that might seem mundane on the surface and highlight it until the viewer is forced to realize how important it is. Like here, where you've shot Katrina's bouquet but managed to have the light specifically hit the cameos of Dad and Wyatt that are tucked in there."

She couldn't help the little glow his praise evoked, shocked that he had noticed the effort that went into creating exactly that angle. "Thank you."

He handed the camera back to her. "Wyn was telling me you have a gallery showing coming up in a few weeks."

Her stomach clenched, as it did whenever the subject came up. This was bound to be the biggest flop in the history of flops. "Yes. In your neck of the woods, actually. Hope's Crossing, Colorado. A friend of Eliza and Aidan Caine saw one of my photos of Maddie hanging at Snow Angel Cove and it just so happens she owns a gallery there."

Though it had been three months since that shocking call from Mary Ella Lange, Megan still couldn't quite believe it was real. She probably wouldn't until she saw her prints hanging in the gallery.

She had dreamed of this kind of opportunity

since the moment she picked up her first camera. Actually, that wasn't quite true. She had never imagined a gallery exhibit in her future then. Instead, she had seen the camera as her ticket out of Haven Point. She had wanted to travel the world, visiting all the places she dreamed of going when she was sitting beside her mother's sickbed, reading old *National Geographic* magazines.

"That's terrific. Congratulations."

"Thank you for bringing it up again. I haven't had a panic attack about it in two hours. Guess it was past time for another one."

His mouth lifted in amusement and she found herself fascinated by that little half smile, probably because it was so rare.

"Why be nervous? Judging by these few photos I've seen, you've got this."

She gripped the camera body, the composite material suddenly cold under her fingers.

"I appreciate you saying that. It's impossible *not* to be nervous. I mean, who am I? I run a hotel in a tiny town in Idaho. My world is small and so are my photographs. Who would ever want to look at them?"

Chapter Six

THE THREADY NOTE of panic in her voice took him by surprise. Megan always seemed so together, as if she wouldn't be fazed even in the middle of a major earthquake. She ran an inn and probably had the capability to handle crises he couldn't begin to imagine.

Here she was, though, suddenly a shade or two paler, her lip trembling at simply the mention of her upcoming show.

He was no expert on gallery showings or the intricacies of the art world, yet he felt compelled to soothe her stress.

"There's nothing wrong with focusing on the small things sometimes. It worked out okay for Norman Rockwell, didn't it? And what about Mary Cassatt? She painted the domestic, everyday events in people's lives and did it brilliantly."

He was ridiculously grateful for the art history class he'd been required to take in college and the random yet salient bits of information he still retained.

Megan gave a small laugh. "I am no Norman Rockwell and certainly no Mary Cassatt."

"No. You're Megan Hamilton, of Haven Point, Idaho. You must have something remarkable to offer, or the gallery owner never would have invited you to do a show there."

She blinked at him, her delicious-looking lips parted in surprise. "I . . . I suppose you're right."

He didn't know if he was or not. It didn't matter, since whatever he said seemed to have temporarily blown away the shadows from her eyes.

"I've only seen a little of your work, and to be perfectly honest, my only photographic experience involves crime-scene analysis, but even I can tell you've got talent. This gallery owner in Hope's Crossing obviously agrees with me."

She gazed at him for a long moment, head cocked as if she were studying a particularly vexing problem. "Thank you," she finally said. "That helps. I suppose I needed a pep talk. I didn't realize how much until right now."

"Glad I could help," he said, and meant it.

As she sat beside him, a subtle, seductive peace seemed to twist and curl between them.

When was the last time he felt truly at peace, free of the demons that pushed him on? It bothered him more than a little that he couldn't remember.

The live band playing on the patio shifted to something slow, quiet, romantic. He couldn't help but notice how she tapped her toe in time to the beat.

"Would you like to dance?"

Again, she didn't quite mask the surprise that leaped into her eyes. "Dance?"

"Yeah. You know the basic concept, I'm sure. Though it can have wild variations, in this case, it's when two people stand together on the floor and move around in time to the music."

"I'm familiar with the term," she said, her voice dry. "I'm only surprised you asked me."

He was regretting the impulse more with every passing second. "You want to or not? It's a simple question."

"Yes. I would love to dance. Give me a moment to put away my gear."

She set the camera bag on the bench beside them, opened it and tucked the camera body and lens into a padded slot. "I need to find somebody to watch my gear. Oh, there's Andie. I'll ask her."

Feeling stupid and wishing he'd never started this, he followed her to where his sister-in-law—pregnant and glowing with it—sat at a table talking to a few women he didn't know.

"Would you mind watching my camera equipment for a few moments? It might be a little bulky out on the dance floor."

"Sure." As she glanced over and caught him waiting nearby, Andie's ready smile suddenly turned speculative.

Crap. He didn't need his family getting the wrong idea about him and Megan Hamilton. He was the last unattached Bailey, and as far as he was concerned, that state of affairs was unlikely to change anytime soon.

This was only a dance—though he couldn't for the life of him figure out why he had asked her in the first place, especially when his shoulder was sulking at him.

He didn't have time to analyze his reasons now, when she was waiting for him. "Shall we?"

"Yes. Thank you."

He held out his left arm, which necessitated her having to move to his other side so she could tuck her hand in the crook of his elbow.

She glanced across him at the sling. "You caught me so off guard when you asked me to dance, I totally forgot about your arm. We don't have to do this, if you think it's too much. I don't want to hurt your shoulder."

"You won't," he assured her. "I'm tougher than I look."

"That would be quite an accomplishment," she murmured.

What did she mean by that? He wasn't the tough Bailey. That honor undoubtedly went to Marshall. Elliot had always prided himself on his mind, though that seemed foolishly shortsighted right now when he was having a tough time stringing more than two words together around Megan.

"Shall we?" he said again, and led her out to

the dance floor. The band was still playing a slow song that made him think of silky sheets and tangled limbs.

"I'm not sure what to put where," she said, her words conjuring up completely inappropriate images in his mind.

"We'll figure it out. We might have to improvise."

"Tell me if anything hurts," she ordered.

"You'll be the first to know."

In the end, he grasped her hand in his and she put her other one on his right shoulder, several inches away from where the slug had scorched through.

She smelled delicious, he couldn't help but notice, of apples and sunshine and a little hint of something he thought might be vanilla.

They didn't speak for the first few moments of the song, a state of affairs he wasn't inclined to change. He was rather appalled at his sudden urge to bury his face in her hair, tug her close against his chest, to hell with his sling, and spend the rest of the evening moving slowly in time to music.

As they moved around the dance floor, he intercepted more than a few curious glances from his family, each of which he deflected with a steely-eyed glare.

So he was dancing with a woman. What was the big deal?

To his relief, Megan seemed oblivious to the undercurrents or all the interested gazes coming their way. She seemed completely lost in the music.

From what he had observed while staying at her inn, Megan was always busy—working on the gardens, talking to guests, even cleaning rooms. At night, he would see her light on next door and guess she was probably hard at work on her photos into the early morning hours.

Even here at this celebration for one of her friends, she didn't stop moving. If he could give her a few moments of peace, he would welcome it.

The band segued into another slow song. Since she didn't seem inclined to end the dance and since he was enjoying having her close more than he wanted to admit, he decided to maintain the status quo.

"Why are you hiding the truth about what happened to your arm from your family?"

Her question, completely out of the blue, made him falter and miss a step.

"Who says I'm hiding anything?"

"Your family. Both your sisters say you are a genius at changing the subject whenever anybody asks you about your shoulder."

He couldn't deny that. "Maybe I just like to keep my business to myself."

"Maybe you enjoy being an object of mystery.

Face it, Elliot. You like being a conundrum surrounded by an enigma wrapped in a paradox, don't you? It's all part of your FBI agent mystique."

"Is it?" He couldn't help a slight smile, amused despite himself. She teased him like no one else.

"You have so many layers, I'm not sure even you know what's beneath them all. Are you in trouble of some sort?"

His smile faded. She had no idea. The temptation to tell her everything took him completely by surprise. He couldn't. Once she started digging, she wouldn't like what she uncovered.

"It's a very long story. I would tell you, but the song is over. Looks like the band is taking a break." He stopped moving and dropped her hand, feeling the chill of the evening for the first time as she stepped slightly away.

"That sounds like the excuse of a man with something to hide."

"Or maybe simply a man who doesn't like blabbing about ugly business in the middle of a party," he countered.

"That's fair, I suppose."

Again, he was shocked by the urge to tell her everything, suddenly. His stubbornness, his mistakes, and the fact that his entire career in the FBI hovered on a knife's edge.

Why Megan? It made no sense. Marshall or Cade would be the more logical confidants. They were both in law enforcement. They understood the hazards and complications of the job and how a few poor decisions could turn an investigation horribly wrong. He had been here for days, though. As Megan said, he had become an expert at disclosing no more than he wanted to about what had truly happened in Denver.

Something about this woman who saw the world through such a unique perspective called to him. He didn't understand it. Hell, he didn't like it much, but it was becoming increasingly clear there was some intangible connection between them that went beyond the fact that he was staying at her inn.

"Well, since you won't tell me all your dark secrets, I suppose I should get back to work. Thank you for the dance. It's been a long time since I've taken the chance to put down my camera for a moment to enjoy one of the many wedding celebrations I photograph around town."

"My pleasure," he answered, and meant it.

Something told him these moments on the dance floor with her would remain a cherished highlight of this evening in his memory.

AFTER WATCHING HER walk away, Elliot turned to find his youngest sister in front of him, bright and glowing and beautiful in her specially designed wedding dress.

"I saw that. If you can dance with Meggie, you can dance with me," Katrina insisted.

He supposed he couldn't argue with her logic. "Great party, sis," he said as he took her in the same rather awkward hold he had with Megan.

"It is, isn't it? It's a little odd to have a wedding reception months after the actual ceremony, but that's just the way it worked out for us."

"I don't have to ask if you're happy with Bowie. Anybody looking at the two of you can see the truth."

"So happy," she murmured. "I never imagined one heart could hold this much joy."

A hard knot lodged in his throat. He told himself he was only a little emotional in the face of his baby sister's overflowing happiness, yet that knot felt suspiciously like envy.

Where was *that* coming from? He didn't envy Katrina and Bowie—or Cade and Wynona or Marshall and Andie, for that matter. As the oldest brother, he was happy his siblings had found love and were creating beautiful lives together.

Love wasn't for him. Hadn't he proved that over the years? He wasn't any good at relationships. As Megan said, he kept too many secrets. Some of that was the nature of the job while some of that was simply his personality, drilled into him from all the years of trying to be the responsible oldest son in a family of wild siblings.

"I wish you could find somebody," she said, then added pointedly, "You and Megan seemed to be enjoying your dance together."

He could feel his muscles tighten and had to force himself to relax before she noticed. "We did."

"Wow. From you, that's practically gushing over the woman."

Her words stung. He had plenty of emotions about all kinds of things; he had simply learned early not to reveal them.

Do your best, Elliot. We're counting on you.

Never a moment's worry, our Elliot. We couldn't ask for a better son.

He forced the past away. "What do you want me to say? Megan is a friend. We danced. That's all there is to it. I'm not in the market for more right now, Kat. Anyway, today is about you and Bowie."

To his relief, she let the subject drop and they talked about other things. They finished the dance and he returned her to her groom.

After another hour of making small talk and visiting with friends of the family, Elliot decided he was done. His arm ached like a son of a bitch, he had a headache brewing at his temples, and he craved nothing more than the quiet and tranquility of his cottage by the lake.

He headed over to Katrina and Bowie to say goodbye.

"I really am happy for both of you, kiddo," he said to Kat, kissing her on the cheek.

He shook Bowie's hand. "Since our father's not here, allow me to stand in for him."

"That sounds strangely ominous," his brother-in-law said with a grimace.

"It should. I said this at the wedding and I'll repeat it now at the reception. You mistreat our baby sister in any way and you'll have the wrath of the entire Bailey family raining down on you. We are a force to be reckoned with."

To Bowie's credit, he looked more amused than threatened. "I think I can hold my own against you and Marshall." He paused. "Your mom and Wyn? They're an entirely different story."

He had to smile. "Damn straight."

After kissing Katrina one more time, he headed over to say goodbye to Charlene, who was standing nearby talking to Barbara Serrano, McKenzie Kilpatrick and a group of other women from town.

"You're leaving?" His mother's frown clearly showed her disappointment.

"Yes. It's a great party but it's been a long day."

He almost used his aching shoulder as an excuse but knew that would only earn him more questions he didn't want to answer.

"Never mind. Get some rest. I'm glad you could make it at all," his mother said. "It's been wonderful having you in town, my dear, even if you do tend to spend most of your time hiding out at the inn, hunched over a computer."

He said his final goodbyes, then headed for

the pathway that would take him back to the inn, only about a ten-minute walk from here.

Apparently, he wasn't the only one escaping the party. He had only gone a few hundred feet along the path that wound around the lake when he encountered Megan moving in the same direction, carrying two bulky bags of camera equipment.

She looked startled when he caught up with her. "Oh. I thought everyone would still be partying for a bit longer," she said.

"You're leaving early?"

"I lost the light and I figured Kat wouldn't need my flash going off every second. I got the cake cutting ceremony. The rest is just the party and there are enough people taking candids with their phones to cover that."

"Here. Let me take something."

"I'm fine. I carry my gear all the time. Anyway, I don't want to hurt your shoulder."

"I've got two, remember? The other one is fine."

She hesitated for a moment, then handed him the longer of the two cases. "If you don't mind carrying the tripod, that would be great. It's not heavy, just awkward."

He hefted it onto his shoulder. "I don't know how you haul all this stuff around."

"This is my workout. Carrying my gear around."

"And cleaning hotel rooms."

"When the need arises, yes."

They moved together along the path and he thought again how lovely it was here in Haven Point. The air was sweet and cool away from the kerosene heaters at the party. The water lapped softly at the shore and the full moon gleamed on the ripples. Across the water, the mountains loomed, solid and imposing and still snow-capped, yet somehow comforting in their bulk.

"Can I ask a stupid question?" he asked after a moment.

"Sure."

"Why did you walk over to Serenity Harbor with all this gear?"

She sighed. "I'll give you a stupid answer. It seemed like a good idea at the time. I figured parking would be an issue, plus every inch of my SUV is filled with framed photographs I'm taking to Colorado tomorrow."

"You're leaving tomorrow for your exhibit? When we were talking earlier, I didn't realize it was so soon."

"The show doesn't open for another week, but Mary Ella needs my prints early so they can figure out where to hang everything."

"At this moment, which emotion is winning? Excitement or panic?"

"Hard to say. Do I have to choose?"

He couldn't hold back his smile. "They can both exist simultaneously."

They walked a few more moments in a not

uncomfortable silence. He could see the lights of the inn twinkling above the treetops.

He was fiercely aware of Megan—each quiet breath, the moonlight catching strands of her hair, the soft, apple-spice scent of her swirling around him.

He wanted to kiss her.

"Is this a good time?"

He started at her words, wondering if she could read his mind. "A . . . good time for what?"

"You told me earlier you didn't want to talk at the party about how you were injured and whatever else is going on with you. We're not at the party now. I have to ask if this is a good time for you to tell me."

"No," he said promptly.

"How about now?" she asked.

He grunted, half-amused, half-annoyed by her persistence. "No."

"Now?"

She would only grow more persistent. He might as well tell her all of it, especially as he could be out of a job in a matter of weeks.

He opened his mouth but she cut him off before he could respond.

"I'm sorry. I'm teasing. You don't have to tell me. I believe we recently removed the section in the rental agreement that says you have to spill all your dirty secrets."

She made him smile. He didn't know how she

115

did it but Megan always seemed to fill the world around her with sunshine. When he was with her, he never felt like a dour, stiff, humorless FBI agent. Mr. Roboto.

"Probably for the best. Who knows what kind of scandalous tidbits you might hear from some of your tenants?"

"You've got that right."

He wanted to tell her. He wasn't sure why but again he couldn't shake the urge to confide in this woman.

"I let my emotions get in the way," he finally said.

She stumbled over a root but caught herself before he could drop the tripod and lunge to her rescue.

She stared at him, eyes wide in the moonlight. "You? *You* let your emotions get in the way?"

"You don't have to sound so shocked. It happens. I'm not some kind of robot, contrary to what you and my family seem to think. Yes, I tend to be serious about some things, but that doesn't mean I have no feelings. Maybe I've only had to become adept at hiding them."

For a moment, he wondered if he had revealed too much. She studied him, those photographer's eyes sharp. "I imagine you have," she finally said. "What happened? Can you tell me? How did you let your emotions get away from you?"

They were almost to their side-by-side cottages.

He could see them just beyond the trees. He was silent for a long time, then finally decided he had come this far—he might as well tell her the rest of it.

"I disobeyed a direct order, interfered in a case that wasn't my jurisdiction, blew up a months-long investigation by another agency and ended up killing a man."

Chapter Seven

SHE BLINKED AT his harsh words. Of all the things she might have expected him to say, such blunt honesty completely astonished her and she had no idea how to answer.

Elliot might come across as rather scholarly. He was a writer with the uncanny ability to convey pathos and heart in stories about grim and difficult events. It was easy to forget he was also a trained law-enforcement officer, that he was, in fact, a very dangerous man.

I disobeyed a direct order, interfered in a case that wasn't my jurisdiction, blew up a months-long investigation by another agency and ended up killing a man.

She swallowed. "Wow. When you screw up, you don't mess around."

"One might even call me an overachiever in that department."

"Yes. One might."

She might have thought he smiled a little in the moonlight before his expression grew grave again.

"The situation was a disaster from the start."

"What happened?"

"I usually investigate fraud and money laundering but for the last few months I've been part of a task force investigating a string of luxury car thefts in the Denver area. It was a well-organized ring that could steal a high-end car, completely alter the VIN numbers and ship it by train to the coast, where it would be sent to China within twenty-four hours. We had an undercover guy on the inside who managed to contact us about a conversation he had been a party to that had nothing to do with our case. He and one of our subjects met up with a worm by the name of Louie Cho, who was in the market for a Lotus for a relative back in China. Turns out Cho let slip he was expecting a major shipment that night and would be able to pay cash the next day."

"Drugs?"

"That's what we thought at first but it didn't take long for us to figure out he wasn't talking about bringing in drugs." Elliot paused and she thought for a moment he wasn't going to tell her the rest. When he spoke, his voice sounded reluctant, as if the words were being yanked out of him one by one.

"He was talking about underage girls, at least fifteen of them, smuggled in from rural China, to be dispersed the next day throughout Colorado. Sex trafficking."

Nausea curled through her at the abhorrent words. "Oh, no."

"Our guy on the inside had a location where they were spending the night. We reported it to the special agent in charge, who relayed the info to the DEA. We started working on a warrant and began assembling a team, ready to go in hot and make a rescue using our intel."

He paused and she could see his jaw harden.

"What happened?" she asked.

"Interagency politics. Within the hour, the DEA shut us down. Turns out that while we were looking into the stolen vehicles, they had a simultaneous investigation into a major heroin distribution ring and Cho was a confidential informant for them. If the FBI raided the place to save a dozen girls who were in the country illegally in the first place, it would jeopardize their case and they would lose all their progress of the last six months. We argued until we were blue in the face. There would be no better time to rescue the girls than right then, before they were dispersed throughout the state. After that, we didn't have a chance of finding them all. In the end, we were ordered to stand down."

"But you didn't." She knew enough about Elliot's stubbornness to guess that, even if he hadn't already dropped hints.

"I couldn't. Our undercover guy risked his life to take a secret video with his phone and email it to me. I saw them. Girls jammed into the back of a semi trailer. These were just kids. Scared girls, some just a few years older than Chloe back there."

Sometimes she couldn't bear thinking about the ugliness in the world.

"I became an FBI agent because I wanted to make a difference. I kept asking myself what my father would have done in my place."

John Bailey had been chief of police in Haven Point for decades. During those brief months she had been dating Wyatt, he had always treated her with warmth and kindness.

The entire Lake Haven community had grieved when he suffered a brain injury after a shoot-out with a burglary suspect.

His family had lost so much—first Wyatt, then John, though Elliot's father hadn't died until years after his initial injury. Instead, he had spent his remaining years in a nursing home, unable to walk or talk.

No wonder Elliot hadn't shared anything about his injury with his family. He was protecting them, she realized, from the ugliness that had touched him.

"What did you do?" she asked.

"For the first time in my fourteen-year career at the FBI, I disobeyed direct orders. I organized the raid, figuring we could rescue the girls then sort it out later. We had a chance, so we took it. The only trouble is, Cho came back unexpectedly, just as we were loading the last girl into the van. He started spraying us with gunfire."

"So you killed him." She couldn't quite believe

121

she could utter those particular words in such a matter-of-fact tone.

For an instant, Elliot's features briefly looked tortured, yet they returned to his usual reserve so quickly she wondered if she had imagined it. "I didn't have a choice. He was firing on us and on the girls. He was going to kill someone."

His jaw worked. "I couldn't get a clear shot without leaving whatever small cover we had with the van. Somehow he hit me in that brief instant."

Though he didn't fill in the blanks more than that, Megan knew Elliot well enough to guess at the rest. No doubt he had risked his life in order to save the others. The Baileys were predictable to a one.

His family protected and served, had done the same for generations. Wyatt used to say it was the Bailey family curse.

"I see why you're keeping the truth to yourself. Especially with your family's history. Charlene would be beside herself."

"She's been through enough. She doesn't need to know."

"So you told her you had bone spurs removed."

"It wasn't a complete lie. I did. I just didn't tell her I also had a slug removed from a semi-automatic weapon fired by a sadistic, homicidal bastard."

Whom he had killed. She shivered a little as

they reached Silver Beach. The moon hung low above the mountains, casting a pearly half-light across the water. The lovely, calming scene seemed in stark contrast to the ugliness of his words.

"You'd better take care of your dog," Elliot said as they approached her cottage. "Sounds like he knows you're out here."

She could hear Cyrus's little *hey-Mommy* bark from inside.

"You can't stop there. Let me put my gear inside and let Cyrus out. Then I need to hear the rest of the story."

"I've told you all the important points."

"You didn't tell me what happened next. Hold on." She hurried up the steps, aware of him following behind with her tripod. She opened the door and was greeted immediately by Cyrus's writhing delight. "Hey, buddy. How was your night? I need a second. Then I'll give you the love."

She set her camera gear inside then took the tripod from Elliot, careful to keep her wayward fingers a safe distance away from him. It wasn't an easy task, especially when she had a powerful urge to tuck them inside his tailored gray jacket.

He had loosened his tie, she saw, something she hadn't noticed on the walk over from Serenity Harbor. He looked sexy and rumpled and . . . tired.

All her insides seemed to have turned gooey and warm. With dismay, Megan turned to the ready distraction of Cyrus, picking him up to give her hands something to do. He licked at her face and wriggled with joy, as if she had been gone months instead of only a few hours.

"Can I grab a beer for you?" she asked, once she had cuddled her dog sufficiently for both of them.

"No. I had a glass of champagne at the party and a finger of scotch. That's more than enough alcohol for me on a given night. There's always a chance I might need to take a pain pill later."

She had a strong feeling he wouldn't, whether he needed it or not.

"Do you . . . want to sit down?"

Her open living room and kitchen wasn't a huge space and she had made it smaller by filling the periphery with planters containing favorite flowers, props used for portrait shots and her kitchen herb garden. She had created a cozy conversation nook with a small sofa and a comfortable armchair positioned by the front window that overlooked the beach, but Elliot made no move to sit there.

"Seems like a shame to waste one of our perfect Haven Point evenings—the rare night when the weather is good, yet the tourists aren't here being stupid."

"I need those tourists," she reminded him.

"Most of the town needs them. That doesn't mean residents can't enjoy shoulder seasons when they're not here."

"Sure. Let's go outside."

As soon as they walked back out to her porch with the dog leading the way, she realized the problem. All she had out here was a porch swing. She would have no choice but to sit beside him.

He was investigating her brother.

Unfortunately, the reminder didn't have the cooling effect she might have anticipated. Luke and his missing wife seemed to have slid to the back of her mind.

After a moment's hesitation, she plopped onto the cushioned swing to a rattle of chains.

"Will that hold us both?" he asked, doubt in his voice.

"Oh, yes. It's secured to the joist."

He hesitated a moment more then sat down beside her. The chains clanked together from the movement but the swing didn't even wobble with the added weight.

The scent of his aftershave, cedar and citrus with a spicy undertone, drifted to her on the night air. They were only inches apart, so close she could feel his shoulders move with each breath.

Megan scooped up Cyrus and held him tightly in her lap. "Then what happened? You disobeyed orders, you rescued the girls and you shot the bad guy. Not a bad night's work, I suppose."

His mouth quirked a little, as if he wanted to smile but couldn't quite manage it. "One would think, right? But here's a little something you might not know about the Federal Bureau of Investigation. They tend to frown on renegades. Outliers. It wasn't the fact that I shot a man, though no one was particularly happy about that. I disobeyed a direct order and ignored the chain of command. In the process, I risked the girls and two other agents in the FBI, not to mention our operative on the inside, though he managed to protect his cover."

"What about the DEA?"

"Oh, they're good and pissed at me. I killed one of their informants. Yeah, he was a scumbag, but he was *their* scumbag. Turns out their case had already been all but wrapped up, even without Cho, so they still managed to make several significant arrests and shut down the drug ring."

"A win all around, then."

"Not quite. I still disobeyed orders, and a man died."

She heard the grim note in his voice and suspected that night still haunted him. Maybe during all these late nights, he hadn't been burning the midnight oil, working on his book, but brooding instead about the life he had taken, no matter that it sounded as if the man provided no value to the world.

"What will happen next for you?"

"I've been suspended for a month and I still have to face a disciplinary review board. I may be done at the Bureau—and that's before you factor in whether my shoulder heals correctly and whether I can still pass all the firing range requirements."

All because he had tried to do the right thing. "Oh, Elliot. I'm sorry. That's so unfair. Isn't it your job to protect the innocent? Those girls had no one else but you! I think you're a hero. I'm only sorry you have chosen not to tell everyone about it. Your family should be celebrating what you did."

He was silent for a long moment. In the dim light on the porch, she saw surprise and something deeper in his eyes.

"Thank you. I appreciate the vote of confidence," he finally said, and the raspy note in his voice made her shiver.

"It won't do you much good. My vote doesn't particularly count. Who cares what an innkeeper in Haven Point, Idaho, thinks?"

"I do," he answered softly.

She gazed at him across the width of the porch swing. In the moonlight, his somewhat austere features looked softer, somehow. He looked younger, less severe. Far more approachable.

Gorgeous.

A low ache of awareness curled through her. It would be so very easy to reach across that short distance and touch him. She was overwhelmed by the urge to tangle her fingers with his and tug him toward her.

She wanted him to kiss her.

The realization swept over her, fierce and shocking and somehow *right* at the same time. What would that mouth taste like? Would he kiss with the serious focus he applied to everything else in his world? He gazed down at her and for an instant she thought she saw something leap into his gaze. A yearning that matched her own.

He wanted to kiss her as well. His pupils dilated slightly and he swallowed hard. His fingers flexed on his leg.

"What time are you leaving tomorrow?"

The abrupt change of topic left her a little disoriented. He was so very hard for her to read. Had she imagined that expression? Or was he simply an expert at veiling his emotions?

Either way, she had to give herself a few moments before she could formulate her stray thoughts into a coherent response.

"Early. Probably before seven. Everything's loaded up into my SUV now. I'll try not to make too much noise to disturb you."

"I'm not worried about that. I'm an early riser."

"I've noticed." He went to bed late and was up early, heading out before sunrise to run around the lake. "I've wondered if you even get any sleep at all."

"Not as much as I need. And the only reason you know that is because you're up at all hours of the day and night as well. Don't think I haven't seen your lights on over here."

That soft, seductive awareness curled through her again to think about him gazing at her cottage from his, maybe wondering about her as he stood at his window. "Things have been a little crazy lately while I've been busy preparing for the gallery opening. They'll settle down now, especially after I go to Hope's Crossing tomorrow to take the prints."

He was silent, the only sound in the night that rhythmic rattle of the chains and the quiet lick of the water on the shore.

"How would you feel about having a traveling companion?"

AS SOON AS Elliot asked the question, he knew it was a mistake. He hadn't meant to blurt it out quite like that, raw and unadorned, but the idea had been stewing since she told him she was leaving for Hope's Crossing the next day.

He should have let it percolate a little more— and then slammed the lid on it and shoved it in a cupboard, never to see the light of day.

What was he thinking? Under what crazy moon did he ever think it might be a good idea to be shut up in a car with Megan Hamilton for eight hours at a stretch as they drove to Colorado together—and then back again?

It would be a huge mistake, especially with this low heat that simmered inside him whenever he was around her.

"You want to go to Hope's Crossing with me?" she said slowly.

Hearing her say the words aloud only reinforced what a wild idea it was. He *did* want to go to Hope's Crossing, but he didn't necessarily need to go right now, with Megan.

"There's a person I would like to interview who might have information about Elizabeth's case."

She tensed. "In Hope's Crossing?"

Her pudgy, smushed-face dog lifted his head and whined at her sharp tone.

"I've been poring through my father's files on Elizabeth's case and found a . . . possible lead. Someone who might have seen her that night."

He chose his words with care. In truth, he wasn't exactly sure *what* this Peggy Burnett might have seen, but he certainly found the brief tip report he had discovered the night before buried in the files intriguing enough that he knew he couldn't leave that particular stone unturned.

"What sort of witness? What does he have to say?"

"I don't know yet. My father's paperwork isn't as . . . complete as I might have wished."

The investigation had huge, gaping holes, but he didn't tell her that. He found them heart-breaking, this further evidence that his father's mental acuity and job performance both had been slipping in his last months as police chief.

Clearly, the sheriff's department had tried to fill in some of those gaps after taking over the case, but for reasons he didn't understand, no one had followed up with this particular tip. The report had actually been misfiled, tucked into the middle of a stack of interviews conducted among neighbors of Luke and Elizabeth.

"I do know *he* is a *she*. A long-haul truck driver who might have seen something that night. I won't really know until I talk with her. I could take a statement over the phone but I always prefer face-to-face interviews whenever possible."

In person, he could ascertain things like body language and facial tics that wouldn't be clear on the telephone. Through that body language, he could also pick up on avenues he needed to pursue, things he wouldn't necessarily sense over the phone.

"And she lives near Hope's Crossing? That's an odd coincidence."

"About forty miles from there. I was planning to talk to her after I return to Denver in a few weeks, but since you're going to the gallery anyway, I could keep you company, maybe take turns driving."

131

Yeah, it was a crazy idea and he didn't know why he had suggested it. Megan looked as baffled as he was.

Whether responding to her unease or just bored with the conversation, her dog wriggled to get down from her lap and curled up on the braided rug in front of the door.

"I'm planning a quick trip down and back but I'll still be gone for at least two days," she finally said. "Don't you have a deadline?"

"Yes. But I've been able to get more done in the last week than I have for months. I'm almost there. I can spare a few days on this case."

With all his experience reading body language and facial expressions, he didn't miss the way she pursed her lips while she considered the idea and drummed her fingers on the arm of the swing.

Did she feel any of this attraction tugging between them? That he *couldn't* read.

After a moment, she released a heavy breath. "I don't see how I can say no. I want you to find the truth about Elizabeth. If there's any chance this witness might have evidence that would clear my brother, I want you to find it."

"I don't know what she might have seen that night," he warned. "It might implicate him more."

"Never," she said firmly, with a faith he found both sweet and troublesome. He didn't want to be the one to break her heart.

"I wouldn't mind a copilot anyway. I'm leaving

132

at seven a.m. Pack light, since I don't have much room, at least until I unload the prints. Oh, and Cyrus is coming along, too. Is that a problem?"

He liked her dog. Who wouldn't, with his easy-going, affectionate manner? "Not with me. He can be our bodyguard."

"Also, I should warn you that I like to listen to loud music when I drive. Cyrus likes it, too. Country, hip-hop, Broadway musicals. His tastes are eclectic."

"Good to know. I'll be sure to take along my noise-canceling headphones so I don't get in the way of Cyrus's jam."

She smiled a little. "Smart."

He rose from the swing to the jangle of the chains. "I guess I'd better go find them and pack the rest of my stuff, then."

She rose as well. "See you in the morning. Thanks for helping me carry my gear home."

"You're welcome."

"Oh, and Elliot?"

He turned back to her, struck by how the moonlight played over her features, making her look almost otherworldly. Some kind of soft, fey creature who had materialized out of his own fantasies to taunt and tempt him.

"I still think you're a hero for what you did. Risking your career and possibly your life to help those girls."

Her words touched him to the core. He found

enormous comfort in them, in knowing she came down so firmly on his side. She was the first one outside the Bureau who knew the story. She didn't condemn him; she saw straight to the principle of what he had done. Sometimes the nuances of a situation belied the customary rules and regulations.

"Thank you."

"For what? Anyone hearing the story should feel the same way. You rescued the helpless, protected the defenseless. Your dad would have been proud of you."

A lump rose in his throat, making it difficult to swallow. Her words were exactly the ones he hadn't realized he needed to hear. "I hope so."

She was remarkable, this woman who had suffered through sadness and loss herself. He wanted to tell her so, but couldn't quite find the words. Instead, he stepped forward, intending to give her only a small kiss on the cheek and wish her good-night, but the moment his mouth brushed her skin, he knew he was fooling himself.

This wasn't a kiss of gratitude or some polite, friendly farewell at the end of the day. He kissed her because he wanted to. He had craved the taste of her for what seemed like forever.

"Oh." Her voice was a soft, silky whisper in the night. It slid around him, binding him to her. When was the last time he had ached like this for a woman? He couldn't remember.

He wasn't sure he ever had.

Her green eyes were wide and startled and . . . aware.

He didn't miss the way her breath caught or her lips parted. She swallowed, her mouth trembling a little, but she didn't push him away. Instead, her gaze landed on his mouth, sending heat unfurling through him.

Helpless, enthralled, he lowered his mouth again. Some corner of his brain knew kissing her wasn't a good idea. All the reasons against it clustered around him, but for once he decided not to listen to common sense.

Her mouth was soft and sweet and tasted like strawberries and champagne from the party earlier. Tantalizing. Seductive. Irresistible.

Only for a moment, he told himself. Until she pushed him away and asked what he was doing. But she didn't do anything of the sort. She kissed him back, tentatively at first, then with more enthusiasm.

He forgot all the reasons he shouldn't be doing this, about Wyatt and about the case against Luke and about the fact that he was a battered, cynical FBI agent and she was soft and sweet and wonderful.

It was a magical, star-kissed night here beside the lake he loved and he could only focus on the woman in his arms and how very long he had ached for her.

Chapter Eight

NEVER, IN HER wildest dreams, had Megan imagined that Elliot Bailey would kiss like this.

She thought of all the times she and his sisters teased him about being so serious, so focused on work. Mr. Roboto, the stiff, humorless FBI agent who only cared about the job.

How could she possibly have guessed that he would kiss a woman like this, with a single-minded intensity that left her shivery and weak. His mouth was hard, firm, and tasted minty. She was careful of his arm, still in the sling, and didn't press her curves against him like she would have wanted. Only their mouths touched, which somehow made the kiss more erotic.

She should stop things.

The warning played through her head but she ignored it. She didn't want this sultry dream to end. A few moments longer, she told herself, and surrendered to the delicious play of his mouth over hers.

After a few moments, Cyrus made the decision for her. At some point he must have wandered over to investigate what they were doing because he barked once from right at their feet, jolting her out of the soft, hazy wonder back into hard reality.

Her fingers were tangled in his hair, her body pressed against him. He was watching her out of those intense eyes, his features focused and intent and gorgeous. What was she doing? Kissing Elliot Bailey as if she couldn't get enough!

He certainly wasn't behaving as if he disliked her now or thought she was silly or foolish. On the contrary. He kissed her with a heat and hunger that completely stole her breath.

She eased away.

In the dim moonlight, his features were in shadow, dangerous and mysterious.

She didn't quite know how to play this. What did one say when the world had just shifted?

She decided a light tone was the only way to go. He couldn't know how that kiss and the emotions bubbling up out of nowhere had shaken her to the core.

"That may not have been the smartest idea ever," she finally said.

He didn't answer, only gazed down at her out of those unreadable blue eyes.

"I mean, we've got an eight-hour car ride tomorrow and now we have all this . . . weirdness between us."

"Weirdness?"

"Things are bound to be awkward now. I mean, how am I supposed to keep my attention on the road now with you sitting beside me, all sexy and brooding? All I'm going to be thinking about is the mind-blowing information that Elliot Bailey sure knows how to kiss."

He looked startled for a moment, then gave a short laugh. "Is that a compliment?" he asked, throwing her own words back at her.

"I guess you could call it that, but it's information I really didn't need to know."

How could she possibly travel to Colorado with him, remembering the solid strength of him against her, the rasp of his stubble on her skin? She would drive them both off the road.

"Would you feel better if I didn't come with you tomorrow? I don't have to go. The last thing I want is for things to be *weird* between us."

That would be the easy way out. She could tell him she needed to concentrate on her upcoming show, not on the very real distraction of this inconvenient and unwanted attraction.

Yet if she did that—chickened out, gave in to her fear and told him she would rather he didn't come along the next day—what might she be giving up? What if this witness held the key to unlocking the entire mystery of Elizabeth's disappearance and clearing her brother's name and reputation? Could she risk letting that chance slip away, simply because she had discovered how much she liked kissing Elliot Bailey?

No. She had been hoping and praying for any opportunity to help Luke put the past behind him. This might be the break they had been looking for. She decided she had no choice but to treat the kiss as nothing more than a casual moment between friends, one that shouldn't have happened.

"Let's see. I once dated your brother, you're investigating *my* brother and you're a guest at my hotel. I would say things between us have been weird since day one. What's one more eight-hour car ride?"

She almost thought he would smile again. His mouth lifted slightly on one side but he smoothed out his expression before he could reveal more of himself.

"I guess you're right. Great. I'll see you first thing in the morning, then. I'll bring my noise-reducing headphones and my laptop and you won't even know I'm there."

She barely managed to hold back a rude snort. Sure. That was likely, that any woman could overlook someone like him. Even before he had kissed her, Megan had always found Elliot Bailey impossible to ignore.

She certainly couldn't reveal that to him. "Perfect. I'll see you in the morning, then."

And probably dream about him all night long.

She sighed and let herself into the house. Cyrus waddled to his water bowl as she sank down onto the sofa, and she tried not to feel abandoned. She could have used a little moral support here, but she supposed it wasn't her dog's job to talk his human through her latest stupid decision.

She shouldn't have let Elliot kiss her. She should have pushed him right off the porch swing and hurried into the house fifteen minutes earlier. If she had, she wouldn't be battling a strange combination of regret and longing.

It had been far too long since she had been kissed so thoroughly, since she had felt cherished and feminine and *desired*.

She dated. It wasn't as if she had put her whole life on hold after Wyatt died. A few years earlier, she had even been involved for several months with a new orthodontist who moved to Shelter Springs. Jon had been funny and kind and tender. Most important, he had been understanding about the chaos of her life, between the inn, her photography and her obligation to help Luke with the children.

She had wanted so badly to fall in love with him but had gradually realized her feelings weren't growing. She liked him and enjoyed his company, but it seemed unfair to keep him on a string simply because she was tired of going places alone.

She had known he deserved better, someone whose heart didn't have these huge jagged cracks in it. He had found love just a few months later when he met a sweet dental hygienist at a conference in Boise. They'd been married six months now. She had seen them at a home-improvement box store in Shelter Springs and they seem deliriously happy together.

In the last few years, nearly every one of her closest friends had become engaged or married. It was almost an epidemic in Haven Point, really. She would have liked to find someone who filled her world with the same kind of joy her friends had found.

That wasn't going to happen for her. She had figured that out after Wyatt died. She had cared about him, yes. Maybe she had even loved him a little, but not with the grand passion she saw in her friends' relationships.

Maybe something inside her was broken.

Maybe she wasn't worthy of love. Her father had certainly tried to drill that message into her head.

Scrawny. Ugly. Worthless.

She pushed away Paul's voice. The man had been gone for decades. When would she finally stop listening to those echoes in her head?

Not everyone was destined for a happy ending with someone else. Sometimes love could be a disaster, all the way around. Hadn't she seen that in many of the relationships around her? Her mother certainly had not chosen wisely. Neither had Luke. Both had suffered terribly because they had given their hearts to the wrong person.

Who could blame her for guarding hers so carefully? The one time she had started to push away the barricades and allow Wyatt inside, he had died.

After that, she built them bigger and higher than ever determined to make her own happy ending.

This gallery opening was her chance to begin the process of achieving her own dreams. She wasn't about to complicate that by letting herself fall for someone so completely *wrong* for her like Elliot Bailey.

EMBARKING ON AN eight-hour drive after a night of little sleep was probably not the best idea she'd ever had.

Oh, she had tried to sleep, but as she had predicted to herself, her mind had raced all night with thoughts of that shocking kiss.

What had Elliot been thinking to kiss her? What had *she* been thinking to let him?

She had no idea how to answer either of those questions.

He'd never given her any hint, in all the years she'd known him, that he might be attracted to her. If anyone had asked her to name fifty men of her acquaintance she thought would ever be interested in her, Elliot wouldn't have even made the list.

They hadn't had a great deal to do with each other, with him in Colorado and her stuck here in Haven Point, but she was close friends with his sisters, which made it inevitable that their paths would cross occasionally. Weddings, major birthday parties, that sort of thing.

He always seemed to treat her with not precisely condescension, just . . . formal politeness bordering on coolness. Never any hint that heat might lurk beneath the surface.

Why had he kissed her?

The question had raced around her thoughts all night, until she'd finally given up answering the impossible. The only theory that held any weight was that perhaps the moonlight and their dance and the confidences they had shared had temporarily made him lose his head, maybe helped along by the two drinks he'd said he had at the party, along with any lingering impact from the last time he took pain medication.

Whatever the reason, she only knew the kiss was something that never should have happened.

The horse was already out of that particular barn, though. There was nothing she could do now but try to catch it and rein it back in.

She carried her small tote bag and Cyrus's supplies out to her SUV. She had removed the back row of seats for more room and the entire cargo area was filled with photographs of differing sizes stacked on their edges—thirty of them, all printed on fine photographic paper and sandwiched between sheets of acrylic to bring out the details and make the colors pop.

At the sight of them, Megan had to fight down panic. This was her best work; she couldn't dispute that. She had carefully selected each photograph to tell a story. Together, she hoped they painted a vivid picture of small-town community life in a sleepy little town on the shores of a beautiful crystal-blue lake.

What if people hated them? Thought them trite, sophomoric? Or worse, had no reaction at all?

No. She caught the negative direction of her thoughts and frowned. She couldn't go there. This was her best work and she knew it had impact. She simply needed to have faith in her abilities and shove Paul Hamilton's voice out of her head again.

"You ready to go, buddy?"

At her feet, Cyrus wagged his stubby little tail.

"I guess that means yes."

He loved car rides, even those rare afternoons when she just took a few hours off from the hotel to drive around the beautiful countryside and take pictures.

Now he just gazed at her with his head tilted and his flat pug face scrunched up.

Cyrus had been injured sometime in his life, before she had adopted him from the animal shelter. The vet at the shelter suspected he'd maybe been run over by a bike or even hit by a car. As a result, his head was always tilted a little to one side, as if giving her a quizzical look. It made for some interesting conversation between them.

Now she opened the second-row door and found room next to the large-frame prints for the dog's crate, then lifted him into it.

Cyrus circled a few times, sniffing the corners in case any other dogs might have trespassed since the last time they used it, then settled in for the ride.

"Looks like there's almost room for me in here."

Her heartbeat accelerated at the deep voice coming from behind her. She drew in a deep breath and uttered an internal prayer that she could survive the next two days without making a complete idiot of herself, then turned to face him.

Elliot stood in the predawn darkness holding a cup of coffee, a small duffel and what looked like a battered leather laptop bag.

He wore khakis, loafers and what probably passed for casual traveling clothes for him: a button-down light blue shirt and a navy blazer.

How would she make it through the next eight hours with him—and then turn around and do it all over again the next day?

She wouldn't worry about that now. When faced with other daunting tasks in her life, she tried to focus only on what was right in front of her, not the huge, overwhelming picture.

Right now, that was settling everybody into her SUV and hitting the road so she could meet up with Mary Ella Lange at her gallery by the end of the day.

"There is plenty of room, actually. You can set your bags on the seat there next to Cyrus."

Elliot found a place for his duffel but kept the messenger bag with him, then leaned in to greet the dog. "Good morning. You ready for an adventure?"

Cyrus gave a snort in greeting but barely opened his eyes.

Was that how Elliot saw this? An adventure? She was tied up in knots about both the gallery show and about having him along on the journey. Megan wondered all over again why she had ever agreed to let him join her.

Luke, she reminded herself. She would do this for her brother's sake. If Elliot could prove Luke's innocence and clear his name once and for all—and possibly find answers to the mystery that had haunted her family for so many years—any inconvenience on her part would be well worth it.

"We're both ready," she answered.

He opened the passenger door, set his laptop bag on the floor, then slid his lean frame inside.

She filled her lungs with one more deep, pine-scented, Elliot-free breath, then climbed in beside him.

Her roomy midsize SUV seemed to have shrunk to the size of a cereal box, and the scent of his soap, woodsy and masculine, filled the interior.

"I'm surprised," she admitted after she started the engine. "I had a bet with myself that you would offer to drive before we even headed out."

"That seems a strange bet. Why would you assume I would do that?"

She shrugged. "Most men of my acquaintance tend to get antsy with a woman behind the wheel. I'm not sure if they like to be in control, if they're misogynists or if it's plain old arrogance, the certainty that they can do it better."

He held up his bag. "I figured I would work while I have the chance, if it's all the same to you. To be honest, I'm hoping to make serious progress on my manuscript today and maybe wrap it up if I can. Whenever you need a break, though, let me know. I'm happy to drive."

"Thanks. I'll keep that in mind."

He was full of surprises. Something told her this wouldn't be the only way Elliot Bailey would leave her discombobulated over the next few days.

She put her SUV in gear, backed out of her parking stall and headed for the highway, hoping this wasn't a huge mistake.

Chapter Nine

WHY HAD HE ever imagined this might be a good idea?

As Megan drove away from the inn, Elliot settled into the passenger seat, wondering if he'd suffered some kind of previously undiagnosed brain injury during the shoot-out, one that was only now making itself manifest.

What was he doing here? And how would he make it through two days of being in her company without doing something crazy—oh, like, say, stealing a kiss in the moonlight, simply because he couldn't help himself.

He sighed, the memory of that kiss taunting him. He could still taste her, heady and delicious.

It was going to be a long two days.

He couldn't back out now. He would simply have to keep his mind on the goal—interviewing a potential witness to Elizabeth's disappearance and possibly moving one step closer to finding out what happened to her.

If he could help Megan out with the driving and perhaps provide a little muscle once they reached the gallery, he would count that as a bonus.

He only had to control this unruly attraction to her for forty-eight hours. No problem.

"I love road trips," she said after a few

moments, "especially that first hour or two, when the whole road lies ahead of you and you haven't had time for boredom to set in yet."

The morning was lovely, he had to admit, as the pines along the road dripped condensation and sunlight streamed through the treetops. This wasn't a bad way to spend the morning, riding next to a lovely woman as they made their way toward the freeway.

Elliot had never been very good at small talk, the little polite, socially lubricating conversations that eased the way at gatherings and around the water cooler at work. He preferred to listen, to absorb, to process information.

A loud mind is greater than a loud mouth, his father used to say, and from the time he was young, Elliot had taken those words to heart.

He never had much patience for talking about inconsequential things and invariably ended up asking questions that were too deep and probing for casual conversations.

But he wanted to hear everything Megan had to say. The woman intrigued him on so many levels.

Yes, he was physically attracted to her. It was much more than that, though. He liked being with her. He couldn't remember the last time he could say that about a woman.

"Did your family go on many vacations when you were younger?"

He regretted the question when her smile

dimmed slightly and she kept her gaze fixed on the road stretching out ahead of them.

"Not really. We went to Yellowstone once before my mom died. I remember we stayed in a tent and saw Old Faithful and roasted hot dogs around the fire."

With a start, Elliot realized that while he knew the basics, he didn't know much else about her past. He knew her mother had died when she was in elementary school and her dad had been in and out of the picture. Her maternal grandmother had basically raised her and Luke in her home on the grounds of the inn, despite the fact that Luke had been a product of their father's first marriage and wasn't even her biological grandson.

When they were kids, Luke had always been pretty closemouthed about his family life. Elliot had never probed, though he'd somehow gained the impression it hadn't been ideal.

"What about you?" she asked in return. "Did the Bailey clan ever hit the open road?"

"Dad took us on fishing trips and the occasional campout but he didn't like to be away from Haven Point that much."

John Bailey had seen his position as chief of police in Haven Point more as a calling than a job. They used to tease him that he thought the whole town would descend into anarchy if he wasn't there to keep the peace. Trips to Disneyland couldn't compete with that sort of obligation.

Charlene had done her best to give them those experiences, though. "Mom would take us a few times a year to visit her family in Wyoming and once she loaded us all up in her minivan and drove alone to the Oregon Coast. She said she was tired of waiting for Dad to carve out a week. It was breathtaking."

"You're very lucky," she said softly.

"Because I've been to Oregon? What I didn't tell you was how exhausting it could be to travel with five kids. I was the oldest, so before we left, Dad told me I had to help Mom with the others. Marsh was okay but Wyatt and Wynona fought the whole way and Katrina turned into a pouty brat the minute we passed the city limit sign."

He felt ridiculously pleased when she smiled at that.

"I love your family. All of them. It was one of the things . . ." Her voice trailed off.

"One of what things?" he asked when the silence became heavy and awkward.

"One of the things I liked most about dating Wyatt."

Elliot's insides clenched at this reminder that she had once been in love with his brother.

"You dated Wyatt for his family?"

"Not only that. He was . . . Well, you know. He was laughter and practical jokes and silly faces. He loved to have a good time and he wanted

151

everyone else to as well. He truly cared about everyone."

"And in the end, it killed him."

Her hands tightened on the steering wheel and Elliot wanted to kick himself. He could be such an ass sometimes. A total failure at social conversation 101.

Yes, Wyatt had died while helping someone else. It had been tragic and heartbreaking. He had been off duty from his job as a highway patrol officer when a fierce and sudden blizzard struck the area of the state where he had been working.

On the job or not, Wyatt hadn't shirked from his desire to help. He stopped to dig out a stranded motorist. He was outside of his own truck trying to push the vehicle out of a snowbank when another vehicle spun out on the same patch of ice and hit both Wyatt and the other motorist.

"I'm sorry," he said. "I loved my brother. If you want the truth, I envied him."

"You did?"

He sifted through his words, not wanting to reveal too much to her. He could still remember his shock at learning from Charlene in one of their regular Sunday phone calls that Wyatt and Megan Hamilton had begun dating, and how pleased they all were about it.

"Maybe she'll settle that rascal brother of yours down a little," his mother had said.

Elliot remembered ending the call and just

sitting in the dark of his apartment in Denver, wondering what the hell he would do if she and Wyatt actually wound up together.

He had ended up going out to a bar and getting drunk, for one of the few times in his life.

He certainly couldn't tell her that, though.

"This may come as a shock to you, but I tend to be a little serious," he said instead.

"You?" She raised an eyebrow and he didn't miss the dry note in her voice.

"I always have been. I take after my dad, I guess."

She smiled. "You and Marshall seem to have that in common, at least until he and Andie found each other."

"Neither of us talked a lot. We used to be able to play Legos for hours without once fighting about which of us needed a particular brick. And then came Wyn and Wyatt. Two little rascals, into everything and never stopping their chatter long enough to even take a breath. Wyn was the sweetest thing and Wyatt was a born stand-up comedian. When he was in a room, everyone else there couldn't help but smile. Even me."

"And me," she said.

Megan was the same way, he realized. She had a unique way of looking at the world that invariably made him smile—on the inside, anyway.

"Do you miss him terribly? Is that why you

haven't found someone else in all these years?"

So much for small talk. As soon as he asked the question, Elliot wanted to kick himself. Did he really want to hear the answer to that?

She was quiet for a long moment and he almost told her to forget he'd said anything. The only sound was the whirring of the tires on the pavement and her dog's snuffling snores from behind them.

Finally she spoke. "That's hard to answer. I miss the future we might have had but I don't know if we would have ended up together anyway. Neither of us was ready back then. I wanted to get out of small-town Idaho, just take my camera and go, while he loved it here and couldn't imagine settling anywhere else."

She wanted to leave? He hadn't known that. He'd always assumed she'd created her life at the inn because that was what she wanted.

"I suppose a corner of my heart will always belong to Wyatt," she went on, "but I haven't spent the last six years in mourning, I promise you that. Mostly, I've been too busy helping raise my niece and nephew to go on many dates."

"Are they the reason you didn't leave after Wyatt died?"

"Luke and the kids needed me. He had been there for me after my mother died. I couldn't abandon him, too."

She had put her own dreams on hold and stayed

in Haven Point. He wondered if that was one of the reasons she stubbornly clung to the misguided conviction that Luke had nothing to do with Elizabeth's disappearance. She probably wanted to believe she had sacrificed all of her plans for an innocent man, not one whose children lost their mother because of him.

He again had that uneasy feeling that maybe he ought to leave the whole mess alone, just let Marsh and his department continue to investigate. Megan would be devastated if his suspicions turned out to be true.

"They seem like sweet kids," he said gruffly. Children who deserved to know the truth.

"They're pretty amazing," she agreed. She sent him a sidelong look. "What about you? Why haven't you married? You're, what, thirty-six now? Heading into confirmed bachelor territory, aren't you?"

"Something like that."

"So why isn't there a Mrs. Elliot Bailey by now? You're not only an FBI agent but a best-selling crime writer. You've got that sexy, dangerous vibe down. I would think you'd have women knocking down your doors."

He snorted. "Oh, yes. I can barely walk outside without stepping on all the broken hearts I've left there."

"I don't doubt it."

"I go out. Just never anything serious."

"Why not?"

"You said it yourself. I have an intense, demanding job and another one on the side. There's not a lot of wiggle room in my calendar for grabbing drinks or going to the movies."

"When something's important enough, you make time."

He raised an eyebrow. "Now you sound like my mother."

"Well, look at it this way. If things go south with your disciplinary hearing, at least you'll have more time for a social life."

He laughed. He couldn't help it. "Sure, my career has imploded, my reputation is in tatters and everything I've worked for over the last thirteen years may be chugging down the drain. But at least I can sign up for a couple of dating services now and finally get my mom off my back."

"There you go. There's always a bright side. Sometimes you just have to look for it."

How did she do it? After everything she had been through—losing her parents, her grandmother, Wyatt—how could she still have such an optimistic view of life?

He didn't know. He only knew he found her delightful. She was like Wyatt, he thought again, someone who brought joy and sunshine wherever she went.

Resisting her would be one of the hardest things he'd ever done.

• • •

WHO WOULD HAVE guessed Elliot Bailey could be a pleasant traveling companion?

By the time she was ready to take a break and let poor Cyrus stretch his stubby little legs, Megan had decided that even though she didn't mind driving, the trip wouldn't have been nearly as enjoyable on her own.

They hadn't spoken much since that surprising conversation after they first set out, but it wasn't an uncomfortable silence. She quite enjoyed glancing over every once in a while to see him working away on his laptop, noise-reducing headphones on and his features intense as he touch-typed far more quickly than she might have expected.

Every once in a while, he would make an exclamation or mutter to himself. She had a feeling he wasn't even aware of it. Every time, it made her smile. She did the same thing when she was in the groove, editing and organizing photos on-screen.

She had listened to a photography podcast she liked for the last few hours and the miles had passed quickly. She would have driven another hour before stopping, but she didn't think Cyrus could wait that long.

"Do you need gas?" he asked, removing his headphones when she slowed down to take the next exit.

"I've still got half a tank but figured I would top it off. Mostly I need to let Cyrus out," she explained.

She pulled into a gas station close to the exit, and Elliot opened his door as soon as she turned off the engine.

"I'll take care of the gas," he said. "You deal with our furry friend."

She headed around the SUV to let Cyrus out. The moment she lowered him to the ground, he went to the nearest tire and lifted his leg.

"Looks like you stopped just in time." Elliot gave her an amused look over the SUV's roof.

"I had a feeling. He has this little grunt he does when he's desperate."

"Reminds me of a couple guys I work with," he said.

Had Elliot Bailey just made a joke? Who would have believed it? The man was full of surprises.

"I'm not sure he's done. I'm just going to take him over to the grassy spot over there and let him run around a little."

"Do you want anything inside? A drink or something?"

"I forgot to tell you I have snacks and some water bottles in a cooler in the back, but I wouldn't mind a cup of ice."

"You got it."

"Oh, and maybe something chocolaty and bad for me."

He gave that delicious half smile. Something else that was bad for her. "I'll see what I can find."

While the gas was still pumping, he headed inside. She grabbed Cyrus's water bowl and one of the water bottles and walked with him to the little patch of grass. She filled the bowl up for him and did a few yoga stretches to work out the kinks in her back from huddling over the steering wheel in one position as he lapped at the bowl eagerly.

More water in his system would mean another stop, sooner rather than later, but she didn't mind.

When he was done drinking, the dog wandered around the small patch of grass with his nose to the ground. After only two or three moments, he plopped onto his stomach and gazed at her with an expectant *what-now?* look.

Megan rolled her eyes. "Seriously? That's all the exercise you want? Five minutes of getting a drink, answering the call of nature and rolling around in the grass?"

He gave her his cocked-head, scowly look that always made her laugh.

"Okay. Your choice. But it will be a few hours before we stop again."

She hooked his leash back on, picked up his water bowl and headed back to her SUV to return him to the crate.

She could use a quick restroom stop, too, she

decided. She was still fifteen feet from her car when she saw a figure sidle up to her passenger seat, give a careful look around, then reach into the open window. When he pulled his hand out, Elliot's laptop bag was dangling from it.

"Hey!" she shouted.

Startled eyes turned in her direction, belonging to a kid who couldn't be more than eleven or twelve.

He stared, frozen, for just a moment, then took off running with the bag. Megan started after him. She had always been fast but quickly realized she wouldn't gain on the thief while hampered by a peripatetic dog with stubby little legs.

She scooped Cyrus up, deposited him inside the open window of her vehicle, then took off after the thief.

She reached him before he could turn the corner of the convenience store. With a mighty burst of energy, she grabbed the hood of his sweatshirt, yanking him back and stopping his progress.

"Give me that," she snapped, adrenaline pumping through her.

"What's going on?"

She was so caught up in the moment, she hadn't realized Elliot must have seen her wild spree as she chased after the boy and had followed them.

"He was trying to steal your laptop." She didn't know if it was the wild burst of exertion or the adrenaline that made her breathless, but she found it pretty disgusting that she didn't have much more energy than her chubby little dog. Maybe she would have to forgo the chocolate bar Elliot held in his hand.

Or maybe not.

"Is that what you were doing?" he asked the boy.

The kid looked around nervously. His sweatshirt was torn and his hair was shaggy, in need of a trim. Her initial assessment proved to be pretty accurate. He looked about eleven or twelve, though he could have been older and just small for his age.

"No, dude. I was just—"

"Were you?" Elliot asked again, his voice harder.

"I was just playing around, dude. Here. Take it."

Out of nowhere, Megan felt a pang of sympathy. The boy had a pinched look around his mouth, and his eyes reminded her of a stray dog that had hung out around the hotel for a few days the month before, until she found a home for it.

"What's your name?" she asked.

The boy's nervousness was now palpable. "Joey."

"You have a last name, Joey?" Elliot asked.

"Why do you need to know? You have your stupid computer bag. No harm done, right?"

"This could be a felony, you know, especially if you have a weapon on you. That's a knife in your pocket, isn't it?"

Fear flashed across his features. He looked like he wanted to take off running. To his credit he stood his ground, though Megan had released her hold on his sweatshirt.

"You a cop?"

"FBI," Elliot replied, just as tersely.

Now the fear twisted into outright terror. The boy's hands started shaking. "Look, let's just forget it, dude. *Sir,*" he corrected. "I made a mistake. It was stupid. I'm sorry. It won't happen again. Please don't arrest me."

Elliot studied him, his features harsh. "What would you have done with my laptop, if you had been a little faster? Pawned it to buy beer or blow?"

"No, man. I don't do that stuff."

"Then what?"

After a long moment, the boy finally sighed. "My brother and me need a computer for homework."

Oh.

Megan's ridiculously soft heart started to melt, though she knew it was stupid and he was probably lying.

Elliot wasn't as easily fooled. "Am I supposed to buy that?"

"I don't care if you buy it or not. It's true. My mom's laptop died and she doesn't have the cash to replace it right now."

"So you wanted to give her a stolen one?"

"All our classes give homework on the computer now. Without one at home, we have to go to the library."

"What's wrong with that?"

"Nothing, except my mom has to work at night since our dad left and I have to babysit my brother and little sister. She's only three and it's too hard to take her to the library all the time, especially at night when she's tired."

He looked down at the ground then up at Elliot. "I'm sorry, man. I shouldn't have taken it. I just saw your bag sitting there in your nice ride and figured you probably had insurance and stuff and could afford another one. I'm sorry. It was wrong. Please don't tell my mom."

"You can't just take other people's things, simply because you want something," Megan said.

"I know. It was stupid. Are you going to arrest me?"

Elliot looked to be considering it. Before he could answer, a woman came around the side of the building, clearly looking for something. Or someone. Her eyes widened as she caught their tableau and her features first looked worried, then protective.

"Joey, what's going on?"

The boy's features paled further as his gaze jumped from Elliot to Megan to his mother. The

163

woman looked tired, with deep circles under her eyes and fatigue lines around her mouth.

"Uh . . ." He swallowed hard, obviously trying to come up with an explanation.

That, if nothing else, convinced Megan he was telling the truth when he explained his reasons for stealing the laptop. He obviously wasn't a very good liar.

"You should be very proud of your son," she said suddenly.

The woman looked confused. "I . . . should?"

"Someone just tried to steal my friend's laptop but Joey helped us get it back. He's a good boy, ma'am."

She straightened a little, losing some of her fatigue. "He is."

"He deserves a reward," Megan went on. "Don't you agree, Agent Bailey?"

He gave her a long look, eyebrow raised. "A reward."

"Yes. For assisting the FBI. It's a matter of national security. A reward is the least we could do." His gaze shifted from her to the boy and back again. She held her breath, hoping he wouldn't call her a liar and the boy a thief, and break a mother's heart.

Elliot always played by the rules. Or at least she thought he did. She was coming to realize there might be much more to him than she had always thought.

After a long beat, Elliot reached into his pocket for his wallet.

He slowly pulled out a twenty. Then, after a moment, he added another and handed them to the boy.

"I can't take that," Joey said, looking appalled.

"Sure you can," Megan said. "Save it. Maybe you can tuck it away and use it for something you need."

"Thank you," the mother said, looking baffled at the entire situation.

"You're welcome, ma'am," Elliot said, with another dry look in Megan's direction. "We couldn't do our job without vigilant, honorable citizens out there, willing to step up when they see something wrong."

Megan had to swallow her smile, delighted beyond words that he would play along.

"Good luck with school, Joey. Something tells me you're the kind of guy who's going to make all the best choices from here on out," she said.

"I sure will." Joey looked astonished, gazing down at the bills in his hand as if they had dropped from the sky.

"See you around," Megan said. "Don't forget your laptop, Agent Bailey."

She ushered him back to the car, leaving a startled boy and his equally baffled mother behind them.

Chapter Ten

"LET ME GET this straight," Elliot said slowly, after they had returned to the SUV and found Cyrus curled up in the driver's seat. "The kid tries to steal my laptop and walks away with no punishment, plus a forty dollar reward."

"You gave him the forty dollars. Don't blame me for that."

"Only because you guilted me into it. What else was I supposed to do, when you were giving me *that look?*"

"What look? I don't have a look."

"You totally have a look. A *we-have-to-do-something* look."

"Okay, go ahead and say it. I'm a sucker."

"You, Megan Hamilton, are a sucker."

She made a face. "I know. I can't help it."

In Joey's case, she knew she was a goner when he matter-of-factly dropped the information about his father leaving the family. She was entirely too familiar with that feeling.

"I'm willing to bet you give away plenty of free hotel rooms to people in need, don't you?" Elliot said as he returned Cyrus to his crate with a little extra scratch behind his ears.

Had Cade told him about their arrangement? The Haven Point police chief knew he could always call her in an emergency. No matter what it took, she would find room in case a woman needed to quickly leave a violent situation or a family had been displaced by fire or even when someone traveling through town ran into car trouble or had insufficient funds to continue on their journey.

"Sometimes," she admitted now to Elliot. "My grandmother had a policy to always help those in trouble."

"And you've continued it."

"Maybe I am a little too familiar with what it's like to feel completely helpless about the circumstances swirling around you."

He gave her a long look, clearly curious about what she had left unsaid. She didn't want to enlighten him further. She had already said too much.

"Anyway, I had a good feeling about Joey," she said, to distract him from digging too deeply. "I think he was telling the truth about his homework situation. He shouldn't have taken your laptop but he obviously thought he had a good reason."

"You could tell that from a thirty-second interaction?"

"I have good instincts about these kind of things."

His eyebrows shot up but he didn't say anything.

"Anyway, you got your laptop back. That's the important thing, isn't it?"

"Thanks for chasing after him. It's password protected and encrypted and also backed up in triplicate, but I would have lost everything I had worked on today on the manuscript. That would have been a shame, since I was able to make some serious progress this morning."

She liked thinking she had a positive impact on his creativity.

"I'm glad. Keep going, since it's working for you."

"Are you sure you don't want me to take a turn behind the wheel?"

"Positive. I don't mind driving. Just give me five minutes to use the restroom. Then I'll be ready to hit the road again."

"I'd better stay here to watch over things, just in case any other miscreants happen by. At this rate, I'll go broke giving out rewards before we hit the state line."

Another joke. If things continued like this, she might begin to suspect Elliot's sense of humor was far more keen than she had ever imagined.

HE AWOKE WITH the odd, disconcerting confusion of not being quite sure where he was in the universe.

He had been working, he remembered, so close to finishing one of the last chapters of his book.

From there, he wasn't sure what happened. He only knew they had stopped moving.

A glance out the window told him they were parked in front of a gas pump, a different one from earlier in the day.

He blinked a few more times and found Megan looking at him, apology in her eyes.

"I'm so sorry I had to stop," she said softly. "I wanted to keep going and let you sleep but I think Cyrus needs to pee again."

Elliot couldn't remember the last time he'd fallen asleep in a moving vehicle. Maybe on that trip to Oregon when he was a boy.

"It's fine," he said, dismayed when he had to clear the sleep out of his voice. "How long have I been asleep?"

A tiny smile played around her mouth. "An hour, maybe a little more. I had the feeling you needed it."

She was right. He hadn't been sleeping well, not since . . . Well, not since the shoot-out. And especially not since coming back to Haven Point and finding Megan living next door to him.

"Thank you. Though I must admit, I'm a little embarrassed. Did I snore?"

Now her small smile grew into a full-fledged one. "A bit. I wouldn't worry about a little snoring. The drooling, now, that's another matter."

He might have been mortified, if he didn't catch the teasing look in her eye.

169

A whine and nails scrabbling on plastic from the back seat caught his attention before he could reply. Her poor dog. He was likely to explode.

"I'll take care of the gas again," he said. "You worry about Cyrus. Maybe you might like to take him for a little walk."

"I was thinking the same thing," she said, climbing out of the driver's seat while he exited the other side. "I noticed a sign when I pulled in pointing to a scenic river trail. We'll just wander there for a moment, if you don't mind."

"No. I can stay here with the car."

"Worried we'll run into another Joey?"

"You never know."

"I'm sure you would be fine if you pulled in front and locked it after you fill up. I imagine you need to stretch your legs, too."

Everything was tight, especially his shoulder. His wound was protesting where he apparently had been leaning against it while he slept.

"Sounds good."

Megan opened the crate and hooked the dog's leash on his collar before lowering him to the ground. Again, the dog didn't wait for grass but lifted his leg against the tire.

"I'm going to need a serious car wash when this trip is done," she said, shaking her head. "It's my own fault for making him wait so long."

"Poor guy."

"I'll swipe my card, then leave you to fill it up," she said.

"I'll pay for this top-off," he said.

She looked as if she wanted to argue but finally shrugged. "We won't take long."

After a moment's hesitation, she pulled out her camera bag, slung it over her shoulder, then took off with the dog leading the way.

He watched them go for a moment, before turning back to take care of the gas.

When the tank was full again, he started up the SUV and drove to a shady spot near the front entrance, within sight of the clerks inside, tucked his laptop bag beneath the seat and out of sight, then climbed out, locked it and took off after Megan and her dog.

The trail curved behind the service station, leading down to a pretty little creek bordered by cottonwood trees. He followed the trail wending beside the river, enjoying the lovely May day. After about ten minutes of walking, he caught up with her. She was leaning across a boulder, her camera lens balanced in front of her as she snapped away at a waterfall that tumbled about six feet, surrounded by colorful spring wildflowers.

He had to stop, suddenly breathless at the picture she made—completely in her element while her dog sat at her feet, content with his world.

Elliot wasn't aware of it but he must have made some sound. She looked up, sensing his presence, and smiled in welcome. "It's beautiful, don't you think?"

How was he supposed to notice anything but the happiness in her green eyes and the way the sunlight picked out coppery highlights in her hair?

"Stunning," he murmured.

He sat down on a weathered wooden bench that had been thoughtfully provided for contemplation. After a moment, Cyrus rose and waddled to him with a jingle of his leash. Elliot obliged by picking up the dog and petting him, to Cyrus's delight.

"If you aren't careful, I'll waste the entire afternoon here shooting. I lose any sense of time and place when I have a camera in my hands."

"It's fine with me." He wouldn't mind sitting here all afternoon, watching her. "And it wouldn't be wasted, if you came away with some nice shots."

"Except I need to be in Hope's Crossing before dark. And the midday light isn't the greatest. It's a morning shot, I think."

She shot a few more frames of the waterfall and the flowers, then started putting her camera body and lens away.

He set the dog down and rose. "I can take that,"

172

he said, holding his hand out for her gear when she finished.

She looked as if she wanted to argue but must have seen she wouldn't win. With a sigh, she handed over the bag and took Cyrus's leash in return while Elliot slung her gear over his left shoulder and took off down the trail.

"Have you always loved photography?" he asked as they made their way back toward the service station.

Her brows drew together as she considered the question. "I suppose I have. My grandmother gave me an early digital camera years ago, when I was maybe eleven or twelve." She gave a short laugh. "I used to walk around the inn, photographing everything. The lake, the gardens, the guests. I was probably entirely too intrusive on people's vacations, but nobody complained—at least not to me, anyway. In those days, I *wanted* to get lost behind a camera lens. It was magic."

Why had she wanted to escape? Elliot wondered again at her childhood with a sickly mother and a father who hadn't been well liked around town. It must have been very different from his own.

"I continued on with photography in high school but really started to get serious about it again when I went away to college."

"Is that what you majored in?"

"No. My degree is in business administration,

but I took a couple of fine art photography electives and loved those more than anything else at school."

She glanced over at him as they walked. "What about you? I guess I don't need to ask what you planned to do when you grew up. I think you were born wanting to go into law enforcement, weren't you?"

"My mom used to say I came out with a badge in one hand and a printed Miranda warning in the other."

She laughed, her features soft in the afternoon light. "That's what I remember about you most. Always so serious, always following the rules and making sure you didn't step out of line."

He didn't like that she saw him in such rigid terms, uncompromising and inflexible. He had a wild urge to show her she was wrong.

"Not always," he murmured.

He stopped on the trail, leaving her no choice but to stop as well. Before he could talk himself out of it, he turned around, leaned down and kissed her.

He meant it only as a joke, to let her know he could be capricious when the mood struck him, but the feel of her mouth, the heat and taste of her, sent all his intentions floating down the creek like leaves swirling in the current.

Whoever would have guessed she fit so

perfectly? She was the perfect height for a man to tuck against him and explore that delicious mouth.

The circumstances weren't perfect. It was midday and they were on a public trail where anyone could stumble onto them at any moment. Beyond that, his arm in its damn sling kept her too far away from him, she was holding a leash and he had a camera bag slung over his good shoulder.

Someday he would like to kiss her when the moment was exactly right. But he didn't really need perfection. He would kiss her in a hurricane if it meant he could taste her again.

After a moment, she slid away from him. Her lips were trembling, as they had the night before, and looked swollen and delicious.

"What was that all about?" she asked, sounding vaguely disgruntled.

"A demonstration that I don't always do what people expect. Once in a while I can be spontaneous. Carpe diem and all that."

"I really didn't need an object lesson."

She sounded so put out, he had to smile. "And if you want the whole truth, I kissed you because I wanted to kiss you—because I've wanted to kiss you again since last night."

She opened her mouth to answer, then closed it again. Cyrus made a snorting noise that sounded suspiciously like a laugh. She glared at him, too, then turned and started marching back along the trail to the gas station.

"Why don't I drive now?" he said when they reached her SUV. "I've been sleeping on the job, when I was supposed to be relieving you."

She looked undecided for a moment, then shrugged. "As long as you tell me the moment your shoulder starts bothering you."

"Sure," he lied. "You'll be the first to know."

"Why don't I believe you?"

Because she understood him better than he wanted to admit?

"I can't answer that. Maybe because you're a suspicious, cynical woman."

"Or because you're a stubborn, hardheaded man who would rather pull out his fingernails himself than admit he's in pain?"

"I guess we'll never know the real reason. I would still like to take a turn at the wheel."

She shrugged and gestured to the driver's seat before she let her dog into his crate.

As was his routine, apparently, Cyrus clicked his nails on the plastic of his crate a few times, turned around in a circle then plopped onto his stomach, looking content. When Megan seemed sure he was comfortable, she opened the passenger door and leaned inside.

"Do you want to grab something to eat before we head out?" he asked.

Her forehead wrinkled as she considered. "I'm

okay snacking for now and don't need anything big. Don't let that stop you, though. Looks like there are plenty of places to eat at this exit."

"I'm good."

She nodded. "Let's make progress while we can, then. I'll bring up some of the snacks from the back, and maybe next time we stop for gas, we can grab a sandwich. Does that work?"

"Fine with me."

She spent a few moments raiding the cooler, finally settling on crackers, sliced cheese and grapes, which she brought up along with chilled water bottles. Once she was settled in the passenger seat, Elliot adjusted the driver's seat and the mirrors for his longer length, then headed for the on-ramp.

"Driver gets choice of music," she told him.

"I'm going to cede that to you. It's your vehicle, and you know your presets."

"What kind of music do you usually listen to?"

"I don't know. It varies, depending on my mood. Mostly classical and some jazz."

She made a face. "Why doesn't that surprise me?"

"Because you know I'm a boring stick-in-the-mud?"

She gave him a sidelong look. "There is a chance—a small one, mind you—that you might not be quite as robotic as I have always believed."

He wasn't sure what he was supposed to think

about that—he did know her words made him happier than was probably good for him.

She tried a few stations on her satellite radio and finally landed on a mellow classic rock station that he actually had as one of the presets in his own vehicle. "I'm afraid jazz or classical might put us both to sleep," she said. "Will this do?"

"Perfectly."

She shifted around in her seat trying to find a comfortable position. "So. What do you do for fun in Colorado, when you're not stopping crime or writing about it?"

Sleep. And sometimes eat. That was about the sum of it.

He really had to make more of an effort to get out more and savor the world around him.

She was a great example of that. With Megan, every moment seemed like an adventure, whether that was watching her niece play softball or chasing after a would-be thief in a convenience store parking lot.

"I read a great deal, mostly other true-crime books and manuals on law-enforcement techniques."

"I may reconsider. Maybe you're stuffy after all."

While he tended to agree with her for the most part, he did his best to defend himself. "I also run and hike and kayak. In the winter, I ski—cross-country and downhill."

"And women? Where do they fit in?"

"I date occasionally. Usually others in law enforcement."

"So you intend to create your own Bailey crime-fighting dynasty. Like father, like son."

"Something like that."

To his relief, she let the subject drop and was quiet for a few miles. "Tell me about this person you're going to see outside Hope's Crossing," she finally said. "What's the connection to Elizabeth's case?"

His fingers drummed on the steering wheel in time to the song on the radio as he tried to decide how much to tell her. He didn't want to reveal *anything*. Usually he preferred keeping information close to the vest, but that seemed impossible when she was so closely tied to the investigation—and when they were sharing a tight space, together on the open road.

"It may be nothing," he warned.

"We have spent seven years of nothings," she said quietly. "What's one more?"

Missing-persons cases could be hell on families. The uncertainty and the fear and the possibility, however remote, that their missing loved one might come back could play hell with any family dynamics.

"Apparently a trucker called in a tip about a month after Elizabeth disappeared. I found it buried in the files. I haven't been able to reach her in person or even find a number, only an address, but according to the tip report and my dad's notes, she said she may have given a ride to a woman who roughly matched the description. There were a few discrepancies. Enough, anyway, that Dad discounted it."

"But you're intrigued enough to follow up."

"I have no idea what I'll find. Maybe one more nothing. It might be a complete dead end, but I can't help feeling it's worth making contact to follow up."

"Why did your father discount the lead?"

Elliot's jaw work. I'm not completely sure. Like I said, it might be a dead end. He had pretty good instincts about most things. Not everything."

"He was a good man, your dad," she said. "I have often wondered if his investigation was too sharply focused on Luke from the beginning. If he had widened his search for other suspects, maybe something would have come up before now."

Elliot bristled at her criticism of his father, though it wasn't completely unfair. In the last few years of his time on the job, John Bailey had begun to make more and more mistakes in judgment.

He could only hope this hadn't been one more.

Apparently done asking him questions for the moment, she picked up her book and began to read. Elliot focused on the drive.

After a few more miles, he became aware of the same strange feeling that had washed over him at random intervals throughout this journey.

Contentment.

When was the last time he had known it? Between the pressures of the job and the stress of book deadlines, it wasn't a feeling he found familiar.

Yes, he knew his world was still in chaos. He didn't know if he would return to a job or learn after his disciplinary hearing in a few weeks that he had ruined his entire career.

At the moment, none of those things mattered. At this particular moment, with Megan next to him, everything in his world seemed right.

Apparently she was no less susceptible than he had been to the steady, calming rhythm of the vehicle tires on pavement. After about fifteen minutes of reading, her eyes began to flutter, opening and closing several times before finally settling on closed.

The book slipped onto her lap and she pressed her cheek against the seat, facing him, and nestled back against the door.

Only when he was certain she was really asleep did he allow himself to shift his gaze from the road at random intervals to sneak the occasional glance at her.

Megan Hamilton was the sort of woman a man would never tire of looking at. It wasn't simply her physical appearance, though he found her beautiful, with her delicate features, high cheekbones and long, sooty lashes.

There was more to it than that. She was a strong, courageous woman with a deep capacity to love.

His chest ached with a soft, fragile tenderness. He had always had a thing for her, whether he had admitted it to himself or not, but over the last few weeks, that attraction had begun to deepen into something more.

He was falling for her.

He frowned at the pavement stretching out ahead, not sure what the hell he was supposed to do about it.

He had never been in love before. Had always figured it wasn't for guys like him. He had the job he loved at the FBI and then the writing that started on a whim but had provided far more satisfaction than he ever imagined.

It had always seemed like enough.

In sleep, she made a soft little sound and wriggled, perhaps trying to find a comfortable position. As she tucked her hand beneath her cheek, he was overwhelmed with the crazy urge to pull over to the side of the road, tug her against him and hold her while she slept.

Elliot forced his attention back to the road. He wouldn't fall in love with her. The very idea was ridiculous. Yes, he had a little thing for her. That couldn't be love. He had spent thirty-six years without a woman touching his heart. What made him think he was ready to start now, with Megan?

Of all the women to tangle him up!

What would she do if this lead went nowhere—or worse, led him to the inevitable conclusion that Luke indeed had something to do with Elizabeth's disappearance?

What other possibility was there? He remembered Marshall telling him Elizabeth had suffered from postpartum depression and some people wondered if she had killed herself. Wouldn't some trace of her have surfaced by now?

The mountains around Haven Point were vast, yes, with plenty of unexplored terrain. There was always a chance she could have walked into Lake Haven with a backpack full of stones. Either way, eventually some article of clothing or a bone or *something* would have surfaced.

The alternative was equally untenable. He couldn't believe Elizabeth was living somewhere, had chosen to walk away from her husband and her children and the life she had in Haven Point, completely without warning.

Megan had faith in her brother. He accepted that and understood it—even admired her loyalty, to some degree. But the facts were the facts. Luke and Elizabeth had a stormy marriage. The police had been called during a domestic disturbance just days before her disappearance.

The couple had financial difficulties and she had been deeply unhappy.

Elliot was almost positive Luke had lost his temper and something terrible had happened, either intentionally or accidentally, leading him to dispose of her somewhere in the vast mountains around the lake—or perhaps in the deep lake itself.

What would happen when he proved his suspicions?

Yes, justice would finally prevail after all these years. Luke would be arrested and go on trial for his wife's disappearance and suspected homicide.

And Megan would despise him for any small part he might have played.

All the more reason he needed to put aside any foolish idea that he might be harboring feelings for her. They wouldn't do him any good. He was a sworn officer of the law to the bone, even if his future at the FBI hovered on a knife's edge. He had a job to do and he couldn't let things like emotions or affection cloud his judgment.

Chapter Eleven

ELLIOT BAILEY SURE knew how to kiss a woman.

They were on a brightly colored quilt next to a gurgling creek with a soft breeze teasing them, sweet with the scent of wildflowers and sagebrush. He didn't have a sling on now and he was using both hands to pull her close, molding her to his muscles while his mouth played against hers, teasing and tantalizing, drawing out all her secret desires.

She didn't want it to end. She wanted to stay right here in this delicious fog and kiss him all afternoon, until the sun slipped behind the mountains and the stars began to pop out, one by one.

"Somebody's stealing your laptop," she mumbled against his mouth.

"Who cares?" he answered back, kissing her more firmly. The scent of leather filled her senses, though she wasn't sure exactly why. When she blinked at him again, somehow he now wore a leather biker jacket instead of his blazer and button-down shirt. It was black and worn, and made him look dangerous, disreputable.

Delicious.

Oh, the girls at the book club would love

to see him like this. Roxy Nash would have a conniption! None of them ever would believe stuffy Elliot Bailey could be so . . . so *bad*.

She wrapped her arms more tightly around him and nuzzled her face into his neck. "Mmmm."

"Megan. Wake up."

"Don't want to," she murmured. Her muscles felt languid, soft, and every part of her hummed with anticipation and aching hunger.

"Megan?"

The voice intruded again, a little more firmly. "I'm sorry. I wish I could let you sleep but we're almost to Hope's Crossing and I don't know where to go once we hit the city limits."

The creek and the quilt and the leather jacket all disappeared like smoke and Megan fluttered her eyes open. Elliot was still here, watching her with a casual expression, not at all the passionate lover.

She blinked. How did he turn it on and off like that? she wondered, disgruntled.

"We just crossed the Hope's Crossing city limits. I don't know where to go," he said.

The import of his words finally shoved its way through her consciousness and she opened her eyes more fully. They weren't on a blanket and hadn't been except for her overheated imagination. There had been no kiss, other than that abbreviated version on the trail earlier. "We can't be here already."

"See for yourself."

When she looked out the window, the first thing she noticed was a large, charming wood-painted sign that read Welcome to Hope's Crossing.

The Colorado resort town was nestled in a pretty valley with steep, forbidding, still-snowcapped mountains in all directions. She could see historic streetlamps, hanging baskets overflowing with colorful flowers and a dynamic, bustling downtown.

None of it made sense, though.

She sat up, scrubbing at her eyes. "How can we be here? We were supposed to grab something to eat."

"We had enough gas to keep going and Cyrus seemed fine, so I didn't bother to stop. You were pretty out of it."

He had driven for at least three hours, without a break. Had she really slept that long? She couldn't quite believe it. On the other hand, she had been living on about four hours of sleep a night for weeks as she tried to get ready for the show, manage the inn and still keep up with her photography bookings. It really wasn't any wonder she had collapsed at the first chance.

"Poor Cyrus. I probably need to let him out."

"Let's head to the gallery first. Then I'll do it. Do you have an address?"

"Yes. It's the Lange Gallery on Main Street. I can look up directions on my phone."

He shook his head. "No need. I know where it is."

She sat up, wondering what kind of snarled mess her hair was in. "Really? You're that familiar with the town. I had the impression you had only been here briefly."

He had told her earlier that he had been there but hadn't given details.

"A few years ago, I had an assignment here for about a week. We were interviewing friends and associates of a man accused of serial murder and multistate insurance fraud. He had lived here briefly during his crime spree."

She shivered, struck by the realization that Elliot spent most of his life surrounded by the ugliest aspects of human nature. How hard that must be for him, focusing on the dark side of people.

Was that one reason he was so quick to believe the worst of Luke, when he had known the man since they were boys?

"What happened? To the suspect, I mean."

"He was convicted on all counts and is currently in the state prison, serving multiple consecutive life sentences."

She did not miss the hard note of satisfaction in his voice.

"You love what you do, don't you?"

Like the rest of his family, Elliot saw his career in law enforcement as more than just a job. It was part of him.

He shrugged. "What's not to love? I get bad guys off the streets and behind bars, where they belong."

That was how he saw her brother. A bad guy who belonged behind bars. The thought left a sour taste in her mouth and she picked up her water bottle from the drink holder and took a long, cleansing sip as he drove to the gallery.

"That's it right there, isn't it? The building with all the flowers?"

As he pulled into a convenient parking space in front, she gazed at a stately redbrick building with flower boxes in front of the windows and a basket of blooms hanging from an awning.

A metal sign above the door read Lange Gallery.

Nerves fluttered through her like monarch butterflies returning north after migration. "I . . . Yes. This is the building."

What was she doing here? She should call the whole thing off. She thought of her humble, everyday pictures hanging in that elegant-looking gallery and those butterflies went wild.

She drew in a shaky breath, unable to breathe. Unexpectedly, Elliot shocked her by reaching out and covering her trembling fingers with his.

"This is going to be great," he said. "I've got a good feeling."

"Thanks," she mumbled, drawing more strength

than she would have imagined from the simple gesture.

"Why don't you go in and find out where they would like us to unload? I'll take care of Cyrus."

She suddenly wanted him inside with her, all that solid, comforting strength to lean on. He was the kind of man a woman could always count on, whether she needed bad guys taken out, a shoulder to cry on or just a supportive hand on hers when she was frightened.

No. She straightened her shoulders. She could do this. After all the weeks of preparation and work, she could make it the final few steps.

"Thank you. This shouldn't take long."

He squeezed her fingers one more time. "You've got this," he repeated.

She would do her best to believe him. Megan checked her reflection one more time in the mirror on the visor. She looked like someone who had just spent eight hours in a car—and who had slept for three of those hours.

She couldn't fix that now. Mary Ella would have to accept she would be disheveled.

She climbed out of the SUV and headed for the front door of the gallery but it burst open before she even reached it.

Mary Ella Lange rushed out, all energy and elegance and warmth.

"Megan! I've been watching for you all day. Oh, I'm so happy you made the drive safely."

The other woman hurried to her and folded Megan into a big hug, which might have felt odd given their short acquaintance but somehow only conveyed the other woman's generous enthusiasm.

"How was the drive?"

"Lovely, actually," she answered, laughing a little. "It's a beautiful time of year to be driving across the western United States. We found some beautiful wildflowers and a waterfall outside a rest stop in Wyoming."

"I'm so glad." Mary Ella glanced at her vehicle. "Oh, you brought a friend with you. How wonderful."

"I . . . Yes." She had no words to describe exactly what Elliot was to her. *Friend* certainly fit, though the very notion still took her by surprise.

It didn't cover everything, though. Not heated kisses beside a tumbling creek or feverish dreams where those kisses were definitely leading to more.

Mary Ella grasped both Megan's hands in hers. "I can't tell you what a buzz your exhibit has created, both here in town and elsewhere. After I sent out the initial press release along with a few of your photos, I've had calls from art critics from around the state, wanting to come to the opening."

Art critics.

Panic felt like a living creature inside her, clawing at her throat. "I . . . That's great," she said weakly.

"And wait until you see the space we set aside for you. I think you're going to love it."

She wasn't sure why, but Mary Ella struck her as a woman who had seen both tragedy and great joy in her life. Megan had liked her from the moment they met at Eliza Caine's house.

"Where would you like us to park? Is there a delivery space behind the building to bring in the prints?"

"Where you are is great. You were lucky enough to nab a prime spot. Let's bring everything in."

The other woman had the demeanor of a kid about to run down the stairs on Christmas morning to see what was under the tree. All Megan could worry about was that she and Elliot had just driven eight hours to deliver an SUV full of coal.

Heart pounding, she returned to her vehicle as Elliot was opening Cyrus's crate, leash at the ready.

"Hi. I'm Mary Ella Lange. Welcome to Hope's Crossing."

He shook her hand. "Elliot Bailey."

"Any relation to the true-crime author by the same name?" she asked.

If Megan hadn't been so nervous, she might have found it rather endearing when Elliot looked flustered.

"He is *that* Elliot Bailey," she said for him.

She looked delighted. "Oh, wait until my husband finds out you're in town. He adores your books! My daughter owns a bookstore in town. If I had known you were coming, we could have arranged a signing or something!"

"It was, um, a spur-of-the-moment thing," he said, looking disconcerted by the attention. "Will you excuse me? Cyrus here needs to find a patch of grass. I think it's rather urgent."

"What a darling dog," Mary Ella exclaimed. "If you're looking for grass, the bead store just next door has a little garden in the back."

"Are you sure it's all right?" Megan asked.

"I promise, it's fine. My daughter-in-law owns it. If you go through the front of the store and explain you have a dog emergency, they should let you straight back without delay."

She almost volunteered to take him. The dog was her responsibility, after all, but Elliot was already leading Cyrus away.

"Is that your dog or his?" Mary Ella asked.

"Mine."

"He's adorable. And, if you don't mind me saying, Elliot Bailey is gorgeous, too. Who knew? He looks so solemn and stiff in the publicity photos on his book jackets!"

She had to agree, though Megan didn't say so aloud.

"Do you want to wait for them to come back before we start unloading? I'm assuming you brought him along for those lovely muscles."

She didn't want to think about his muscles or her entirely too vivid dreams about them.

"Something like that," she said. "We can start unloading some of the smaller pieces. Then Elliot can help out with the bigger, bulkier prints."

"Sounds like a plan."

She opened the back of the vehicle and she and Mary Ella grabbed several wrapped prints each and began carrying them inside the gallery.

"We're going to set you up in this space here," the woman said, leading her to a large room behind the main section of the gallery.

Her name was already there, printed on a placard over the door.

Megan Hamilton. Fine Art Photography.

Oh, dear heavens. She never should have agreed to this.

She drew in a breath, pushing away the negative thoughts. She knew where they came from—the chaos of her childhood.

She had talent. In her heart, she knew she did. Mary Ella believed it as well, otherwise she never would have offered Megan this amazing opportunity.

Somehow she had to find a way to get out of her own way and enjoy the accomplishment.

"What do you think?" Mary Ella asked.

"This all looks amazing," Megan exclaimed. "I still can't really believe this is real, that I'm not dreaming."

"It's real," Mary Ella Lange assured her. "And you're going to be a smash. Trust me on this."

She would try, Megan resolved, though it might be among the hardest things she'd ever done.

"I want to unwrap everything right now," Mary Ella said, all but clapping her hands together in glee, "but let's carry the pieces in first."

Elliot met them at the door. "I'm here to help. What would you like me to do with Cyrus? It's a warm day, probably too warm for him in the car."

"Oh! I should have told you that you could leave him next door," Mary Ella said. "There are always a few dogs running around back there to keep him company. But behind the desk there is just fine."

Elliot found a spot for the dog, looping the handle of his leash under the chair so he had room to explore but not to wander and possibly knock down high-dollar sculptures. Then they all returned to her SUV for another load.

Mary Ella carried a large print inside on her own, leaving Megan alone with Elliot.

"She seems nice," he said.

"She is lovely. I thought so the first time I met

her, at Eliza and Aidan's for Jamie and Julia Winston's engagement party. I liked her before she ever asked if she could show my work at her gallery."

She did like Mary Ella but was reserving judgment about her husband, a crusty billionaire named Harry Lange, who owned the local ski resort and lodge.

"Not only nice, but she obviously has superior taste," Elliot said.

It was the perfect thing for him to say. She drew in another breath and felt the last vestiges of her panic float away on the soft, lovely May afternoon.

"Thank you. I needed that."

He smiled, looking so gorgeous it took her breath away. "Anytime."

His arm was back in the sling but it didn't seem to bother him as he carried in a couple of the larger prints.

Soon they were all inside and Mary Ella was practically bouncing off the walls in her eagerness.

"Okay. Now the grand unveiling. Are you ready?"

Ready as she would ever be. Megan nodded and held her breath as the other woman ripped off the first paper.

Chapter Twelve

NONE OF THEM said anything as Mary Ella removed paper wrapping after paper wrapping and set the framed prints around the room. Three dozen of them, her very best work.

By the time each had been revealed, Megan was so nervous, she felt sick to her stomach.

"Oh, Megan," the gallery owner breathed.

She finally allowed herself to meet Mary Ella's gaze and found her expression so radiant that Megan's fingers itched for her camera. She could capture the other woman here, in her element, surrounded by art.

"These are spectacular. So much better, even, than I imagined."

A weight the size of her SUV seemed to lift off her.

"Thank you," she whispered.

"Beautiful," Elliot agreed gruffly, and again she had to catch her breath at the sincerity in his voice.

She looked at her work, trying to see these familiar prints through their eyes. She had a few favorites. A trio of elderly fishermen out on a weathered, colorful wooden boat, their features wrinkled and sun-worn as they cast their lines out onto the lake with steam rising up around them into the morning air.

Elliot's new niece Gabi hugging Katrina and Bowie's dog, their faces squished together and both beaming with love while the sweet light of dusk gathered around them.

A pair of little boys in muddy jeans, hair drenched with the rain that poured down around them, one saluting while the other pulled down the flag at the elementary school—a lucky shot she had captured after going to the school to pick up Bridger and Cassie one day.

"Oh, I was excited for the opening before," Mary Ella said. "Now I'm utterly feverish with anticipation."

She had another week before she had to panic about that, Megan told herself.

"I'm so glad you like them," she said.

"I do. And everyone else will, too. Trust me." The other woman gave her a sharp look and suddenly turned maternal. "You've had a long drive and should rest. There's nothing more we can do this afternoon."

"There isn't?"

"I'd rather organize the display when we're fresh. Why don't you check into the lodge, relax for a few hours, maybe have a lovely dinner at one of our restaurants here in town? I can highly recommend my daughter Alex's restaurant, Brazen. I promise, you won't be disappointed.

Then we can meet back here tomorrow morning to discuss the details of the exhibit and how to show every print to best advantage."

As much as she might like to move forward and finish what she had come here to do, Megan sensed Mary Ella was right. They would have better results in the morning.

"What time would you like me here tomorrow?"

Mary Ella pursed her lips. "Why don't we say eight? Is that too early? That way we should be able to wrap things up by noon and you can even head home when we're done, if you want— though of course you're welcome to stay another night at the lodge, if you'd like."

"Eight works."

"You know how to get to the Silver Strike, right? Go down Main Street, turn left and drive until you see the sign for the ski resort. It's about six miles from here up a box canyon. You'll see the resort as soon as you drive as far as you can."

As part of her compensation for the gallery showing, Mary Ella had arranged a room for her at her husband's ski resort.

"We can find it, I'm sure."

That reminded her. She needed to talk to them about getting an extra room for Elliot. Wouldn't it be her luck to show up at the lodge and find out they only had one room available?

This was a ski resort community. She imagined that their tourist cycle was similar to Haven

Point's, with May considered shoulder season—too late for winter recreation and too early for the summer tourists. They must have a room—and even if the lodge was full, surely Elliot could find a hotel room somewhere.

She wasn't going to worry about that. She hadn't been expecting him along on this trip. If he couldn't find a room, they would have to make do.

"Thank you for everything," she said to Mary Ella. "We'll see you bright and early tomorrow."

She picked up a patient Cyrus and left the gallery owner with more hugs and assurances about how well the exhibit would do ringing in her ears.

"Now what?" Elliot asked as they walked out into a lovely Colorado late afternoon.

"Why don't we check into the lodge? I can take Cyrus for a walk and some much-needed exercise. Then we can figure out where we want to go to dinner. I've heard good things about the restaurant Mary Ella was talking about. Brazen. When Jamie Caine found out I was coming to his hometown, he insisted I couldn't miss it."

Jamie was marrying her dear friend Julia Winston. If someone had told her before Christmas that the two of them would get together, she would have thought them crazy. They seemed an unlikely pair—the sexy pilot and the reserved librarian. Now that the idea had sunk in and she had seen them together, they fit perfectly.

"Sounds like a plan." Eliot said as he opened the door for Cyrus and let the dog into the now-empty back seat.

"You drive, since the seat and mirrors are already set for you."

Hope's Crossing was charming, she thought as Elliot drove through the downtown area and followed Mary Ella's directions toward Silver Strike Canyon, where the ski resort and lodge were located. The scenery was spectacular and the town had obviously made an effort to focus on aesthetics.

When they arrived to check in, they found the lodge had plenty of available rooms.

"I've got two connecting rooms on the first floor. Would that work for you?"

"That sounds good to me," Elliot said. "What do you think?"

She thought she hadn't given this enough consideration. The idea of Elliot sleeping only a thin wall away left her slightly breathless.

"Sure. Thank you."

He insisted on carrying in her bag and Cyrus's crate to her room, waiting until she unlocked the door before carrying them inside.

"I'm going to see about renting a car for the morning while you're at the gallery."

"You can drop me at Lange Gallery and use mine, if you want to."

"It would be easier to have my own transportation. I'll check into it. And while I'm making arrangements, what about dinner? I can call for reservations. What time would you like to eat?"

"You have work to do. I don't mind grabbing room service or even going down to the on-site restaurant by myself."

"I'm fine, as far as work goes. I made far more progress than I expected on the drive. I've heard good things about Brazen. It's in a converted firehouse and it's supposed to be amazing. It would be crazy to drive all this way and miss the chance to eat there, if it's at all possible to get a reservation."

"I suppose you're right."

"I'll give the restaurant a call and let you know."

"Sounds good. Thanks."

"I'll be in touch."

They shared a slightly awkward moment when he was leaving. If he had been any other friend, she might have hugged him or given a kiss on the cheek, but she was afraid to do anything more than hold the door open for him.

She really had a terrible crush on Elliot. How mortifying was that? Now she had to spend an entire evening in his company, just the two of them, eating in a romantic restaurant.

How would she possibly be able to keep things in perspective and remember they were merely friends—and that was all they could ever be?

She had no idea. She simply would have to do her best.

THIS WASN'T A DATE.

Elliot stood outside Megan's hotel room door, letting those words play over and over in his mind.

Yes, they were going to dinner at an elegant restaurant. Yes, he had dressed up a little, ironing a fresh shirt, putting on his blazer and shaving away the day's stubble. Yes, he'd even used a little bit of aftershave, which was rare for him.

That didn't mean this was anything *like* a date. They were merely two friends sharing dinner in a lovely Colorado resort town.

And one of those friends happened to be wildly attracted to the other one.

He couldn't let himself think about that. He would simply have to work hard all evening not to remember how delicious her mouth tasted and how perfectly right she felt in his arms.

This was stupid. He had spent the entire day with her. What were a few more hours?

He finally knocked, put on his stiff, formal FBI face and waited. When she answered the door, all his good intentions flew right out the window. She had pulled her hair up in a loose bun and had put on a little more makeup than she usually wore. She wore a soft black dress with a colorful silky wrap over her shoulders against the spring chill and she looked gorgeous—not just pretty, but take-his-breath-away stunning.

Who the hell was he fooling here? He had it bad for her. "You look, um, lovely." Did his voice sound all strangled and tight to her, too? He could only pray it was his imagination.

"Thanks. So do you. How's your arm? You're wearing the sling again. Did you overdo today with all the driving and hauling in prints?"

"It's fine," he lied. He didn't want to tell her about the pain that ricocheted from his shoulder to his fingertips. Better to simply ignore it. He had taken ibuprofen earlier and expected it to start kicking in anytime now.

She gave him a careful look, obviously trying to gauge his sincerity. He did his best to shield his emotions, meeting her scrutiny with a polite smile. "Are you ready to go?" he asked. "We're still a little early."

"I'll be ready as soon as I take care of my dog. Come on, Cyrus. Crate up."

The pug scowled at her, his head cocked, but headed into the crate, circled a few times, then settled in.

"I didn't think about Cyrus when we were discussing dinner reservations. Will he be okay on his own while we're gone?"

"He'll be fine. Earlier, I took him for a long walk around the lodge and he's worn out. I wouldn't be surprised if he slept the entire time we're gone."

"See you, bud," he said to the dog, who opened one eye, snorted, then closed it again.

"He loves you," she commented.

"Is that what you call that? How can you tell, from a single snort?"

"Better than a growl, which is what he gives most of my dates." She cut the word off and quickly corrected herself. "Most of the men he sees me with."

Was she having a hard time remembering this wasn't a date, too?

He cleared his throat. "Shall we?"

Megan grabbed a small purse off the bureau that held the television set, then picked up a room key and led the way out into the hall.

"Look at those stars," she exclaimed when they walked outside the lodge and started toward her SUV.

"They must have a dark skies rule up here in the canyon to limit light pollution." He had noticed all the exterior illumination in the parking lot and around the lodge were downlights, intended to reduce skyglow.

"Oh, that sky is magnificent. Doesn't it make you feel small when you see those millions and millions of stars overhead?"

205

"Yes," he said gruffly.

"I love looking at the stars in Haven Point, but there's something magical about seeing the night sky from another perspective. I always dreamed of shooting the stars from every continent."

He had seen other night skies in his travels. He didn't think she would appreciate his perspective that few places compared to the beauty and majesty of their shared hometown.

"You drive," she said as they approached her vehicle. "You know where the restaurant is, plus the seat is still set for your long legs."

"Sure. Here. Let me grab your door."

"I've got it," she said. They both reached for the door at the same time and she pulled it open. He was standing too close and the door smacked his injured arm before he could move it out of the way.

He sucked in a quick breath that he quickly tried to hide with a cough. She was too observant, though.

"Oh! I'm so sorry."

"It's fine," he said, though he had a feeling his voice probably sounded about half an octave lower than normal.

"You're lying," she said flatly. "That would have hurt, even if you weren't recovering from a gunshot wound. You're in pain, aren't you? Did you take something for it?"

"It's fine," he repeated.

Megan frowned. "Tell me something. Did Charlene give all of you Bailey kids lessons on how to be stubborn or does it just come naturally?"

He had to smile as the pain began to recede. "A little of both. We learned by example from both of our parents, which also would indicate we're probably genetically predisposed to stubbornness."

"I don't doubt it." She shook her head, though he didn't miss the little smile playing around her mouth. "We don't have to go out, you know. There's always room service. Or we could order pizza."

He found both of those ideas appealing, but something told him it would be dangerous to spend too much time alone with her in one of their elegantly appointed hotel rooms.

More than likely, food would be the last thing on his mind.

"We were lucky enough to swing a last-minute reservation. We shouldn't let it go to waste."

"I suppose you're right."

Was it his imagination or did she look disappointed? He didn't let himself even entertain the possibility as he walked around the vehicle to the driver's side.

Her phone rang as he pulled out of the parking lot and turned toward town.

He could tell by the way her face lit up as she

looked at the display that the caller was someone she loved. What would it be like to see her face glow like that when he called?

"Sorry. Do you mind if I get this? It's my niece."

"Not at all."

She sent him a quick smile then answered the phone. "Hey, Cassie. How's my favorite fourth grader?"

He couldn't hear what her niece said, but he could tell by the way Megan's smile slid away that she found it concerning.

"Oh, honey. I'm sorry. But if your dad says you can't wear makeup yet, you can't wear makeup yet. He's your father and he gets to make those kinds of rules."

She paused. "No, I don't remember how old I was when I started wearing makeup. I'm pretty sure I was older than nine and a half, though. I was at least twelve. Maybe even thirteen."

She was silent. "I know it's frustrating when all your friends are doing it, but there will be plenty of time for wearing makeup, trust me."

The conversation went on in a similar vein until they pulled up to the restaurant, when Megan sighed. "He's not a mean dad, honey. He loves you."

Elliot really didn't want to eavesdrop on her conversation with her niece but he couldn't help it, considering they were sharing a small vehicle.

"I'm afraid I can't do that," Megan finally said firmly. "If you want to talk to him, you're going to have to do that yourself. I can't intervene in this one. No. I don't think your mother would have let you wear makeup at this age, honey."

They continued for a few more moments, before Megan finally ended the conversation. "I have to go, Cass. I'm sorry I can't be more help, but you'll be old enough for makeup and boys and all kinds of things, before you know it."

She hung up her phone and returned it to her purse. "Sorry about that. She never met a dead horse she didn't want to beat."

"How old is Cassie now?"

"She's nine and would like to be twenty-five. Usually she's the sweetest girl, but she can sometimes be feisty about certain things."

"Growing up without a mother must be hard."

He said the words casually but she still sent him a swift, censorious look. "And hard on Luke, having to raise two kids by himself with the cloud of suspicion hanging over him for years."

"Sure. That, too."

He shouldn't have brought up Elizabeth. The reference to her forced a shift in the mood, as if clouds had drifted past that spectacular night sky.

"It can be terribly painful for a girl," she finally answered. "Not having a mother, I mean. I still miss my mom every single day, and she's been gone twenty years."

His heart ached at the hollow note in her voice. He should have remembered that Megan *also* had spent her adolescent years without a mother.

"I'm sorry," he murmured, feeling like an ass.

She shrugged. "I had my grandmother. She helped make life . . . bearable after Mom died. And I try to do the same thing for Bridger and Cassie."

"Sounds like Luke is a strict father."

She sent him a slit-eyed look. "He sets clear rules and enforces them. In my mind, that makes him a *good* father. Cassie is not even ten years old. A lot of her friends on the softball team are a year older, and a few already wear so much makeup, they look like circus clowns."

"What would happen if she disobeyed him?"

Her expression grew unnaturally still and she said nothing for several seconds. "You mean, would she disappear one day like her mother?" Her voice was as low and lethal as a rattlesnake.

"I didn't say that."

"No, but you insinuated it. I didn't realize a simple phone call from my niece would result in an FBI interrogation."

"It's not an interrogation," he protested. "I was just curious about Luke and his parenting methods."

Her icy expression plainly conveyed her disbelief. "I'll say it again. My brother is an excellent father. Extraordinary, really, when you consider what our—" She caught her words, making him wonder what she wouldn't say. "When you consider everything he's had to do on his own. Yes, he sets rules, but not unreasonable ones, and he's not inflexible either. He loves his children and would never do anything to hurt them—especially not take their mother away from them, leaving them with so many unanswered questions, no matter how troubled she might have been."

He really shouldn't be let out in polite company. He winced, feeling like an idiot and wishing he had kept his mouth shut.

"I'm sorry. Megan. I shouldn't have brought it up. My mother always said I take after my dad in that way—the proverbial dog with a bone. I can't rest until I've chewed things to bits."

She gripped her bag more tightly and gazed out the window, not giving him an inch.

"Do you want to forget dinner and go back to the lodge?"

After a long moment, she turned back to him. Her features looked resolute—and also perhaps a little sad.

"No. I'm starving and I've heard too many good things about the place. Let's make a pact that we won't discuss Luke or Elizabeth or their children for the remainder of the evening."

Relief pulsed through him. "Deal. Any other topics we should keep off the table?"

"My gallery opening," she said, so promptly he knew it must have been at the forefront of her mind. "I'm terrified about it and my stomach clenches every time the subject comes up."

That was harder for him to concede. He found her work amazing and she had no reason to be nervous about even discussing it. He could respect her wishes, though.

"Got it. Anything else?" he asked as he pulled into the valet parking.

"That covers things on my end. What about you?"

He considered his options. "If it's all the same to you, I would rather not talk about my job right now. Or my deadline. Or my family."

She gave a short laugh. "That doesn't leave much left on the table. The weather, maybe. And our favorite baseball team. We're quite a pair, aren't we?"

He wanted them to be, more than he dared admit to himself.

"That leaves plenty to discuss." He opened her door and helped her out, then handed the keys to the valet. "And if all else fails, I have a conversation app on my phone that might come in handy."

She stared at him. "Why would you need a conversation app?"

He hadn't meant to reveal that and now he squirmed a little, not sure how to tell her he bought the app because he was lousy at small talk. Sometimes he was so focused on the goal—usually extracting information from a source—that he didn't remember how important subtlety and finesse could be in his line of work.

"I'm afraid that to answer that question, I would have to talk about my job, which we've both agreed is off-limits."

Now she gave a full-fledged smile that lifted his heart. "In other words, you could tell me, but then you'd have to kill me."

Did she have any idea how contagious her smiles were? "Something like that," he murmured.

"This should be an interesting evening, then. I can't wait."

Chapter Thirteen

TURNED OUT, THEY didn't need an app or any other kind of conversational help. They did fine on their own.

They talked about movies they liked, their favorite ice cream flavors, places she dreamed of visiting and about some of the challenges she found in running the inn. She did ask about some of the cases he had written about, though she didn't consider that technically breaking their agreement, since she wasn't discussing his current book.

After their rocky start, the evening turned out to be thoroughly enjoyable.

At the end of the meal, Megan set down her spoon and wiped the corners of her mouth with her napkin, fighting the urge to lick clean the bowl of her fruit bedecked crème brûlée. "I'm just going to come out and say it. That was the most delicious dinner I've had in years."

"An excellent choice," he agreed. "Everything was pitch-perfect. You'll have to tell Mary Ella tomorrow how delicious we both found her daughter's restaurant."

"I will."

It had been an exhausting day, with the long journey and then their time at the art gallery and dinner, yet she found she didn't want the evening to end.

When he put his mind to it, Elliot could be every bit as charming as Wyatt had been. More, maybe, if she were honest.

Wyatt had been like a puppy, happy all the time, eager for attention and constantly in search of the next entertainment. She had so desperately needed that at the time, just months after her grandmother's death when she was reeling from the loss and from the sudden responsibility of inheriting the inn.

It had been a terribly hard time and she had felt so alone. Luke had been too busy with the contracting business he had started and with his new wife and their new baby to be much help.

She hadn't wanted to run an inn. That had never been her dream. Too much of her high school years had been spent making beds or working the front desk. Beyond that, after an internship at a Boise-area travel magazine, she had just been offered a job as assistant to a *National Geographic* photographer. All her dreams had been about to come true—and then Gran got sick and she had come home to care for her and had felt stuck.

Wyatt had suddenly tumbled into that tough, joyless world, exactly when she needed him.

He had been sweet and kind and funny, the perfect antidote to her grim circumstances. Then, just as her feelings had started to deepen, Wyatt had died on a lonely stretch of snowy highway while doing what he loved best: helping other people.

Elliot was very different from his brother. More serious and introspective, less impulsive and rash, yet still inherently kind.

If she was not very careful, Megan was afraid she would find it entirely too easy to lose her heart to him.

No. She couldn't let that happen. All she could see ahead on that path was heartbreak and pain.

Besides. She had her future mapped out and it didn't include a sexy FBI agent.

She had put her dreams on hold for her entire adult life, first to care for her grandmother, then to help Luke with the children. In a few years, Luke wouldn't need her help with Bridger and Cassie nearly as much as he did now. Soon Cassie would be able to keep an eye on Bridger when Luke was on a job site and would be able to take on more responsibility.

Megan had it all figured out. When that day happened, she would find someone competent to run the hotel and would take her camera to all those places she and Elliot had talked about. Iceland. Paris. Japan.

Falling in love with *any* man was not in that master plan at all. Falling in love with Elliot would be a disaster on so many levels.

"What's wrong?"

She shifted her mind away from her grim thoughts to find him watching her closely. He was a man who saw entirely too much, an FBI agent trained to sift through expressions and body language to the truth, no matter how carefully she tried to conceal it.

"Nothing." She forced a smile. "I was only thinking it has already been a long day and we're in for another one tomorrow."

"I suppose you're right. We should head back to the lodge."

"Right. Cyrus is waiting, too."

It was rather terrifying, how badly she didn't want the evening to end.

To Megan's surprise, a few moments after Elliot requested the bill, the chef herself came out to their table.

Mary Ella's daughter Alex Delgado was younger than Megan might have guessed, around the same age as Elliot. She was pretty and blonde, with a winsome smile and Mary Ella's same green eyes.

"Thank you for the wonderful meal," Megan said as the chef approached. "I don't know when I've had anything better."

"You're very welcome." Alex accepted the praise with a warm smile. "I'm glad I had the chance to meet you before your gallery opening. My mom has been raving about your work for months. Between you and me, she's acting as if she's discovered a new planet."

That wild burst of panic churned through her again but Elliot placed a calming hand on her arm, as if sensing some of her emotional tumult and understanding she needed reassurance. The gesture, so perfectly timed, sent a soft, seductive warmth to push away the panic.

"Thank you," she murmured, not knowing whether she was speaking to Alex or Elliot.

"You're very welcome," the chef said with a smile. "And I wanted to tell you, your bill has already been paid."

She frowned in confusion. "By whom? Your mother?"

Alex shook her head. "My cantankerous step-father beat her to it. Apparently he's a big fan of both of yours. He insisted we put your dinner on his tab, and when Harry Lange wants something around Hope's Crossing, few people argue with him."

"That's very generous of him," she said. "I don't know what to say."

"You don't need to say anything," Alex said with her mother's same warm smile. "You've made my mother very happy, agreeing to have your first gallery opening here—and what makes my mother happy makes Harry happy."

"Thank you."

"It was an extraordinary meal," Elliot said.

"Truly memorable. I'll be dreaming about those scallops for a long time."

She grinned at him. "Come back anytime."

She talked to them for a few more moments, then excused herself when diners at another table called her over to gush about their meal.

After the chef left, Megan sat in stupefied silence for several seconds, then shook her head. "I have no idea what that was all about, but I suppose I have nothing left but to be grateful."

"My dad used to say, the only thing better than a delicious meal is a delicious meal where somebody else picks up the check."

The memory of John Bailey made her smile. "You must miss your father very much."

To her surprise, his expression darkened slightly. "Let's just say, I miss the father I remember, the one from about four years before he died."

She did a quick mental calculation that made her frown. "I don't understand. He only lingered in that nursing home for three years after he was shot."

She had visited him often and had found a strange peace in spending time with him, listening to music together, talking to him about problems she was having rebuilding the inn.

The brain injury he suffered in that shoot-out with an armed robber had left him unable to care for himself, without even the most basic of skills.

He could no longer talk but she hadn't minded. Even without conversation, John had exuded an air of calm and peace that had comforted her. She wanted to think she had provided a little comfort to him as well.

She had adored John Bailey, had once wanted so badly for him to be her father-in-law. He had been kind and loving and wise, one of the most decent men she had ever known.

She didn't need a therapist to tell her she had been seeking a substitute father figure in her world. She had sometimes wondered if the chance to truly belong to the boisterous, loving Bailey clan had been at least half of Wyatt's appeal to her.

The thought wasn't a new one but it still felt somewhat disloyal—though certainly less disloyal than the idea that she might be falling for Wyatt's brother.

"It's a long story," Elliot said now in answer to her, "and probably one of those topics I should have thrown in the old off-limits bucket."

"Your father is an off-limits topic?"

He looked torn for a moment before composing his features again into that serious, almost stern expression. "For now. I'll tell you at some point, but I would rather not ruin the evening talking about sad things."

Though she was still curious, she nodded her understanding. John Bailey's injury had been heartbreaking for everyone in Haven Point.

"We don't have to leave, if you'd like coffee or something."

"I'm fine. It's been a long day and I imagine you're anxious to get back to Cyrus."

"I suppose you're right."

He helped her into her wrap. Then they walked outside into the lovely mountain air to retrieve her vehicle from the valet.

Like Haven Point, Hope's Crossing was a mountain community at a high elevation, which meant the evenings turned crisp and cool the moment the sun went down. The lodge was even higher in the mountains, and she was wishing for more than her light wrap by the time they made it inside the building.

When she opened her door, Cyrus gave his little snort in greeting.

"I know, baby. I missed you, too," she said. She immediately went to the crate to let him out and he did little happy spins while she petted him and smiled.

"I get the feeling you two like each other," Elliot said with a smile.

"A bit," she admitted. "Do you need to go out, buddy?"

The dog padded to the door and stood there expectantly.

"Need me to do that for you?" Elliot asked. "I don't mind taking a walk to stretch after that meal."

"Let me grab a warmer coat and we can all go."

She put on the only other coat she'd brought along, a suede, lined jacket she loved, then found Cyrus's leash and hooked it onto his collar.

"This shouldn't take long," she said to Elliot. "I don't mind. I like to walk."

Something else they had in common. Though she suddenly wasn't entirely sure it would be wise to spend more time with him given her growing feelings—especially in the romantic moonlight—she didn't know how to get out of it. She certainly couldn't say, *Hey, Elliot, why don't you stay here? I'm afraid I'll get carried away and do something stupid.*

She could handle this, she told herself.

Cyrus toddled ahead of them, in an obvious hurry to get outside now. The moment they hit the cold night air, he hurried to a convenient bush and peed for what seemed like hours.

"When a guy has to go, I guess he has to go," Elliot drawled.

She had to laugh. "We're lucky he made it this long. I have a puppy pad in the room but he likes old-fashioned grass."

The evening was lovely, that peculiar soft night that could only be found in the mountains, when the air was crisp and clean and stars glittered in a vast blanket overhead.

"Dinner is over. Does that mean we can now

talk about all the off-limits things we tabled earlier?" she asked.

"Are you in such a hurry to bring the rest of the world in and destroy the beauty of this evening?"

He had a point. Here, she could pretend the two of them were alone, that all the conflicts and stumbling blocks between them didn't exist. For tonight, Elliot could simply be a handsome, somewhat too-serious man whose smile made her toes tingle—instead of the FBI agent who had the potential to ruin her brother's world.

They wandered along a pathway through the resort lined with evenly spaced waist-high downlights that illuminated their way but didn't add light pollution to the sky.

"It's so beautiful here," she said.

"Could you see yourself living here?"

She considered. "I don't know. Maybe."

"If your life had taken a different course over the last decade, where do you think you would be right now?"

"Not in Haven Point. That was never in the plan. I wanted to be living abroad somewhere, or at least stationed in a bigger city I could use as a launch point to other destinations. I wanted to be a *National Geographic* photographer and explore the world. Instead, I'm an innkeeper in a small Idaho town."

"I can see you now, the intrepid traveler with nothing but the clothes on her back and a bag full of camera bodies and lenses."

She loved that romantic image. She always had, though sometimes she wondered if she loved the idea of being free of her commitments, able to come and go as she pleased, more than she did the actual dream of being a photographer.

"And Cyrus. Don't forget Cyrus."

He smiled. "If you had a ticket anywhere in the world, where's the first place you would like to go with your camera?"

"How do I pick just one?"

"Okay. Top three. In no particular order."

He seemed genuinely interested, there on the dark down-lit path. How long had it been since someone had asked her about her dreams?

"I've always wanted to go to Africa. Maybe just spend a few months in the veldt, living in a hut somewhere and photographing everything I see, from daybreak to sunset. Village life, exotic animals, the stunning scenery. Everything."

He nodded. "Where would be the second place?"

She laughed a little wildly. "There are too many options!"

"I told you, they don't have to be in any particular order. Surely you have a bucket list."

She considered before answering. "I suppose I

would have to say Iceland, for the landscape. It's stark and raw and beautiful, the kind of place I think I could shoot in every season."

"And finally?"

"Probably some remote island in the South Pacific, simply for the contrast. I've never been scuba diving, but I would want to start so I could shoot the variety of sea life in the coral reef."

"I hope you get the chance to shoot all of that."

Again, the sincerity in his voice warmed her. She never would have imagined Elliot could be so supportive of her dreams. "Thank you," she murmured, more drawn to him than she dared admit. What could possibly be more attractive to a woman than a strong man who believed in her?

Their meanderings led them around the lodge to a viewpoint where they could look out and see the town of Hope's Crossing, glittering below the mouth of the canyon. Above them, the Milky Way spread out, a vast stunning glitter of sky.

"It's so beautiful here."

"Too bad you don't have your gear out now."

"I do love night photography. If you have a friend with a high-powered flashlight, you can have him paint an object with the beam of the light and shoot a long exposure. Oh, I guess you saw a few of those in the photographs we took to the gallery today. The one of the old barn north of the lake and also the one of the Lights on the Lake boat parade last Christmas."

"I loved both of those. I wish I'd had time to really study all your work. Maybe I'll drive down from Denver after the opening to spend an afternoon at the gallery."

She gazed at him, stunned by his words as a soft, seductive warmth unfurled in her chest. "You would really do that?"

"Why do you sound so surprised? We're friends, aren't we? That's the sort of thing friends do for each other. Or at least that's what my robot training manual tells me."

She winced. "I'm sorry we've teased you about that. I don't think you're a robot."

Silence stretched between them, taut and heavy and brimming with things unsaid. She was fiercely aware of him, the heat and strength and power of him.

"Meg," he began, his voice strained.

He felt it, too, this connection between them. Her gaze met his and the awareness in his eyes stunned her.

He wanted to kiss her again. She wasn't sure how she knew so completely, but she had no question.

She had two options, as she saw it. She could turn away from him and return to the hotel to spend a restless night alone in her room, tossing and turning. Or she could give them what they both wanted.

It wasn't really a choice at all. The impulse was simply too great to ignore. She had to taste him one more time, before this surreal interlude ended.

Chapter Fourteen

WITHOUT TAKING TIME to think it through further, she crossed the short distance between them, wrapped her arms around his neck and pressed her mouth to his.

He didn't move for a moment, his mouth warm against hers and tasting of chocolate and wine from dinner. Anticipation swirled around them, as if the night and the stars and the wind were all watching and waiting to see what they would do. After a long moment, he pulled her to him tightly and kissed her with a ferocity that stole her breath.

Oh, yes. He wanted to kiss her. That was more than clear now.

How was it possible that he could manage to restrain all this passion and heat in most of his life, could hide it away and appear restrained and formal to the rest of the world? She liked thinking few other people in the world ever had the chance to see this side of him. It was a delicious secret she wanted to tuck away against her heart, that Elliot Bailey was a sensuous, passionate creature beneath his stiff layers.

She pressed her curves against him, loving his hard strength and the feel of his hands on her back, in her hair, against her cheek.

She wanted him. All of him.

Why not take him back to her room, where they could be warm and comfortable, where she could explore all those muscles and see if they could lose control together?

A tiny voice of reason told her that would be a really lousy idea, would complicate what was already an intensely tangled situation.

She told that voice to shut the hell up and tightened her arms around his neck.

Once she had watched a documentary about a cenote in Mexico that looked from above like an ordinary small, calm body of water. Dive deep enough, however, and you could find a wild underground river, complete with rapids and waterfalls and hidden currents.

Elliot was like that, with all this *life* seething below the surface. She wanted to dive as deeply as she could into him to discover everything he kept from the rest of the world.

She wasn't sure how long they kissed before she felt a tug against her hand and realized it was Cyrus moving around on his leash, ready to go back.

Reality wormed its way through her subconscious and that warning voice grew louder.

As much as she wanted this kiss to go on and on—and possibly lead to more—she knew it would be far too dangerous.

Every moment she spent with Elliot, in his

arms, a few more of those barriers around her heart weakened and he wriggled his way closer. She couldn't afford to let him inside.

Falling in love with anyone wasn't in her future. She had already decided it. Falling in love with Elliot would be disastrous. She couldn't let a few magical kisses sneak beneath her defenses and lead her into doing something foolish beyond belief.

She stepped away, already colder outside the circle of his arms.

It took her several beats to grab her tangled thoughts enough to form a coherent sentence.

"So apparently the two of us don't have much self-control on moonlit nights."

His mouth quirked up into that rare almost-smile she found entirely too appealing. "Can you blame us, really? A star-filled sky, a lovely May evening and an even more beautiful woman beside me. Even a robot would find you impossible to resist."

How could she ever have thought him a robot? He had a deep morass of emotions lurking beneath the surface. He had simply become an expert at holding them all at bay.

"What are we doing here, Elliot?"

He raised an eyebrow. "I hate to state the obvious, but if you don't know, I must be doing something wrong."

"You know what I mean. This thing between

us . . . It's crazy. Completely impossible. Every time we kiss, I tell myself it's got to be the last time. Then it happens all over again. I can't think straight when you kiss me. I'm beginning to think you're my Kryptonite."

"Kryptonite."

She couldn't read his expression in the moonlight but it didn't matter. She didn't need to. He was probably thinking she sounded ridiculous. Which she did.

"You just have this sexy, brooding, dangerous injured-warrior thing going. I can't seem to resist it."

He gazed down at his arm. "Who would have guessed a bullet and a shoulder sling could work so well?"

He didn't need a sling and he knew it. He only needed those intense blue eyes that made a woman want to tell him all her secrets.

"You can add it to your arsenal of FBI interrogation tactics. I tell you things I have no intention of revealing."

"I'll keep that in mind. I'll make sure I'm wearing the sling when I talk to the trucker tomorrow about Elizabeth."

He had to bring that up again, to insert the world back into this moment. She shivered and wrapped her jacket more snugly around her. "You could always forget the interview tomorrow."

She didn't know why she said it. The words

slipped out, maybe in part because she resented being reminded of everything between them.

His sharp intake was audible, his eyes like polished chips of agate in the moonlight. "Why would I do that?"

Oh, her big mouth. That was exactly what she meant when she said she couldn't think straight when he kissed her. He scrambled her brains and she ended up blurting out stupid things she didn't mean.

"Nothing. Never mind."

"No. Why would you say that? Why would I forget the interview tomorrow, when I've come all this way?"

She gripped Cyrus's leash harder. "I don't know. It's just . . . some part of me wishes you would . . . drop the investigation into Elizabeth's disappearance. That you could accept that she left on her own and that Luke had nothing to do with it."

The moment she said the words, she regretted them. His features turned stony and he eased away from her farther. The night suddenly felt frigid, as if an icy wind had just blown out of the mountains and trailed bony claws down her spine.

"Is that why you kissed me? Were you hoping to distract me from digging further into the case?"

Her face flushed. "That's ridiculous."

"Is it?"

How was it possible for the soft, sweet tenderness between them to so quickly chill to this cold anger? "I kissed you because I wanted to kiss you. Obviously, it was a mistake for both of us."

Did he really suspect her of trying to distract him away from the investigation like some . . . femme fatale? Trade her emotions, her *body,* to protect her brother? Hurt warred with the anger and she felt a ridiculous lump of emotion lodge in her throat.

"Come on, Cyrus." Before she could do something monumentally stupid, like burst into tears in front of him, she gripped her dog's leash and turned toward the lodge with her little pug trotting close behind.

After a moment, she heard him sigh and follow her.

"I'm sorry," he said when he caught up. "I shouldn't have said that."

"Why not? You're obviously thinking it. Why hold back? Might as well get the truth out there. Yes, Elliot. The only possible reason I could ever want to kiss you would be to persuade you to drop the investigation and leave my brother alone. Is that what you wanted to hear?"

HE WAS AN ASS. No question.

Elliot walked with Megan in silence. The easy camaraderie they had shared earlier had

233

disappeared on the breeze, replaced by this tight, awkward tension. When would he ever learn to keep his mouth shut?

Is that why you kissed me? Were you hoping to distract me from digging further into the case?

His own words felt ugly and small. He didn't even know why he had said them. He didn't believe that. She had kissed him because she wanted to, as she said. The same reason he'd kissed her earlier in the day.

It was a stupid thing to say and he wasn't even sure why he had. Was he trying to sabotage this attraction between them before it had a chance to bloom into something real?

Not that anything could come of this. She had made it clear she wasn't interested in more than a few kisses. Maybe that was why he overreacted, because he wanted so much more and had the sudden grim realization that it was impossible.

Even her dog seemed to pick up on the seething tension between them. As they walked toward the hotel, Cyrus started dragging his feet, dawdling enough that Megan finally picked him up about a hundred yards from the hotel entrance and carried him the rest of the way.

How could he restore the easy peace between them? He had no idea.

"I was able to rent a car for tomorrow," he said when they reached the corridor outside their rooms. "I'll use that in the morning. I expect to be done by noon and can return the car here at the lodge. Then we can head back to Haven Point whenever you're ready. Does that work for your plans?"

"That's fine." Her voice was clipped, tight. "I don't expect to be done at the gallery before that."

"If I'm going to be later than noon, I'll let you know."

He was almost tempted to suggest he could drive the rental all the way back to Haven Point, if she preferred not to spend any more time with him. Some part of him was afraid she might take him up on the offer.

When they reached her door, she had her key card out already, as if she couldn't bear to spend a moment longer than necessary in his company.

He couldn't leave matters like this between them, marred by this heavy, aching awkwardness. How could he scale the wall his suspicious words had erected between them?

She unlocked her door and pushed it open, then set Cyrus down. The dog went immediately to the water bowl. With the dog settled, she turned back to him. "Good night," she said stiffly.

Elliot sighed. "Megan. Forgive me. Please. I shouldn't have said what I did. I don't think that."

"You must believe it on some level, or you wouldn't have said it."

Perhaps it was easier to let her go on thinking that. The alternative was to bare his heart. After a lifetime of hiding any deep emotions, that course of action filled him with something that felt suspiciously like panic.

"I'm . . . not good at this. I suppose that's obvious."

"At what?"

"Relationships. At least the . . . messy kind."

Instead of smoothing things over, he was making things worse. He could see it in the way she folded her arms across her chest and lifted her chin. "I'm sorry you find things between us messy. I'll remind you that you kissed me first last night, Agent Bailey."

Had it only been last night? He could hardly credit that. It seemed a lifetime ago that he'd first tasted her. "You're right. I kissed you first and I insisted on coming with you to Colorado."

He didn't know what was happening here. This thick knot of . . . angst in his chest was completely foreign territory. He didn't know how to explain it to himself, forget about explaining anything to *her*.

"You have to understand. I have spent my entire adult life working hard to keep every relationship casual and uncomplicated. I haven't wanted anything to get in the way of my career."

He had been the oldest son in a large family, and had taken that responsibility seriously.

Set the right example for your brothers and sisters, Elliot.

We need to be able to count on you.

What would we do without your common sense, son?

His parents had been loving and kind but had buried him under the weight of their expectations.

He had tried. He had studied hard, had graduated top of his class in criminal justice and been recruited into the FBI. From there, he had set out to be the best agent he knew how to be.

The structure had felt comfortable to him. He had always been working for the next commendation, the next promotion. Expectations piled upon expectations.

When he dated, he chose women who didn't threaten that focus, who were happy with infrequent, casual encounters.

He thought that was enough, but lately—maybe when he had found himself facing a flurry of bullets a few weeks earlier—he had realized that in all that hard work and concentration, he hadn't left much room for *life*.

"This . . . thing . . . with you is anything but uncomplicated. Or casual, for that matter."

He drew in a breath, wondering if he were making another mistake, if he should keep his mouth shut and let things remain awkward and cool between them. It might be easier that way, in the long run.

He couldn't. He missed the warm rapport of earlier in the day. He wanted it back.

Sometimes life had to be messy and uncomfortable and *honest*. Sometimes a man had to embrace the chaos. He had accepted that, too, a few weeks earlier when he had disobeyed orders for the first time in his career.

"I am beginning to have feelings for you," he finally blurted out. "Feelings I don't quite know what to do about."

She lifted her gaze to him, shock and something else, something he couldn't read, in her eyes. "You . . . what?"

He sighed. "Actually, that's a lie. I'm sorry."

Confusion warred with the shock in her eyes. "What's a lie? That you have feelings for me? Or that you don't know what to do with them?"

He would have to tell her all of it, no matter how embarrassing. Somehow it didn't seem honest to keep from her this secret that had weighed on him for years.

"I, um, lied when I said I was beginning to have feelings for you." He cleared his throat and avoided her gaze, focusing on her cranky-looking dog instead. "There is no *beginning* about it. My, um, feelings are not necessarily new."

The mistrust in her eyes transformed into something else, astonishment and disbelief and no small measure of arrested fascination.

"They're . . . not?"

Why had he gone there? So what, if he kept

secrets? This was one he should never have revealed to her, of all people.

He wanted to escape the hotel room but knew he would still have to face her the next day. Hell. He had come this far. Why not blunder through the rest?

"You might as well know the truth. The entire time you were with Wyatt, I was crazy with jealousy. I tried to be happy for my brother that the two of you had found each other, but the whole time, I felt like I was burning up inside. Why do you think I didn't come home much during that time?"

She lowered to the edge of the bed, staring at him as if he had suddenly sprouted wings. "You were always so cool and stuffy to me," she whispered. "I figured you couldn't stand me, that you thought Wyatt deserved better."

"No. I'm sorry you thought that. I was doing my best to keep my . . . attraction to myself."

She still looked at him doubtfully. "Wyatt has been gone for a long time. All these years, you've never given any sign of this attraction you claim to have."

"When would you have suggested I do something about it? Six months after Wyatt died, Elizabeth disappeared and you were tangled up in that. Then my father was shot and that didn't seem the time either."

"Then my inn burned down."

"Right. And you were up to your elbows trying to rebuild. Given everything that's happened, I just figured things weren't meant to be between us. Fate was making that pretty clear."

"You don't strike me as a man who puts much stock in fate or kismet or anything else woo-woo like that."

"Maybe not. Maybe it was simply a coincidence when the inn's rental cabins were the first things to come up on the search engine when I was looking for a place to stay for a few weeks. I knew I would likely run into you while I was here trying to finish my book. I just never imagined I would find you living next door."

"I . . . don't know what to say."

He shifted closer to the door. Yeah, he shouldn't have opened his mouth. He had been hoping to ease the awkwardness between them but had only introduced far more. Sometimes honesty *wasn't* the best policy, though his mother would probably disagree with him.

"You don't have to say anything. In fact, it would probably be better if you didn't. I don't even know why I told you, other than to explain that I'm not always in my right head when it comes to you. Why don't we both pretend this conversation never happened?"

She snorted. "You might be able to do that, but my imagination isn't nearly that advanced."

Unexpectedly, he felt some of the tension ease

and he even managed a smile. "Don't sell yourself short. I've seen your portfolio, remember? It takes a keen eye and a creative brain to capture the world as you do."

She was quiet for a long moment, still sitting on her bed. She looked tired and vulnerable and beautiful.

"For the record," she finally said, not looking at him, "you're not the only one who might have . . . an attraction here. You're a hard man to ignore, Elliot."

A low heat uncurled inside him. "What do you suggest we do about it?"

"Not find ourselves in the moonlight again, to start."

"Check."

She smoothed down her skirt and swallowed. "I'm . . . attracted to you. I can't deny that, Elliot. But anything between us is . . . completely impossible. You see that, don't you?"

What was he supposed to say to that? Before he could come up with an answer, she went on.

"I mean, look at us. We couldn't be more different. You're all about focus, control, while I'm an artist, impulsive and scatterbrained. I don't think three moves ahead like you do."

He had his impulsive moments. Kissing her, for instance. And blurting out his feelings for her.

"Neither of us is in a good place for a relationship right now," she went on. "I know I'm not, anyway. After years of putting my dreams on hold to take care of my grandmother and Cassie and Bridger, I finally have the chance to see my dreams of being an art photographer come true. I don't have much room in my life for the . . . messy."

She was right. A relationship between them made absolutely no sense on paper.

That didn't make him want her less.

"Okay." He forced the words out. "We're agreed. We might be attracted to each other but that's as far as we will let things go. We'll lay off romantic dinners and walks in the moonlight from here on out."

An oddly wistful look crossed her features, and then she nodded. "Probably for the best."

She paused. "I do have room in my life for a friend. I would like to think we still have that."

He could count on one hand the people he trusted enough to consider good friends. Somehow over the last week or so, Megan had slipped into that number.

"Of course," he answered.

She looked tired, he thought again. A true friend would be cognizant of everything she had at stake right now in her life. They had another big day starting in the morning and she would need sleep to give her the strength to deal with it all.

"Get some rest. I likely won't see you in the

morning as I'm heading out early, but I'll be in touch with you at the gallery."

"Sounds good."

He stood somewhat awkwardly in the doorway, then thought friends would probably have no problem with a small kiss good-night either. He moved toward her and kissed her softly, imprinting the taste of her on his memory.

"Good luck at the gallery tomorrow. I'll see you around midday."

"Sounds good. Night."

"Good night."

He drew his hands into fists to keep from reaching for her and forced himself out of the room.

As soon as he unlocked his door and was in his own room, Elliot tossed his key card on the desk and stalked to the balcony, desperate for the cool mountain air on skin that felt hot and itchy.

What the hell was he thinking, to tell her all that? What was *wrong* with him? He wasn't the kind of guy to talk about his feelings. She was bringing out sides of him he didn't know how to handle.

He scrubbed his face. His whole world felt like it was in shambles right now. His job, his personal life, even the writing. His book should have been wrapped up days ago but he kept struggling with the ending.

For the record, you aren't the only one who might have . . . an attraction here.

Her words echoed around inside his head. What did she mean? She hadn't elaborated, obviously eager to end the conversation before things could get even more awkward.

Now that he had kissed her and discovered the magic of holding her in his arms, he didn't know how he could shove all that away.

He would simply have to try.

She had asked if they could continue with their friendship. If that was all he could have of her, he would do his best to forget that her mouth tasted of sugar and cinnamon and about the sexy little breathless noises she made when he kissed her.

And while he was reaching for the impossible, he might as well grab that moon out there and deliver it to her on a room service cart.

Chapter Fifteen

THE NEXT MORNING Megan cringed as she caught her reflection in the rearview mirror while she backed out of her parking spot at the lodge.

If she ever wondered what people meant when they described someone looking like death warmed over, she only had to remember this moment.

Beneath her sunglasses, she had deep hollows under her eyes and pinched lines of fatigue bracketing her mouth. Her skin looked sallow and even her hair seemed to have lost its usual shine.

This was what a long drive followed by a sleepless night could do for a woman.

Blast that Elliot Bailey anyway.

What was he thinking, to drop a bombshell like that on her after she had already had an exhausting day? And then to casually walk away as if what he said meant nothing? Did he really think she would be able to sleep a wink, with his words playing in her ears over and over again?

I'm beginning to have feelings for you . . . No, there is no beginning about it. My feelings are not necessarily new . . . The entire time you were with Wyatt, I was crazy with jealousy.

She still didn't know whether to believe him. It seemed utterly impossible.

Could he really have been trying to hide his growing feelings for her during those months she dated Wyatt? He had given no hint of it. Quite the opposite, actually, as she had told him. The few times circumstances had put them all together, Elliot seemed to have gone out of his way to avoid talking to her.

She had always thought he considered her beneath his attention. The silly friend of his younger sisters who had started dating Wyatt.

Would he ever have told her, if they hadn't traveled together here to Colorado? Or would he simply have let her move on with her life while he did the same?

As she drove the winding canyon road toward the gallery—with steep mountains on one side and a beautiful reservoir on the other—some part of her couldn't help wishing he had never told her.

While her heart might embrace the possibilities, her head told a completely different story.

So what, if he was attracted to her? Or if she had begun to feel the same way, for that matter? Both of them knew nothing could come of it.

How could it? He believed her brother capable of killing his wife. By default, that also meant she was naive or worse for believing in Luke's innocence.

She couldn't help wondering if it would have been better if she'd never found out everything that lurked beneath the surface. Ignorance was bliss, right? At least she might have been able to squeeze out a few hours of sleep the night before instead of wondering about the man who was only a connecting door away.

The morning was cool but warming as the sun came up. Puffy white clouds floated past, tangling in the mountaintops around Hope's Crossing.

Few people were out and about on Main Street as she approached the door of the still-closed gallery, though she could see a steady stream of people going in and out of the bookstore/coffeehouse down the street. Nearby, a café called The Center of Hope looked to be doing a bustling business.

Megan knocked softly on the door of the still-closed gallery and only had to wait a few seconds before Mary Ella answered.

"Good morning!" the other woman exclaimed. "Oh, it's a glorious one, isn't it?"

"Yes. Beautiful." She walked into the gallery, wondering if Mary Ella would think she was hung over if she kept on her sunglasses.

The thought instantly escaped her mind when she spotted a man in his early seventies, handsome and stately, with a shock of silver hair.

She had the impression of power somehow, that

indefinable sense of command some men carried. Before Mary Ella even spoke, Megan guessed his identity.

"Megan, I would love you to meet my husband, Harry Lange," the gallery owner said with a smile that clearly conveyed a deep love for her husband. "I talked him into coming in today to help us."

Help them? Weren't they simply deciding where the photos would hang?

And why on earth would the woman ask her powerful billionaire husband to help them?

Before agreeing to the showing at the woman's gallery, she had done her research and knew that Harry Lange was one of the wealthiest men in Colorado. He owned a ski resort, for crying out loud, and many other real-estate holdings around the state.

"Harry, this is Megan Hamilton."

The man strode to her and held a large hand out. "It's a pleasure." His voice was brisk and firm, a man not used to having to explain himself.

While Megan adored Mary Ella already, she decided to reserve judgment about whether she liked the woman's husband.

"Thank you in advance, then," she said. "And thank you very much for dinner last night. I understand you covered our meal."

He waved off her thanks. "It was my pleasure. I'm only disappointed you didn't bring Elliot

Bailey with you today. There's a man I'm sure is fascinating at dinner parties."

She didn't know quite how to answer that. Elliot *was* a fascinating conversationalist, when he chose. He could also be remote and self-isolating.

"I'm sorry he won't be joining us, either," she lied. "I'm afraid he had other business to attend to this morning."

Clearing her brother's name. At least she could cling to that hope.

Harry shrugged. "It's all right. In truth, I wanted to come to the gallery this morning specifically to meet you."

"Harry." The gallery owner's tone was disapproving.

Apparently her brain wasn't firing on all cylinders this morning. She could blame Elliot for that, too.

"To meet . . . me? Why?"

Mary Ella glared at her husband. "I told him not to bother you. I told him specifically. We have work to do, and if he intends to distract you, he should stay home. Those were my exact words. Obviously, my husband usually does whatever he wants to do."

Despite the gallery owner's glare, Megan could see deep affection between the two of them. It made her chest feel achy and tight.

Harry Lange looked suitably chastened, though

she couldn't help thinking it was a show, mostly to please his wife.

"You're right, my dear. I apologize." He inclined his head to Megan. "Your work is lovely. As usual, my wife's taste is impeccable."

"I . . . Thank you." She had no idea what else to say. What a curious man. He obviously had an agenda, some reason for coming to meet her, but she didn't have the first idea what it might be.

"Where should we start?" he asked Mary Ella.

She sniffed, appearing not at all fooled by his contrite act. "You can start by grabbing some coffee for Megan while she and I discuss our plan of attack. After that, I might let you help us hang a few pictures, if you behave yourself."

"Certainly, treasure of my heart. Whatever you need." After asking Megan how she liked her coffee, he headed for the workroom of the gallery, and Mary Ella gave her an apologetic look.

"I'm sorry. He's mostly harmless, though he does tend to stick his nose into things that aren't his concern. We shall just ignore him. How was your evening? You had dinner at Brazen. I hope my daughter treated you well."

"It was an unforgettable night," she said, aware Mary Ella could have no idea the scope of that particular understatement.

They chatted about the meal and about her impressions of the town until Harry came back with coffees for all of them, then went to work discussing the placement of the photographic prints for maximum impact.

After a few hours of work, they were about half-way done hanging them all. Some of Megan's anxiety over the coming show had begun to give way to a certain pride at what she had created.

Mary Ella left to take a phone call in the back room from a potential buyer of a sculpture she had on display in one of the other exhibits. As soon as she was out of earshot, Harry, who had been telling her some of the history of Hope's Crossing, quickly turned the subject.

"I understand you own the Inn at Haven Point. Tell me about it."

Though his words were casual, she sensed more than simply a passing interest, judging by the sudden intensity of his expression and his tone.

"It's a lovely place, set on the shore of Lake Haven. We had a fire a few years ago but have completely rebuilt it and now have twenty well-appointed en suite rooms."

"So more of a boutique hotel than a traditional B and B inn."

"Semantics. It's always been called the Inn at Haven Point and we've stuck with the name."

"I understand you have a beach?"

"Yes. Silver Beach. Back in the Victorian era, when the lake and the abundant mineral springs were a big tourist draw, an ancestor of mine brought in several tons of sand. It's still there. In fact, I have five rental cottages along the beach that are filled all but a few weeks out of the year."

She didn't add that she currently lived in one or that the mystifying enigma who was Elliot Bailey lived in another one.

"What is your occupancy rate for the inn itself?"

"We're about ninety percent. Summers are almost always full, booked out weeks in advance. Winters are busy as well, with all the skiing and snowmobiling in the area. Spring and fall used to be our slow seasons, but now that Caine Tech has an active facility nearby, we are often full during those periods, too."

Harry asked a few more questions about the inn overhead and her employee turnover rate.

"I can't imagine you find all this interesting," she finally said.

"It is to me." He paused. "I don't see any reason to pull my punches. No doubt you've figured this out by now. I would like to buy your inn."

She stared, certain she heard him wrong. "Excuse me?"

"I guess I ought to ask you first if you're interested in selling, should the right buyer come along."

The inn had been in her mother's family for five generations. Though running it had never been her dream, she had handled the day-to-day operations since she was twenty-one, when her grandmother was first diagnosed with cancer.

Sell it. She could barely process the idea.

"I . . . haven't given it any thought."

"You should. Think about it, that is. From all my research, it's clear Haven Point has all the hallmarks of an emerging destination, especially since Caine Tech has located a new facility there. You've got abundant natural recreation with the lake and the mountains—and now a vibrant tech company for a neighbor. All those things bode well for those of us in the hospitality industry, wouldn't you say?"

Megan couldn't seem to gather the tangled threads of her brain together enough to answer him. Somehow she managed to nod. Or at least she thought she did, what with her face frozen and all.

"It's a hot location, and by happy coincidence, I'm looking for a new challenge," he said quickly, then turned away with an air of feigned innocence, just as Mary Ella walked back into the room.

The other woman wasn't fooled. She put her hands on her hips and glared at him. "You did it, though I expressly told you not to. You told her you want to buy her inn."

"We're only having a conversation," Harry said, looking unrepentant. "Haven Point would be an excellent fit for Lange Properties. Through

253

extensive research, I've decided it would make more sense for me to buy an existing operation, rather than try to compete with something that's already doing it right."

Doing it right? Most of the time, she felt as if she was barely keeping her head above water.

"You've got a nice operation there. I had a couple of representatives check it out for me on the sly and everything they've told me confirms what I suspected, that this would be an excellent investment for my company."

He had sent people to stay at her inn to spy on her operations? She didn't know whether to be flattered or insulted.

"I've shocked you, haven't I?"

Somehow Megan managed a raw-sounding laugh. "You could say that. I came here expecting to hang some photographic prints, not to field an offer to buy my family's inn."

"Is your heart in it? Running the hotel, I mean?"

Was it? She didn't know how to answer that. Before the fire, she had hired Eliza Caine to run the inn for her. That was going to be her chance to gain a little freedom, to perhaps travel a little or spend more time with Bridger and Cassie. Then when the inn burned almost to the ground, everything had changed.

She had swallowed her resentments for years, shoving them down with hard work and effort and the energy she had thrown into rebuilding the inn that provided employment to two dozen people who needed it for their livelihood.

"I don't know where my heart is," she whispered now to Harry. "It's what I've done since I was eleven, when my grandmother took me in after my mother died. It's been my career since I graduated from college."

He gestured to the framed prints around them. "You've got a gift here. I don't think anybody would blame you for wanting to pursue that gift."

To hear her own thoughts put into words so clearly almost made her cry. Megan had to choke back the tears burning in her throat.

"I don't hate running the inn."

"You don't have to hate something to nurture a dream of doing something else," Mary Ella said softly. "Please don't worry about this right now. Let's focus on the show opening. Then you can sit down with my stubborn husband and have an in-depth discussion about the particulars of his offer."

"I'm sorry I hit you with this out of nowhere," Harry Lange said. His bold features somehow looked much kinder than she might have expected. "Give it some thought. For the record, I think you would find my offer more than acceptable."

He named a number that widened her eyes and had her reaching behind her to the ladder for support. "I . . . Wow. You're joking."

It was enough to keep her comfortable for the rest of her life, enough that Luke, a quarter owner despite his protestations that he wasn't even her grandmother's true grandson, wouldn't have to scratch and claw to make his contracting business a success.

He could build houses to his heart's content while she finally could follow her dreams.

"At that price, it's a steal."

"Now you've done it," Mary Ella said to her husband with a chiding frown. "You've made my artist speechless. People around here are used to you and your blunt ways, but Megan has no reason to think you're even serious."

"I am completely serious. Think about it. I'll have my people work up an official offer. Then we can go from there."

Dazed, she turned back to hanging photographs, wondering how she was supposed to think about anything else now.

Sell the Inn at Haven Point! She had never even considered it. Before the smoke even cleared on that horrible day the inn burned down, she knew she had to rebuild. It was a historic landmark, a relic from the time when Lake Haven drew people from the entire western United States to partake of the healing waters in the area.

It had historic and cultural significance. More than that, the inn played a vital role in Haven Point.

Every town needed at least one solid, respectable hotel for its visitors. Her neighbors and friends relied heavily on the tourism industry, from restaurant owners like the Serranos to bike rental places and downtown merchants.

Those visitors would always be an integral part of the region's economy, even now that Caine Tech had moved in—and they would always need a place to stay.

But there was no reason *she* had to be the one running the inn that provided it.

As she worked with Mary Ella to hang her remaining photographs, a thousand possibilities crowded through her mind.

Her thoughts were in chaos and she had to take a moment to breathe, to focus on the task at hand. She needed to talk to someone about the offer, someone wise and introspective, someone who considered all angles before making any decision.

Elliot.

"SON, I DON'T know what in the hell you're talking about."

Elliot stood on the front porch to the address he had finally found after the most frustrating of mornings, frowning at a thin scarecrow of a woman with black-dyed hair, bright red lipstick and a trio of yapping Chihuahuas at her feet.

He wanted to pound his head against the door in frustration—not because of the dogs and their noise but because he was coming to realize this had been a mistake from the beginning.

The morning had been a complete waste. First he'd had a flat tire in the rental car. Then the GPS had directed him twice up the wrong canyon fire road before he found this one.

Now he was here and the woman was looking at him like he had just landed his flying saucer on her lawn next to what looked like an entire battalion of garden gnomes.

"You're not Peggy Burnett?"

"You've got the right woman. I'm not denying that. But I got no idea why you'd think I might know anything about any missing woman from some Podunk town in Idaho. Why would I?"

"I have a police report with the name Peggy Burnett on it and this address. It says here that you called in a tip to the Haven Point Police Department seven years ago, claiming you had information about a missing poster you saw at a truck stop outside of Boise."

The woman gazed at him for a moment, then guffawed loudly, as if he had just invited her to join him in that flying saucer.

"Well, why didn't you say so in the first place? That explains everything. Come on in."

Elliot stood warily on the porch. He wanted to tell the strange woman he would rather have this conversation outside in the sunshine, where she had less chance of reaching for the pump-action shotgun he could see inside the door.

On the other hand, she seemed harmless enough, if a little odd. He had come this far. Why stop now?

The house wasn't quite as run-down inside as the outside would have led him to expect. It was comfortable, even homey, with a leather sofa set and a flat-screen TV that was almost as big as the one he had at home.

"Now, you say you're with the FBI? Let me look at that badge again."

He had brought along his credentials, though technically he wasn't supposed to use them while he was under investigation or while he was on unofficial business. Flouting yet one more rule, he showed her his ID again.

"I am an FBI agent, but as I said, I'm working a personal case unconnected to the Bureau. I only showed you my credentials so you would know I'm a legitimate investigator."

"I would have guessed you were legit. The squeaky-clean haircut gave it away before I ever opened the door. I figured you were either with the FBI or a Mormon. Or maybe both."

He flushed. "Appearances can be deceiving," he said stiffly. "You can't always count on every-one with a shorter haircut to be honest."

"True enough. My first husband looked like

Johnny Cash but he couldn't play the guitar worth shit."

She brayed with laughter. "Sit down, FBI. What can I do you for? You say this is about some missing woman and you're looking for information about a tip called in from a Boise truck stop?"

"Yes. As I was combing through police files, your name popped up on a tip report as someone who reported you may have seen the woman at the truck stop around the time she disappeared. Does any of that ring a bell?"

Peggy picked up a cigarette from the holder next to her and puffed on it. "Not with me. I don't know what the hell you're talking about."

So why had she wasted his time by bringing him inside her house? He rose, intending to leave again, but she shook her head.

"Hold on. Hold on. I may not know what you're talking about, but it so happens I have a daughter named Peggy, too, only she goes by Peg. And for the record, I never wanted to name her after me but my husband at the time—the Johnny Cash look-alike—had a grandma with that name and loved it. So here we are. Anyways, she was driving long-haul truck up until about three years ago. I seem to recall she had a route that took her that way. If anybody knows anything about some missing woman, it probably would be her."

For the first time since he knocked on the door, he began to feel a glimmer of optimism that this whole thing hadn't been a colossal waste of time. "Is there any chance I could speak with her?"

"You sure could, if she were here, but she got married four, five years ago and moved to Rock Springs, Wyoming. Name's Peg McGeary now. She got tired of being on the road, so now she drives the big machines at the mines down there. You ever seen those things? They got tires bigger than my whole house! I have no idea how a little girl like my Peg could handle something that big. I mean, this is a girl who was afraid to ride a bike without training wheels until she was nine years old."

"Is that right?"

He didn't really care about how old the woman might have been when she learned to ride a bike, but sometimes learning these sorts of details helped him assess the character of a possible witness.

"You ought to see her now. Tough as leather. Can I get you a beer?"

As it was just past 10:00 a.m. and he didn't much like beer anyway, he shook his head. "No. But thank you. Would you be able to give me your daughter's contact information, Ms. Burnett, so I can try to reach her and follow up on this?"

Her brow furrowed as she considered. "I don't

see why that would be a problem. Let me just give her a call first, to make sure she doesn't mind me handing out her personal information to every good-looking FBI agent who stops by the old place."

She seemed to find her own words hilarious because she broke out into that deep-throated guffaw again. This one ended in a raspy cough and she sipped at a glass beside her containing a clear liquid that appeared to be water, though he couldn't be quite sure.

Peggy picked up a cell phone from the table next to the water glass and gave a voice command to call her daughter. A moment later, she held the phone to her ear.

"Hey, Peg. You're never gonna believe what I got sitting in my living room right now. An honest-to-God FBI agent. That's right."

She gave that whiskey laugh again. "Fox Mulder. Right here in my living room."

She paused. "Ha ha. Very funny. No, I'm not under arrest. He's looking for you."

Elliot gave an inward wince. The last thing he needed was for Peggy Junior to go on the defensive from the outset. He'd never get anything out of her.

Her mother quickly put her mind at ease. "I'm just kidding. Apparently he's investigating a missing-person case and thinks you might know something about it. I guess you called in a tip or something back when you were driving long-haul."

She was silent for a moment, listening to whatever her daughter was saying, then shook her head. "You know what I know, honey. Here. I'll put you on speaker and you can talk to him."

Peggy monkeyed with the phone for a minute. "There. I think that did it. Can you hear me?"

"Hello?" He heard a woman's voice that sounded remarkably similar to her mother's, even down to the smoker's rasp.

He hated being put on the spot like this and hated speakerphones, too. "Hello, ma'am. My name is Elliot Bailey. I should tell you up front that, while it's true I am an agent with the Federal Bureau of Investigation field office in Denver, this is a private matter, not official FBI business."

"You moonlighting as some kind of private dick?" she asked.

He didn't quite know *what* he was doing, nor why he had been so driven to track down leads in Elizabeth's case.

"Something like that. I'm looking into the disappearance seven years ago of a woman from Haven Point, Idaho. Elizabeth Sinclair Hamilton. Your name came up in the police files among the many tips, and I'm wondering if I could speak with you about it."

"Elliot Bailey. That's a coincidence. Any

relation to the Elliot Bailey who writes books?"

He could feel his face heat again. He never quite knew how to respond when people recognized him from his books.

Not for the first time, he wondered why he hadn't used a pen name when he sold his first manuscript. His editor and his agent had pushed him to use his own name, against his own reservations. If he had gone with his gut, he could have completely avoided these awkward moments when people made the connection.

"Yes. Quite a close relationship, actually. I am also *that* Elliot Bailey who writes true-crime books."

"You're shitting me!"

"No. I'm really not."

"I love your books!" she exclaimed. "Wow. I can't believe I'm talking to Elliot Bailey. I'm reading one of your books right now. *The Dark Lands*. I've been sleeping with my lights on since I started it. And you want to talk to *me* about a case! This is the most exciting thing that's ever happened to me!"

He didn't want to disappoint the woman, but all he wanted was more information. He glanced at Peggy Senior, listening avidly to their conversation. He didn't want to have this conversation on speakerphone, but he didn't want to miss this chance to speak with a possible eyewitness.

"Do you remember calling a tip line to the town of Haven Point about a hitchhiker you picked up sometime about seven years ago?"

"Sure. I remember. How could I forget? I went into the same truck stop I always used on that route and first thing I saw was this woman's face staring at me from a missing poster. She looked familiar right away, and when I looked closer, I knew why. She looked a lot like this woman who had asked me for a ride at a truck stop outside Boise a few weeks earlier."

She paused, and when she spoke again, she sounded reluctant. "I picked her up, even though it was against company policy. I felt sorry for her. She looked like she had been messed up good and I sure as hell knew scared when it was staring at me across the cab of my truck."

Elliot was aware of a weird tingling in his spine, the same feeling he always had when he was onto something.

Across the room, Peggy Senior sat forward in her chair.

He wanted to talk to the woman's daughter in person. On the speaker of a cell phone wasn't ideal for catching nuances in tone and expression—beyond that, he didn't necessarily need her mother listening in to every word.

He thought quickly. "Listen, I'll be passing through Rock Springs later today on my way back to Idaho. Any chance you might have time to meet me for a quick interview late this afternoon or possibly early evening? It probably wouldn't take more than half an hour, just long enough to go over what you remember in more detail and possibly show you a picture of the missing woman to try jogging your memory. I can come to your house or meet you somewhere, if that would make you more comfortable."

"Seriously? Will you autograph some of your books while you're here?"

He scratched his cheek, feeling awkward and weird again. "Uh, sure. I could do that."

"Well then, I'm happy to talk to you. My shift is done at four. I can meet you any time after that. Does that work?"

He did some quick mental calculations for distance and speed and figured the time frame would mesh perfectly.

"Yes. It works. Where should I meet you?"

"You can come to my house," she said after a moment, then gave him an address in Rock Springs. "And just in case you had any ideas, I should tell you that while your books might scare me, you don't. My husband will be here—and by the way, he's six-six and can bend concrete with his bare hands."

If he had nefarious ideas in mind, her husband's size wouldn't matter a damn. Elliot would take him out in the first few seconds, maybe as soon as he answered the door. First neutralize the threat. Then he would have all the time he needed for anything else.

Good thing he didn't have nefarious ideas in mind.

The series of thoughts crossed his mind in about three seconds, long enough for him to think again that maybe he needed to get out of the FBI. The minds of normal people didn't go in those kinds of crazy directions, thinking about neutralizing threats and looking for defensive vulnerabilities.

"I can't guarantee exactly what time we'll hit town but it should be early evening. I can get your phone contact info and reach out as soon as we get closer and have a more firm idea of our ETA."

"We?"

"I'm traveling with a friend and her dog." He wanted to think Megan was still a friend but he wasn't quite sure.

For some reason, Peg seemed to find his words amusing. She chuckled as she gave him her address and related her phone number so he didn't have to obtain it from her mother's phone.

"Thank you," he said after jotting it down.

"No problem. I'll try to see what I can remember this afternoon about her," Peg said. "I can't wait to tell all my friends Elliot Bailey is coming over to my house!"

• • •

THE MOMENT HE returned the rental car to the desk at the lodge, his phone buzzed with a text from Megan.

Ready when you are.

He tamped down his instantaneous and highly inappropriate reaction to that. What was she ready for? Probably not the same thing that had popped into his overactive imagination.

He texted back. Give me ten minutes. I'll knock on your door.

OK, she answered back.

He hurried through the lodge and back to his room, where he packed his toiletries into his small duffel. Eight minutes later, he picked up his duffel and laptop case and headed next door. She opened at once, her few cases piled up neatly just inside the door.

He knew instantly something was up. She had a weird, tightly wound energy, her eyes murky with emotions he couldn't read.

"How did your day go?" he asked.

She didn't answer for a long moment. When she did, her voice sounded strained. "Long story. I don't think I'm ready to talk about it yet."

Her answer didn't satisfy his curiosity in the slightest. Something was wrong and he couldn't stand not knowing what.

"Is there some problem with the exhibit? We don't have to rush away if Mary Ella still needs you. I don't mind staying another night."

"No. Everything is fine at the gallery. We managed to hang almost everything and the rest will be easy enough for Mary Ella and her team."

"That's good."

"It's going to be beyond my wildest dreams, Elliot. She has done a magnificent job. The only thing left for me is to make sure we have the correct captions on the prints and show up on opening night."

It must be something else, then. What had caused her wild, jittery edges?

He wanted to push her to tell him, until he remembered they had an eight-hour road trip ahead of them, with plenty of time to talk.

Whether he wanted it or not.

"Can I carry something for you?"

She held Cyrus's leash in one hand and gestured to her tote at her feet with the other. "This is it. I took Cy's crate down earlier."

He already had two bags and it would be tough to manage a third. "Trade me. You take my laptop bag and I'll get both duffels."

She looked as if she wanted to argue, but finally shrugged. "Thank you."

They had nearly reached her now-empty SUV in the parking lot when she seemed to remember his errand that morning.

"Oh. I can't believe I didn't ask this yet. How did your interview go?"

He wanted to tell her everything, about Peggy Senior and Peg the truck driver and the unexpected stop he now wanted to make in Rock Springs, Wyoming.

He didn't know where to start. He could only remember Peg's words.

She looked like she had been messed up good and I sure as hell knew scared when it was staring at me across the cab of my truck.

The woman Peg had picked up had been afraid, bloodied. Ever since hearing that, one question had been chasing itself around and around his head.

Was Luke Hamilton the architect of both those things?

"The interview went fine. We can talk about that on our way."

But first, he would have to figure out how much he wanted to tell her—and how to keep from spilling more of his own secrets in the process.

Chapter Sixteen

SELL THE INN.

As Elliot loaded their duffels and Cyrus's crate into the now-empty cargo area of her SUV, Megan couldn't seem to think about anything but Harry Lange's incredibly shocking offer to purchase the Inn at Haven Point.

The amount he had offered staggered her. She never dreamed the property could be worth that much. She supposed she should have guessed from the amount of taxes they paid each year, but she had never seriously considered selling it before.

How could she do it? Split the profits with Luke and the kids and walk away?

She had tried to call her brother earlier, with no success. Her call went straight to voice mail, and after a moment's reflection, she had decided not to leave a message. How could she adequately convey over the phone the shocking offer from Harry Lange?

She managed to put it away long enough to deal with the essentials of embarking on a road trip. He pumped gas while she went into the convenience store to pick up a few snacks for the road.

"Are you ready to go, then?" he asked, when they were both back in the vehicle.

"Yes. I think so. I'll drive first."

She had so much pent-up energy, she was afraid she would go a little crazy if she were sitting in the passenger seat doing nothing. At least behind the wheel, she could focus on something outside herself.

Traffic was light as she drove through Hope's Crossing and headed northwest toward Idaho and home.

"How did things go at the gallery today?" Elliot asked after they were on the highway. "Are you feeling good about the preparations for the exhibit?"

So much for not thinking about the tumultuous morning. She sipped at her water bottle, trying to decide whether to discuss it with Elliot. Why not? He was a relatively impartial party who might have some insight into what she should do.

"I met Mary Ella's husband today. Harry Lange."

"Ah. The guy who owns the ski resort and paid for our dinner. The one his stepdaughter said is hard to say no to."

"That's the one." She didn't know how to go on. It still seemed too incredible to believe.

"What's the problem? Was he an arrogant jackass? Some of these billionaires can be."

How many billionaires had he met? She had to wonder. "He was actually very helpful. He worked with us to hang many of the prints for the showing and seems knowledgeable about art and design."

"That's good."

"Yes." She drove another mile before she told him the rest. "He wants to buy the inn."

He stared. "Your inn?"

"Of course my inn. What other inn would I be talking about?"

He gave a rueful laugh. "Good point, I guess. Do you think he was serious?"

"He seemed to be. I couldn't say for certain, since I only met him this morning. Anyway, it's a little hard to judge a man's sincerity when he has just given you news that knocks you to the ground."

"Did he talk specifics or was this one of those maybe-someday kind of things?"

"He listed a number. I'm still reeling from it."

He digested that as the road stripes passed under her tires.

"Are you going to do it?" he finally asked. "It would give you a chance to pursue photography seriously. You could travel, as you've dreamed."

"I don't know. There's so much to consider. It's a bit of a landmark in Haven Point. New owner-ship could come in and change everything."

"Which wouldn't be your concern anymore if you sold it."

That was true enough, except Haven Point was

still her home, a place filled with her friends and neighbors.

"I can't think about this right now—and I could never make a decision anyway until Luke has the chance to weigh in."

"Luke? Does he have a share in the inn?"

"Twenty-five percent."

"I thought the inn is from your mother's side of the family. His stepmother."

"My mother's family ran it, and my grandfather's father before him. It's been in the family for generations. I am the last surviving one of my mother's side."

"But Luke still has a share of the inn, though he was from your father's first marriage?"

"He was six when our father married my mom. My grandfather was already gone but my grandmother loved Luke instantly and always treated him as if he were her own grandson. She tried to leave him a larger share of the inn but he refused. He didn't want any of it, but I insisted."

They had engaged in epic fights about it after her grandmother died. Finally she had simply had the paperwork drawn up, giving him a quarter share and his children shares that almost equaled another quarter. She was still the majority owner, as her grandmother wanted, but she couldn't really make a decision without them.

It was the very least she could do for Luke,

who had protected her and watched out for her from the moment she was born.

"So where did you leave things with Lange?" Elliot asked now.

"I told him I needed time to think. I told him he could come up with the formal offer and I would take it under consideration after speaking with my partners."

"Partners?"

"Luke, Bridger and Cassie."

She didn't want to talk about this now. Her mind felt as if it were spinning in a hundred different directions. The exhibit, the offer from Harry and Elliot's shocking words the night before, that he had feelings for her—and they weren't new.

She couldn't deal with any of it right now. She forced herself to take a deep breath, then let it out slowly.

"How about your day?" she asked, mostly to distract herself. "How did your interview go?"

"Interesting and frustrating." He didn't answer for a long moment, though she felt his steady gaze on her as she drove. "How do you feel about a stop in Rock Springs on our way home?" he finally asked.

She pictured the little hardscrabble Western town, with its working man's vibe. "I know a place that serves up a good steak."

The corner of his mouth lifted into a half smile.

"That might be the place for dinner, but I need to make another stop first."

By the time he finished telling her about Peggy Burnett Senior and his phone call with her daughter, Megan was able to tuck away her stress over Harry Lange's offer.

She didn't know what she would do about that, but for now she could focus on this, a possible break in the case of her missing sister-in-law and the mystery that had haunted her family for far too long.

MEGAN WAS ASLEEP as they drove into Rock Springs.

They had switched drivers two hours earlier when they stopped for gas. The moment they were on the road again, she had turned away from him, tucked her hands under her chin and, judging by her even, steady breathing, drifted off almost instantly.

She hadn't stirred since. Poor thing. Had her night been as sleepless as his?

Now, as he rolled into Rock Springs, she sat up and looked around. "We're here already?"

He couldn't help his smile, charmed by the sleepy note in her voice. "You were out."

"Sorry."

"Don't be sorry. You needed it."

He pulled into a gas station in order to punch Peg McGeary's street address into the navigation system, but figured he might as well fill up the tank while he was there. "Do you want to let Cyrus out for a moment? We made good time and we're still a little ahead of the time I told her we would be here."

"Good idea."

Twenty minutes later, he followed the directions on the GPS through a neighborhood of well-kept, modest homes. He found Peg's house and pulled into the driveway.

"I think it might be best if you wait in the car while I go speak with the possible witness," he said after a moment.

He had thought about it for the last few hours, remembering Peg's words.

She looked like she had been messed up good and I sure as hell knew scared when it was staring at me across the cab of my truck.

What if Peg's information firmly pointed the finger at Luke being somehow involved in his wife's disappearance? For the first time since he had started pursuing the investigation seriously, Elliot found himself battling reservations.

He wanted answers, but he didn't want to break Megan's fragile heart.

"Why don't you want me to come with you?"

That wasn't it. He was startled at the humbling realization that he wanted her with him everywhere. She filled a spot he'd never realized had been hollow all these years.

"I don't know what she's going to tell me," he finally said. "You may not like what you hear."

"I want to know what she has to say, Elliot. Please."

His instincts told him he should insist she let him question the woman alone but something made him hesitate. He didn't know how to refuse her. She had come all this way with him. It seemed wrong to keep her out here in the vehicle alone.

Besides that, Peg might feel more comfortable with another woman along.

"You can come in, but I have to ask you to let me ask the questions."

"Of course."

She opened her car door. Because they had only been traveling a short distance from the service station to Peg's house, Megan hadn't put Cyrus back in his crate but held him on her lap. Now she set him on the ground. "What about Cyrus? I don't feel good about leaving him in the car."

"Bring him along," he said.

The front door of the house opened before they even made it up the steps of the porch.

Peg McGeary didn't match up to anybody's stereotype of a female truck driver. She was petite, pretty, with streaky blonde hair to her shoulders and an athletic frame.

"Hi there," she greeted them with enthusiasm.

"I've been so excited all afternoon, I could hardly focus at work."

"Thank you very much for agreeing to speak with us on short notice," Elliot said.

"Are you kidding? This is the most exciting thing to happen to me since . . . well, ever. And who's this little cutie?" she asked with a smile for the dog.

"This is Cyrus," Megan said. "Sorry to bring him along, but he's been cooped up in his crate for two days."

"My backyard is fenced. We've got a sweet old Lab back there. If he doesn't mind other dogs, you're welcome to let him off his leash to run around while we talk."

Megan looked torn, as if she didn't want the dog out of her sight, but she finally nodded. "He would like that. He loves making new friends."

"Right through here. He should be good outside." Peg led them through a kitchen with dark-stained cabinets and what looked like gourmet appliances. The kitchen smelled of caramel and chocolate, enough to make his mouth water.

"Thank you. This is very kind of you," Megan said after Peg opened the door for her onto a nicely landscaped backyard where a black Lab, muzzle turning white, snuffled a greeting.

Peg dismissed that with a wave of her hand. "We dog lovers need to stick together."

She ushered them back to her living room, where Elliot noticed four of his books spread out on the coffee table.

"Can I get you something?" Peg asked.

He shook his head and Megan did the same.

"Then please. Sit down," she said. "I can't believe it. Elliot Bailey, right here in my living room."

Before they could sit, a giant of a man with dark hair and a big bushy beard came into the room, hovering protectively beside the woman who was probably half his size.

"You're the FBI agent?" he asked.

Elliot reached out to shake the man's hand. "I am. Elliot Bailey. But as I explained to Peg on the phone, I want to be clear I'm not here in any official FBI capacity. I'm looking into a case unrelated to my work at the Bureau."

"Are you working on a book?" Peg asked. "Oh, I can't believe I might get to be in one of your books."

Elliot looked uncomfortable. "I'm not planning to write a book about this case either. I'm only researching to find answers. The woman was a friend of mine and I would like to know what happened to her."

"Well, if we're talking about the same woman, I would guess some son of a bitch beat the shit out of her and she finally got tired of it and took off."

AT THAT BLUNT pronouncement, Elliot could feel Megan tense, and he cursed his own weakness. He should never have let her come into this interview. This was exactly what he had feared, that the information Peg McGeary had to offer might further implicate her brother.

It was too late now. She was here. She would never agree to go back to the car now. The only option was to get through this as quickly as possible.

"I'll get out of your way so you can talk," Peg's husband said. He kissed his wife's cheek, then gave Elliot a hard look that plainly conveyed his willingness to get rough if necessary in defense of the woman he loved. "I'll be in the man cave if you need me."

"Thanks, babe."

The man touched his wife's arm softly on his way out of the room in a gesture of support that Elliot found extraordinarily sweet, especially coming from someone who looked like he could crush small kitchen appliances with his bare hands.

They all sat down, Elliot and Megan on the sofa, Peg facing them on a matching love seat.

"Why don't you start at the beginning," he said after the man had left. "Tell me what you remember about that night."

"You're going to sign my books, right? You won't forget?"

His face, predictably, turned hot. "Uh, sure. I'll sign them when we're done."

He reached into his pocket for his digital tape recorder. "Do you mind if I record our conversation? Again, this isn't a statement on the record. I'm not working this case in any official capacity, but I would like to have it for future reference."

"Fine with me. Record away. Sure, I broke some rules by picking up a hitchhiker, but I don't work for that company anymore and they can't do anything to me. I have nothing to hide."

He pushed RECORD on the device and set it down on the coffee table next to his book. "All right. What can you tell me about that night?"

"As I recall, I had only been driving long-haul for about a year and was taking a load of mattresses from Texas to a furniture store in Pendleton, Oregon. I got a late start that trip after some trouble at the warehouse, then had some weather delays, so it was probably six or seven by the time I got close to Boise. I was tired, looking to grab something to eat, so I pulled into this truck stop outside Boise."

"Any chance you remember the name of the place?"

"Of course I do. I only stopped there every time I went through. L.J.'s, about thirty miles outside Boise. I don't like the big travel centers and always tried to avoid them. You wouldn't believe the kind of crap that goes down at those places. Pills, girls. Even guys, if you're into that. Not for me. I liked the smaller, cleaner places, like L.J.'s, where they remember you from week to week and where I didn't have to deal with the jerks."

He could only imagine how tough it must have been for a young, attractive woman in the good-old-boy network of truckers.

"Then what?"

"I filled up with gas and walked inside to use the ladies' room. This woman was in there, washing up at one of the sinks. She had a nasty bruise on her cheek and looked like she had been crying."

"Do you remember what she was wearing? What she looked like?"

"It's been years. My memory is a little foggy, I'm afraid. I know she was blonde, a few inches taller than me and probably weighed maybe 120. She had dimples. I remember that, and a scar on her cheek, about an inch long."

Next to him, he felt Megan sit up straighter. Elizabeth had a scar like that from a playground accident when she was young.

"She seemed real classy, other than maybe she looked like she'd fallen on hard times, you know? Kind of bedraggled and such."

"Was this the woman you saw?"

He handed over the photograph he had brought along, a large picture of Elizabeth holding a baby in a little pink dress. He assumed it was Cassie. Elizabeth was smiling, but even in the nearly decade-old somewhat grainy image, he thought he could see a certain sadness in her eyes.

Peg McGeary took the picture and studied it for several moments. "Her hair was shorter. Choppy, like she'd taken scissors to it herself, and she looked a bit older than this. But, yeah, I'd say this looks like the same woman. I can't be a hundred percent sure, you understand. Maybe ninety. I've traveled a few miles since then."

Ninety percent was pretty damn certain.

His spidey senses tingled. "You spoke with her?"

"Not at first. She was still there in the john after I came out of the stall, just standing, staring at the mirror like she was in a fog or something. I asked if she was okay and she looked at me like she didn't even speak English for about a minute. Funny thing—have you ever seen anybody nod and shake their head at the same time? She did something like that."

She demonstrated by wiggling her head around, first up and down, then side to side in a gesture of utter indecision. "I guess she couldn't quite make up her mind how she was. Or maybe she didn't want to say. I asked her if she was afraid of someone. She didn't want to answer me for a long time but finally whispered yes. I remember I asked her if she wanted me to take her to the police station. She got really upset about that and said no, she didn't want to go to the police—she just wanted to get out of Idaho for a while but she didn't know how."

Beside him, he could sense Megan's growing tension as Peg rolled on, oblivious to it.

"A guy I was dating hit me once," the other woman said. "I ended up kicking him in the balls, pulling a knife on him and threatening worse, then getting the hell out of there. I didn't look back, not once. I don't stand for men who hurt women."

"Neither do I," Elliot said flatly.

"The lady was so upset, I felt sorry for her. I wanted to help. I'm a sucker that way. I told her where I was going and asked if she wanted to ride with me."

"She went with you?" Megan asked.

"She seemed real conflicted about it. She started ugly-crying, you know? Big sobs. When she calmed down a little, she said something about how it was probably better for everyone that way, if she was gone. I didn't know what that meant but she sounded like her mind was made up, so I grabbed us a couple sandwiches and paid for my fuel. Then she climbed into my rig and we headed to Oregon."

This was huge.

The back of Elliot's neck prickled like it did when he was closing in on answers. Battling with his tingling instincts was a grim knot of dismay in his chest. How had his dad missed a major tip like this that would have busted the case wide open?

And Cade and Marshall? Their officers should have picked up on this, too. Yes, the tip sheet had been shoved into the wrong file and some of the information didn't match up exactly, but it was all pretty damn close.

"Did she tell you anything?" Elliot asked. "Why she was on the run? What she might have been afraid of? Why she needed to leave?"

"No. And I'll admit, after a few miles, I started to think maybe picking her up wasn't the smartest thing I've ever done. Besides the fact it was against company rules and I could have been fired for it, she was acting strange. Real agitated, you know? Kept saying she had made a big mistake. She had to go back. She had to fix things. That sort of thing. I was already behind schedule and didn't think I could spare the time to go back, but I offered to pull over to let her out or drop her off at the next stop. I wanted her out of my cab at that point. I didn't need some junkie freaking out on me."

"A junkie?" Megan asked, features tense. "You think she was on some kind of drugs?"

"Can't say for sure but she was sure acting like it. All agitated and such."

Peg sipped at her drink again, forehead furrowed with the effort to remember events from years ago.

"I asked her if she wanted me to stop, and after maybe two or three minutes of fretting like that, she calmed right down like somebody flipped a switch and said no, she didn't want me to stop. She needed to keep going. It was better for everyone. She said that again. Next thing I knew, she curled up on the seat and fell asleep—the hard kind of sleep, like she hadn't closed her eyes in months."

"What did you do?" Elliot asked.

"I was tempted to pull over and dump her at the next truck stop but I didn't feel right about that. I mean, I didn't want to take any chance the guy who had messed her up would come looking for her. I didn't know what to do, so I finally decided to just keep going. I stopped for gas outside Pendleton, Oregon, a few hours later and had to shake her awake to check on her. Took me about five minutes before she opened her eyes. I told her where we were, told her I was heading up to Portland and she was welcome to keep going with me. She said no, she had made a mistake and needed to go back."

"She said she was going back?" Megan interjected, eyes wide.

"Yeah. She was really upset about it. Crying and everything. Kept saying, 'What have I done? What have I done?' I told her I could arrange a ride back Boise way with a trucker I trusted and she said no. She was going to call someone back home to come get her. She thanked me for my help, climbed out of my truck, and that was the last I ever saw her. Right after that, I took a different route for a bit that took me to the East Coast. I didn't think of the woman again until months later when my route changed again and I made it back to L.J.'s and saw that missing poster."

This was the part he didn't want to face, the ugly, uncomfortable truth he would rather tuck back into the files. "You explained all this when you called the Haven Point Police Department?"

"I tried to. The man I talked to was real nice. He took my name and information, then never followed up. I thought he would call me later and he never did. I called again a few weeks later, next time I was passing through, and got the runaround again."

"Do you remember what you were told by the police department?" Elliot forced himself to ask.

"Like I said, the guy was very nice and said he would keep my information on file. He thanked me for calling but said the timeline didn't match up and the description I gave didn't sound like their missing person."

"But you think otherwise?"

The intensity of Megan's voice seemed to make the other woman uneasy. "I can't say for sure it was this Elizabeth Sinclair woman you're looking for. Like I said, I'm ninety-percent sure. That's the best I can give you."

"Thank you. This is very helpful," Elliot said.

Peg shrugged. "You want my opinion, I think what happened is, she called her knuckle-dragger of a husband to come get her in Pendleton and he was so pissed at her for running away from him that he made sure she couldn't do it again. I know the type. They can't stand it when a woman finally says *enough*."

She sipped at her drink. "I don't know if you've driven that route, but there are a lot of places between Boise and Pendleton where you could dump a body." She unexpectedly grinned, which he found extremely disconcerting, given the topic of conversation. "But then, maybe I read too many true-crime books by great writers like Elliot Bailey. It's always the husband."

Elliot couldn't look at Megan, though he didn't need to. He knew she would be biting her lip against the urge to defend her brother.

"You've been very helpful," he said again. "Thank you for agreeing to speak with us."

"You're welcome. It's my pleasure. I really hope I'm wrong. I hope you can find the woman. She struck me as a lost soul, for what it's worth."

That was the sense he had gained through the course of this informal investigation, too. Elizabeth had been troubled, just as Megan said in the beginning. "It's worth a great deal. I think your information will be very valuable to the investigation. Thank you again."

She gestured to the books. "You can thank me by signing my books. I've got two copies of your latest. I'm going to mail it to my mom, since she loves your books, too."

Feeling awkward and aware every second of Megan beside him and this overwhelming need to tuck her against him and protect her from every ugly possibility, he hurried to sign the copies of his books. When he finished, he reached into his pocket for his wallet and extracted one of his business cards.

"Here's my contact info. If you remember any more details from that night, please don't hesitate to reach out."

"Really? With your cell phone number on it and everything?"

She seemed completely overwhelmed, as if he had handed her a candy bar with Willy Wonka's Golden Ticket inside.

"Anything. The smallest detail you remember could have major value in an investigation like this."

"I know. I read enough of your books to know how investigations can crack open when you least expect it."

"That's right."

"Let me go get your cute little dog for you," she said.

She opened the door and Cyrus trotted in, looking perfectly at home.

"Do you two want some cookies for the road? Rocco makes them and they're fabulous, trust me. He's training to be a dessert chef at one of the hotels in town and I'm lucky enough to get to eat all his experiments."

Elliot had a hard time picturing her big, tough-looking husband training to work with delicate pastries, but he supposed everybody had a thing.

"That's very kind of you. Thank you."

She stuffed several cookies from a container on the counter into plastic bags and handed them to Elliot.

"I'm really glad you called," Peg said as she walked out on the porch with them. "I've wondered over the years what happened to her. If you solve the mystery, will you please keep me posted?"

"I'll do that. Thanks," Elliot said.

As they walked to Megan's SUV, he was aware of her vibrating with tension, like a lit bundle of firecrackers, ready to go off at any moment.

She kept Cyrus with her again instead of putting him in his crate, as if she needed the comfort of her pet. Somehow she managed to hold back until they had both climbed into her SUV, with Elliot in the driver's seat again.

The moment he turned the key and backed out of the driveway, words burst like those fire-crackers exploding into the night sky.

"I told you she left on her own. I knew it. I *knew* it! I've been saying it for years. She was a desperately unhappy woman who was struggling with depression and was self-medicating."

He headed toward the interstate, his mind whirling from the interview and the implications of it. "And I was right about Luke," Megan went on.

"He had nothing to do with it. She left completely on her own and vanished hundreds of miles away from home."

He had to point out the part she seemed to be avoiding.

"What about her injuries? How do you explain those? Luke admitted all along the relationship was stormy."

She cuddled her dog closer. "I don't know how she got hurt, but I promise you, it wasn't my brother's fault. He would not have hurt Elizabeth. I will not believe that for one single instant. My brother would never raise a hand against a woman. Never. Not after what we—" Her voice trailed off and she pressed her cheek to Cyrus's head.

"After what you—?" he prompted.

He wasn't sure she was going to answer him. She kept her features angled away for a long moment before she finally turned back to him.

"After what we saw at home."

Elliot stared at her, shock firing through him, hot and fierce. "You lived in an abusive home?"

She curled her hands again, knuckles white.

"My father was a son of a bitch. Everybody knows that. The town drunk. I'm sure your father spoke of him."

He barely remembered her father. They had lived in Sulfer Springs, one of the poorer areas of Haven Point, and Paul Hamilton had worked at the boatyard. He knew his father hadn't liked the man, which was a rarity for John Bailey, who had tended to give everybody the benefit of the doubt.

If he remembered the details correctly, her father had ended up getting plastered at one of the roadhouses on the highway and wrapping his car around a tree when Elliot and Luke had been in high school. That would have been a few years after her mother died. That couldn't have been easy on her.

"Not everybody who drinks beats his family."

"True enough. I guess we lucked out." She said the words in an emotionless tone that gave him a clearer picture than if she had ranted and cursed and regaled him with horror stories.

"You know Luke and I have different mothers, right?"

"His mom died when he was pretty small, right?"

Megan nodded, gazing straight ahead at the gathering dusk. "She had a miscarriage and didn't get treated and somehow ended up with an infection that turned septic. That's the story I heard, anyway. Luke wasn't quite six. Four months later, Paul married my mother. I came along about nine months after that."

She sighed. "My mom was older and wanted a family. That's what my grandmother told me years later, once when I asked why my parents hooked up. Paul was decent enough when he was sober. A good provider. He could be charming. Funny. Generous to his friends. But he wasn't sober often."

He didn't know what to say. Her childhood couldn't have been more different from his own.

"My mom was almost forty and . . . not necessarily what some would call pretty. I thought she was the most beautiful woman in the world. I've had time to think about it over the years and I think he married her because her family had money from the inn and he needed a mother for Luke. I think she married him because she thought she was running out of options for a family of her own."

She was quiet for a long moment. "It wasn't a happy marriage."

"Your father hit her?"

She finally nodded. "When he was drinking, which, as I said, was most of the time. Luke would try to protect me from hearing it. The verbal abuse was worse than the physical abuse, I think. It wore her down, sucked away her confidence."

She sighed and petted the dog in her lap. Did

she realize Cyrus had fallen asleep a few miles back? Elliot didn't think so.

"My mother died of cancer when I was eleven," she went on, echoes of old pain in her voice. "Sometimes I wonder if she would have fought harder if things had been better at home."

He swore to himself, sick inside. He had great sympathy for women who were victims—though he had to admit, that sympathy tended to shrink a bit when they allowed their children to witness it.

"After my mother died, my grandmother kind of took over custody of Luke and me. I don't think she and my father ever had an official custody arrangement but he didn't argue and we just moved into the inn with her."

"That must have been a change."

"It was wonderful," she admitted. "He died a year later in a drunk driving accident. You probably know that. Fortunately, it was the best possible scenario because he didn't take anyone else out with him."

He remembered that, when Paul Hamilton had wrapped his pickup around a tree. He had tried to comfort Luke and hadn't quite known what to say—especially as Luke had shown so little emotion over his own father.

What kind of friend was he? He should have guessed. All the clues had been there, as he looked back over his friendship with her brother.

Luke had never wanted them to hang out at

the Hamilton home, only at the Bailey place. He hadn't talked much about his home life at all— hadn't *wanted* to talk about it—so Elliot hadn't pressed. He *had* figured out early that Luke had little respect for his father. Now he understood it better.

Elliot had always planned a career in law enforcement. Even as a youth, he should have been perceptive enough to pick up on something that now seemed so very obvious.

He turned his gaze to the woman beside him and something seemed to shift inside him. Amid that kind of ugliness, how was it possible that Megan could hold on to her beautiful, kind spirit? The artistic, compassionate soul, able to see the good in everything around her?

Emotion clogged his throat and he had to clear it away before he could speak. "I'm so sorry you had to live through that."

"I don't need your sympathy," she said stiffly. "I'm only telling you this because you need to understand. After watching the abuse that my mother suffered—and probably his own mother, though he may have been too young to remember—Luke would never raise a hand to a woman. *Never.* I know he wouldn't. He's not capable of it, Elliot. Whoever hurt Elizabeth— whomever or whatever she might have feared—I know it was not my brother."

Chapter Seventeen

HOW WAS SHE supposed to process everything that had happened that day? Megan's head spun, her thoughts racing. The day had been a roller-coaster ride and her equilibrium still felt as if she were spinning and twisting.

Their drive yesterday along this same route seemed like another lifetime ago!

Was it possible this Peg McGeary could be the break they had been searching for all these years? The case had been cold for years. Could Elliot really have found the one person who could finally lead them to answers?

She hated having to tell Elliot about how difficult things had been at home the first eleven years of her life. It was something she had tried hard to put behind her.

She always told herself those years did not define her. Yes, it had been horrible to witness her father mistreating her mother. Every child deserved the security of knowing her parents loved each other, would always take care of each other.

Luke had been the one to watch over her. The two of them had survived together and even thrived after they moved in with her grandmother, where they were safe.

Megan wanted to think her grandmother's love had healed many of her scars.

It was a part of her life she didn't like thinking about and never talked about, but she had had no choice but to share it with Elliot. He had to know the grim reality she and Luke had lived with during their childhood.

"I know you want to think that," he said, his tone so gentle it almost brought tears to her eyes. "But you have to see it from my perspective. As a law-enforcement officer, I'm aware that most studies show that those who grew up in abusive households are more likely to be abusers themselves."

"Most. Not all. Not my brother."

"You can't be certain. You don't know what goes on behind closed doors."

"I know what I've seen all my life and what I saw of their marriage from the outside."

Luke had been a patient husband trying to deal with a difficult woman. She had seen it over and over.

"More than once I saw Elizabeth on the verge of hysteria and Luke was never anything but patient and kind to her. Even in situations where he had every right to respond with anger, he managed to hold on to his calm, no matter how tough she made it."

"Doesn't sound like they were very happy together."

"Before the kids came along, they were. I think Elizabeth really struggled with being a mother, especially of two children. Bridger had colic and that didn't help anything. She was depressed and angry all the time. Her dreams didn't match up with her reality and she took that out on Luke."

She paused. "I asked him once how he could keep from retaliating, how he clung to that control. I'll never forget his answer. He gave me a sad kind of smile and said it was easy, really. He simply asked himself in every situation what our father would do. Then he did the exact opposite."

Elliot appeared to digest that as he drove another few miles.

"I wish I'd known back then," Elliot said finally. "About what things were like for you two at home."

She cast him a sideways look. "What could you possibly have done?"

"I don't know. What if I had told my father what was going on?"

He would have, too. Elliot had always been the sort who would try to protect anyone he thought was in jeopardy.

"It wouldn't have done any good," she said, though the idea of it warmed her. "My mother never would have pressed charges. She was a sweet woman in many ways and I loved her dearly. But over the years, I've come to . . . accept her weaknesses. My mother wanted the pretty picture. She wanted everyone in Haven Point to think she had the perfect marriage. She could never accept that it was only an illusion, even when she had two black eyes and a broken wrist."

She didn't blame her mother. Not anymore, at any rate. She put the blame squarely where it belonged, at the feet of Paul Hamilton.

"You must think I'm the worst sort of friend," Elliot said.

"Why? Because you didn't know? How could you have?"

"I should have figured it out somehow. If I had picked up on the signs, I might have been able to get Luke to confide in me and tried to involve the authorities."

Luke would have hated that, his friends knowing the truth. Her brother could be so stoic about things. He buried his feelings deep, probably because their father had preyed on any hint of weakness.

"Don't blame yourself, Elliot. Luke never would have talked about it to his friends. He didn't want to talk about it with *anyone*. Gran tried to get us into counseling after my mother died but Luke never wanted to go."

Her grandmother used to say Luke was a young man who knew how to keep himself to himself. Not for the first time, she wondered how someone like Luke, reserved and composed, could have fallen for a drama queen like Elizabeth Sinclair, who was never happy unless she was the center of attention.

"He always told Gran he was dealing with things in his own way," she said. "Anyway, none of that matters right now. The important thing here is that Elizabeth left on her own. She caught a ride with a trucker and headed out of Idaho. Peg just confirmed that. What I don't understand is why none of this has come out before. It seems like basic police work. Why would the Haven Point Police Department not follow through on a solid tip like that?"

"Good question."

Was it her imagination or did he look uncomfortable as he drove?

"Why do you think the police department didn't at least take down her statement?"

He faced forward, eyes on the road ahead of them, but she didn't miss the muscle that suddenly flexed in his jaw. "During an ongoing investigation, sometimes tips get missed. I'm assuming that must be what happened here."

She gave him a closer look. "But you're not sure, are you?"

"Not completely, no."

He drove about a mile before he spoke again. "You were honest with me when I could sense you didn't want to be. In return, I feel I have to make a confession."

She gazed at him, baffled by the grim note in

301

his voice and aware of a sense of foreboding. "A confession."

"My father's performance the last few years he was on the job was . . . uneven."

He said the words in a voice devoid of expression, but she could sense they had great significance, though she didn't quite know what. "Uneven? What does that mean?"

If she hadn't been watching closely, she might have missed the guilty expression that flashed briefly over his features.

"In retrospect, we suspect—Marshall, Cade and I—that Dad was suffering from early-onset dementia the last year or so of his service. Cade was concerned enough about Dad during the few months before the shoot-out where Dad was hit that he was ready to report him to the authorities and ask for a performance review. The point became moot when my father was shot and suffered a brain injury."

He glanced at her. "Please. I would ask you not to share that information with anyone. It could jeopardize every single case he worked on that last year—and they were all clean convictions. Cade made sure of that."

She was both touched by his trust in her and staggered by the information. Wyn or Katrina had never said a word to her. How tragic. John Bailey had been such a good man. Everyone in town thought so.

"Dementia. Dear heavens."

"I know. It would have been horrible. It's also impossible to confirm now, since Mom chose not to have an autopsy after he died. Cade is the one who worked closest with him those last few years. He said Dad's behavior was inconsistent. One day he would be fine and totally on his game. The next he would put his car keys in the coffee maker then spend the whole day looking for them."

He was quiet. "Again, I would ask you not to say anything. If you do, I'll have to deny I ever said it."

The ramifications of the information he had shared with her were huge. Catastrophic, even. Was it possible that his father had dropped the ball into the investigation of Elizabeth's disappearance?

"That's why you're looking into the case, isn't it? You're trying to find exactly what we did today, track down leads your father might have missed."

It wasn't malicious on his part, some effort to go after Luke and make him pay for a crime he didn't commit. He was genuinely trying to find answers.

Elliot was the oldest son. The steady, reliable one, the FBI agent who had thrown everything into being the best. Did he feel responsible for fixing his father's mistakes now?

"I'm so sorry about John. He didn't deserve that, after all his years of dedicated service to the people of Haven Point."

His hands tightened on the steering wheel. "He didn't."

"You do see that Peg's testimony could be exactly the link we're looking for. This could exonerate Lucas, after all this time—after all the whispers and sidelong looks and veiled innuendos."

She hugged Cyrus, who woke up, looked around, then closed his eyes again.

"We still can't prove anything. We only know Peg picked up a woman she has tentatively identified as Elizabeth. While it might answer a few questions, it also raises more. If it was Elizabeth, what happened to her after Pendleton? I've looked at Luke's phone records and haven't seen a phone call from Oregon that night, but I would have to look more closely."

"He was in Haven Point all night with Cassie and Bridger then had an alibi for the rest of the day, working with a homeowner. That's on record. How could he have loaded up the kids, driven the four hours to Pendleton, killed Elizabeth, ditched her body somewhere on the way back and made it home in time to be at the job site first thing in the morning?"

He tapped a finger on the steering wheel. "Good question."

"If Lucas can prove he was nowhere near Oregon, someone else was responsible for her disappearance. Or she simply decided to stay away. Admit it! This makes it less likely than ever that Lucas was involved."

When he said nothing, she ground her back teeth. "You stubborn man! Admit it! You, along with everyone else, have been wrong all these years!"

A muscle worked in his jaw. "We can't prove anything at this point. But I will admit, if we had some way to verify Peg's story and her identification of Elizabeth as the woman she gave a ride to that night, it's an important clue."

Her growing elation subsided into familiar frustration. "How could you possibly verify something that happened so long ago?"

"Good question. I don't know. I could check for other eyewitnesses at the service station in Pendleton."

"From more than seven years ago."

"That's right. It won't be easy. Maybe even impossible."

Where did this leave them? With more questions than before. She cuddled her dog, her mind racing over Peg's statement. If only the Haven Point Police Department had followed up earlier, perhaps they could have found out about the trucker's story earlier. Maybe Elizabeth would have been found years ago.

She couldn't be resentful, though. How difficult it must have been for a proud man like John Bailey to suffer the effects of early-onset senility. She couldn't be grateful he'd suffered a debilitating brain injury but the alternative would have been equally heartbreaking for the family.

"I'm sorry about your father," she said softly. "He was a good man. I know how you and Marshall and Wyn must hate having something like that tarnish his legacy."

He gazed at her for a long moment before turning his attention back to the road. "You are remarkable," he said gruffly.

Megan could feel her face heat. "I'm not anything close to remarkable."

"I disagree."

Before she realized what he intended, he reached across the car and covered her hand with his. She couldn't resist turning her hand and tangling her fingers with his, heart pounding at the sweet, tender intimacy of the moment.

His hand was warm, his skin roughened, but she wanted to stay like that the entire drive, safe and cherished and content, next to the man she—

Her mind shied away from the thought but she forced herself to face the truth.

She was in love with Elliot Bailey and the knowledge completely terrified her.

What had she done? She wanted to bury her

face in Cyrus's fur and hide away from Elliot's too-perceptive gaze.

How could she have been so stupid? All these years, she had tried to take care of her heart, to keep it safe. She had loved Wyatt, though he had been taken from her before they ever really had a chance to see what might grow between them.

Now she could see it for what it was. Wyatt had been laughter and sunshine. He had made her laugh at a time when she desperately had needed that. Only a few months earlier, Megan had returned to Haven Point to help her grandmother after Dorothy had been diagnosed with Stage III stomach cancer. She had been afraid for her grandmother and selfishly feeling sorry for herself because she'd had to return to Haven Point right as her dreams were coming true.

Into that dark time, Wyatt had seemed like a bright ray of hope.

When Wyatt died, she had been devastated. She wasn't sure she'd smiled for a year after his death.

They were only in the beginning, lighthearted stages of love. A year later when Elizabeth disappeared, she saw through her brother's eyes what real loss was. Luke had spent the last seven years going through the motions for his kids. All the joy and light had been sucked out of his world. He was only now beginning to live again.

Megan had vowed she couldn't let that sort of

bone-deep love into her heart. She wasn't strong enough to survive the loss of it.

She couldn't let Elliot kiss her again. Every time he did, she slid further and further into love with him, that dark, terrifying place she never wanted to go.

What if she was too late? What if she had already come too far to claw her way back to where it was safe?

She pulled her hand away now without a word and buried her fingers in Cyrus's fur. As always, her dog was steady, reliable, loving.

All she and Elliot could ever share were those stolen kisses. Her head knew that, even if she had yet to convince her heart.

She wanted to cry for all the heartache that waited for her when they finished this road trip, but she was afraid that if she started, she wouldn't be able to stop.

ELLIOT DROVE THROUGH the northwestern edge of Utah, passing only the occasional car and sometimes a big rig.

He usually enjoyed this part of the drive. Some people considered it stark, even desolate, but the wide open spaces always seemed to give his brain room for introspection.

Those times he drove it on his way home to Haven Point from Denver, he often found himself almost in a meditative state as he passed farms and ranches and the occasional cluster of houses springing up in the middle of nowhere. He could work through troubling cases, forge connections, follow pathways, plot books.

This time, that productive calm was nowhere in evidence. His thoughts were a jumble of chaos.

Though he kept his attention focused on the road, he still slanted the occasional glance at the woman curled up in the seat beside him. She slept on her side facing him, her hands folded together under her cheek to make a pillow, like a child in a painting. The sun had set an hour ago, but in the dim light from the dashboard, he could make out her features clearly—delicate cheekbones, dark lashes fanning her cheeks, her soft, sweetly shaped lips parted slightly.

He rubbed at his chest, at the sudden ache there.

This trip had been a mistake, from the get-go. Had he actually been stupid enough to think he could have any hope of resisting her when he spent every waking moment with her for the past two days?

What kind of idiot ever thought that was a good idea?

For years, he had been telling himself his attraction to Megan would burn itself out someday. It wasn't as if he obsessed about her or anything. In Denver, he would go months without thinking about her, yet every time he had returned to Haven Point, he would wonder if he would see her while he was home. If this would be the time he came home and found out she was dating someone else or if he would finally figure out a way to test the waters and see if she could ever return his interest.

After the last few days, he had come to realize he was completely deluded if he actually thought he could extricate his heart from her grasp.

He replayed their conversation of the night before, when he had told her he had feelings for her. Did she have any idea what an understatement that was? He was in love with her, had probably been in love with her for years. He had simply been too stupid and stubborn to see it.

What good would it do to admit it now, to himself or to her? He would have to make some decisions about his life and his future, things he wasn't sure he was ready to face.

He did know that every time he thought about a future without Megan in it, he saw a wide, empty space he found more desolate than the high desert could ever be.

THE SUDDEN ABSENCE of motion jarred her awake. For a moment, she had that wild panic of not knowing where she was. Then her conscious mind processed the familiar lights, colors, sights, and she realized they were at a service station.

Oh, the joys of road trips—long expanses of time interrupted only by the need for fuel.

Cyrus yipped and wriggled around on her lap, making her suddenly aware of how achy her muscles felt from holding him for hours.

"I can't believe I fell asleep again. Where are we?"

"Mountain Home. I wanted to keep going, but the gas gauge was getting low and I didn't want to risk it. Plus Cyrus has been restless a bit for the last fifteen minutes. I figured he needed a stop. I'm surprised he didn't wake you earlier."

"So am I. I feel like I slept the whole way today. I'm sorry I left all the driving to you."

"I didn't mind. You must have needed rest."

She had slept only a few hours the night before, too consumed with his words that ran through her mind again and again on the same soundtrack.

"You take care of Cyrus and I'll pump the gas," he said, falling into the pattern they had developed over this rapid-fire trip.

"You've been driving. You probably need to move more than I do, don't you?"

"It was a pretty easy drive with little traffic. We made good time."

It was only nine, she saw, about an hour earlier than she expected to be reaching this point— probably because he had basically driven straight through from Rock Springs without stopping until now.

Cyrus was all but dancing on her lap with his legs crossed. She quickly climbed out of the vehicle, grabbed his leash from the back seat and set him down.

"Are you hungry?" Elliot asked from across the width of the vehicle. "I can grab a couple sandwiches from the fast-food place here, if it's still open."

She wanted to tell him she could wait until they were back in Haven Point but her stomach chose that moment to grumble loudly.

"I should probably eat, since I didn't have much lunch and breakfast was only coffee."

"Don't forget, we still have Rocco's cookies. I had a couple of them earlier and, I've got to say, I think he has a big future as a dessert chef."

She had to smile, though she still felt achy and wrung out. "They seemed like a great couple. The woman truck driver and the husband cookie maker. I love the role reversals. And she's got great taste in authors."

He flushed, which she found rather adorable. "If you say so. Why don't you take Cyrus over to the dog park? I'll grab some sandwiches and take them over there. We can let him run around a bit before we hit the road again."

"Sounds good," she said, then turned to walk in that direction with her dog.

ELLIOT DIDN'T LIKE talking about himself or his work. That was an entirely new perspective she had gained over the last two days. He was embarrassed by his own success and deflected every conversation that came back to his books.

That wasn't the only perspective of Elliot Bailey that had shifted.

She couldn't believe she ever thought him cold, emotionless. He wasn't. He was only excellent at hiding those emotions.

She would miss him desperately when he returned to Denver. The future without him seemed as colorless and cold as Silver Beach in January.

How would she say goodbye?

She threw the ball a few times for Cyrus, who went along with the program for a few moments but quickly lost interest and seemed content to sniff the perimeter of the fence, scenting out all the other dogs who had come before.

She was sitting on the picnic table and watching him at it while the cool May evening settled around her when Elliot came toward them carrying a plastic bag containing a couple of wrapped hoagies. He had taken time to bring Cyrus's water bowl, too, a thoughtful gesture that touched something deep inside.

She was completely helpless to resist him.

"Go ahead and start on your sandwich. I'll fill this for Cyrus."

"Thank you."

She took the bag from him and pulled out her sandwich. When he returned with the filled water bowl, he set it down for the dog, then pulled her keys and his phone out of his pocket and placed them on the table. Just as he was going to sit down, he looked down at the table and made a face.

"I forgot the drinks. What can I get you?"

"One of the bottled waters in the cooler would be fine. They should still be cold, since I added more ice at the hotel before we left."

"That works for me, too."

He picked up the keys and turned to head back to the SUV.

"Make sure you lock up again," she teased. "We don't need a repeat of what happened yesterday, with the little laptop thief."

At her words, he smiled, bright and genuine and so completely unexpected that it took her breath away.

"Right. We can't have that."

That was a memory she would tuck away forever, the utter shock on his features when she had insisted he give the boy a reward. She had many memories from this trip she would cherish. Kissing him on the trail the day before. Walking with him under the starry sky.

Falling in love.

He was still at her SUV, the hatch up as he looked through the cooler, when the table suddenly buzzed. It was his phone vibrating with an incoming text.

She didn't mean to look at it. She wasn't snooping on purpose. It was simply an instinctive reaction to look down at any phone alert.

Finished first read of the ms. Fantastic, as usual. Another bestseller! Edits to follow in a few days.

When did he finish his book? It must have been the day before while she was driving—or maybe his night was as sleepless as hers and he'd wrapped it up in the early hours.

Yay! What a rewarding feeling that must be, to know he'd created something that would keep people like Verla and Peg reading late into the night.

The table buzzed a moment later with a follow-up text, and she glanced down, again by instinct. This time, it took a few seconds for the words on the screen to register fully, and then she had to set down her sandwich.

Not to nag, but when will you send me Elizabeth's book?

The words took a moment to penetrate. When they did, the one bite of sandwich she'd managed to swallow seemed to congeal in her stomach. A vast wave of acrid betrayal washed over her, sucking away her oxygen.

Elizabeth's book? The book he swore over and over again he wasn't writing?

How many times had he told her he was only investigating the case to tie up loose ends? She had trusted him. The idea that he might use her family's pain—Luke's, Cassie's, poor little Bridger, who didn't even remember his mother—for his own gain left her fighting tears.

He had lied to her and to others. Even earlier that day, he had told Peg that he was only investigating Elizabeth's disappearance to find answers.

She couldn't seem to catch her breath, heartsick at him and at herself. She had known in her heart she shouldn't let herself love him. If she hadn't fallen for him, would she be feeling so very betrayed?

What about his feelings? Had he lied about that, too, when he said he cared for her, that he had been attracted to her for years? Maybe he was only trying to weaken her defenses, to leave her vulnerable and needy so she wouldn't be angry with him over writing Elizabeth's story.

She had trusted him. How could he do this to her and to her family?

She had wondered why he was so passionate about digging into the case. Now she knew. Regardless of his assurances, Elliot planned to exploit her family's pain for his writing career and she didn't have the first idea how to stop it.

He returned a moment later and she couldn't face him as he set a water bottle on the table in front of her, the sides dripping with condensation. "Here you go. I had to dig a little but I found a cold one, in the bottom of the cooler."

It took her several attempts to make her mouth move to form a response. "Thanks," she mumbled.

"Everything okay?"

She wanted to weep, suddenly, to rail and cry and beg him to reconsider. She couldn't. She refused to break down in front of him, especially right now when her feelings were so red-hot. She wasn't her father, all hot fire and anger and hurtful words. She would wait until she was composed before confronting him about the lies.

They had an hour ahead of them before they would reach Haven Point and she had no idea how she would be strong enough to endure the drive without exploding.

"Sure," she managed to answer. "Why wouldn't it be?"

WHAT HAPPENED?

One moment, Megan had been looking at him with warmth and gratitude for the sandwich. The next, she had completely shut down. All he had done was take her some food and go look for a water bottle. Harmless enough. Where had things gone off the rails?

He tried to make conversation as they ate but gave up when she seemed determined to answer in monosyllables.

It had been an eventful few days, he told himself. Maybe she was simply tired of the chaos and ready to be home in her little cottage on the lake. He couldn't really blame her for that.

His supposition was confirmed when she finished quickly, then stood up with Cyrus's leash in hand. "I'm going to load him up," she said.

He stood as well, wrapping up what was left of his sandwich. His hunger had somehow disappeared, frozen out by her cold reserve.

"I'll drive from here," she announced, without giving him a chance to say otherwise. "Go ahead and work, if you need to."

"I don't," he said. "I finished my manuscript last night and sent it to my editor."

If he had expected her to congratulate him, he was doomed to disappointment. She only lifted her mouth in a pale imitation of her genuine smile. "Guess it's time to get started on the next one, then."

"I don't know what I'm going to write next. Maybe I'll take a break."

"I'm sure you'll come up with something," she answered, her voice unusually caustic.

He frowned, wondering again what the hell he had done.

After a few more of his attempts at conversation fell flat, she turned up the music in an outright attempt to avoid conversation.

He went over the day's events and couldn't come up with one obvious thing. While he could have turned the music down and forced a conversation, he figured she had a right not to talk to him if she didn't want to.

They made it back to Haven Point as the moon was cresting the Redemption Mountain Range across the lake. May's full moon was called the Flower Moon—one of those inane facts stuck in his head.

She pulled up in front of her cottage. "Thank you for coming with me, and for taking your turn at the wheel."

The coolness in her voice conveyed a clear message. She was angry—and it angered *him* that he had no idea why.

"Are you going to tell me what I've done now that we're back or leave me guessing?"

In the glow of that flower moon, her features looked beautiful and fragile and as distant as the stars. "I'm not sure what you mean," she said, her voice stiff.

"Seriously? You want to play the ignorance card? You have hardly exchanged three words with me since we left Mountain Home."

"I was listening to music."

"You were avoiding conversation."

"Maybe I didn't have anything left to say to you."

He nearly staggered backward from the impact of that direct hit.

"Wow. Okay. I guess that's it, then."

"What do you want from me, Elliot?"

"An explanation would be nice. I would think I deserve that, at least after what we . . . after everything. What did I do wrong?"

She looked at him for a long moment, then gazed out at the lake, where the flower moon played in the ripples.

"It's not what you did. It's what you're about to do."

"I wasn't aware you were psychic."

"I'm not. Robots act predictably. They do what they're programmed to do. I should have seen that before."

Her words wounded with tiny, sharp daggers. "You must know, then, that I'm about to pull out my hair, trying to figure out how everything suddenly changed. Is it because I kissed you? Or because I told you I had feelings for you?"

"You don't have to pretend, Elliot. I'm another source to you. You're very good at what you do. You'll say whatever you have to in order to get the information you want."

Those daggers sliced harder, deeper. "I haven't lied to you. Not about anything."

Her mouth tightened. "Oh. Haven't you? I saw

the text from your editor, okay? I didn't mean to snoop but it flashed on the screen of your phone when you were pulling water bottles out of the cooler at dinner."

"What text?" He frowned. "I didn't know Joe had been in touch."

"Yes. You'll be happy to know, I'm sure, that he's already read the manuscript you turned in and loves it. He's sure you've got another bestseller on your hands. Oh, and he can't wait to read the next book you're doing on Elizabeth. You know, the one you've been telling me and everyone else all along you had no intention of writing?"

He pulled out his phone and scrolled through the notifications. As she said, Joe praised his latest book—at least he had that—and made a reference to him writing Elizabeth's book.

When he had first come to Haven Point and began looking into the case, his editor had pushed him what was next after he finished *Blood Vengeance*. Elliot had told Joe he intended to take a break for a few months. In their conversation, he had casually mentioned he was pursuing some leads in a local cold case.

After Elliot shared a few details with him, Joe had been intrigued enough to suggest it would make a great next project, especially because of his personal ties to the case, his friendship with both the victim and the suspect.

Elliot had told him outright the publishing house would be doomed to disappointment because he had no intention of ever writing about Elizabeth.

Obviously, Joe was still lobbying hard. Elliot understood how Megan could read the text and come to a different conclusion. He couldn't blame her.

It hurt more than he wanted to admit that she didn't trust him, that she jumped to conclusions without reason. Didn't the past few days between them count for anything?

"Next time you decide to be angry with me, you might want to get my side of the story first," he said, striving for calm.

"What side of the story? It's obvious you've been playing me from the beginning. You told me you didn't plan to write a book about Elizabeth's case, but you were only saying that because you thought that's what I wanted to hear."

"I told you that because it's true. I thought about it, yes, when I first started looking into the case. That wasn't my core motivation but the possibility was real. I didn't lie to you, though. I knew early on that I never could."

"Because writing about the case would mean exposing your father."

"That, yes. But more important, I won't write the book because I don't want to hurt you or your family. You've been through enough. I won't make it worse."

Chapter Eighteen

DESPITE THE FURY and sense of betrayal that had shifted from white-hot to cold, simmering red, Elliot's words seemed to reach straight into her heart.

He sounded so sincere, so earnest. She wanted to trust him, but how could she—especially now, when she had spent the past hour carefully reconstructing all those barriers around her heart?

"You don't believe me, do you?"

She couldn't answer, her heart aching.

The memory of the tender moments they had shared the last few days seemed to crowd her mind. Elliot was a good man. Her heart told her he was. If he said he wasn't writing a book about Elizabeth's case, she knew he wouldn't lie to her.

That didn't change the central issue, that regardless of the evidence, regardless of how persuasive she was in defending her brother, Elliot had made up his mind that Luke had somehow caused Elizabeth's disappearance. How could they ever get past that?

"I wish you trusted me. Since you don't, I'll have to prove it."

He stalked to the door and down the porch steps, each footstep as sharp as a gunshot on the wooden planks. Cyrus whined, alert to the tension between them and perhaps even aware of the ache expanding in her chest.

She stood for a moment in uncertainty while a soft breeze blew off the lake.

Finally, she grabbed her dog and carried him up the steps to her own cottage. The moment she set him down, he waddled to his familiar bed and pulled out his favorite toy, shaking it back and forth as if to remind it the boss was back.

She couldn't even muster a smile. She was cold, suddenly, though the May evening was pleasant. After a moment of shivering, she hit the switch for the gas fireplace and sank into her favorite armchair, wanting to wrap her arms around herself and weep.

She had known the pain in store for her if she allowed herself to love him. That was the reason she had fought so hard against it.

What was she supposed to do now? Her heart felt bruised, achy. Broken.

She should be doing something. Unpacking her things, perhaps, or starting a load of laundry. She couldn't make herself move to deal with inconsequential things right now, when her emotions felt so heavy and raw.

Before she could convince herself to do more than sit here and brood, her door burst open as Elliot came back without knocking. He crossed to the chair where she sat and threw down onto the coffee table a manila folder bulging with a thick stack of papers.

"There you go."

She stared at the stack. "What's this?"

"Every scrap of paper, every file, every phone number I found in Elizabeth's case. The whole thing. I can't give you the official case files from the sheriff's department, but this is everything I've been working on myself."

"I . . . What am I supposed to do with them?"

"Whatever you want. Give them to Luke. Put them in a scrapbook. Burn them, if you want. I'm done with this case. As far as I'm concerned, Elizabeth left on her own free will."

"You believe Peg," she whispered.

He shrugged. "She is convinced Elizabeth is the woman she picked up that night and drove to Oregon. If she's right, that means Elizabeth left Haven Point on her own and made her way to that truck stop."

His words slid over her, warm and soft like one of the hand-knitted shawls McKenzie Kilpatrick sold in her store.

This was exactly what she'd wanted—for him to believe her. She wanted to wrap the feeling around her, to stay there cocooned in the safety of trust.

Sweet relief washed over her. She felt as if she'd been fighting a battle alone for a long time and finally had someone standing at her back.

His next words, however, made it clear that someone wouldn't be Elliot.

"I'm not saying I believe Luke is wholly innocent, Megan. You have to understand that. Peg reported that Elizabeth was afraid and bleeding, which would indicate someone hurt her. I don't know if that person was her husband, but given her previous police report, that's the logical conclusion."

"Except she was lying when she filed the report."

His expression plainly conveyed his doubts. "While I admire your faith in your brother, faith is not the same thing as fact."

He tapped the papers. "Whatever the case, there were countless eyewitnesses placing him here in Haven Point that evening and again the next morning. I don't believe he could have driven to Pendleton, killed her, disposed of her body someplace that no hunter or hiker has stumbled over the last seven years, then made it back here to fit the timeline we have for his movements."

"He didn't do it. That's what you're saying."

He looked down at the papers, then back at her. "That's what I'm saying. I'll tell Marshall about Peg and give him her information and suggest the sheriff's department follows through and see if they can find any other eyewitnesses from that night. I'll also pass along my belief that Lucas wasn't involved."

He paused. "You do know what this means, right?"

"What?"

"This now becomes a federal case, as it crosses state lines. If there were any evidence a crime has been committed, which right now we don't have, the FBI would take over the case."

"Would you take charge?"

"No. I'm too close to things and it's not a Colorado issue, as far as we know. Any further investigation would probably be handled by the Boise or Portland field offices. I've got good friends in each and will make sure it's handled well."

"Thank you for that."

He studied her, his features remote again. She had hurt him by her mistrust, she realized. Would he be able to forgive her? Did she *want* him to?

"I'll remind you, there is no law against a person picking up and moving somewhere else. She has every right to leave Haven Point and start a new life somewhere else if she wanted. If there is no evidence any laws have been broken and no proof that someone deliberately harmed her, there will be no further investigation. Not officially by the Bureau and not unofficially by me."

He was walking away? His sisters called him a bulldog, tenacious and tough, fiercely committed to justice. He had risked his own career—and his *life*—to rescue those girls.

Elizabeth had been his friend. After all his digging into Elizabeth's case, would he really be able to accept not finding more answers?

"Just like that?"

"Yes. Just like that." He stood in the doorway, one hand in a fist against the jamb, the other shoved into his pocket. He studied her for a long moment, his features distant and somehow . . . sad. "What choice do I have? Even we unfeeling robots sometimes know when to give up."

Was he only talking about the case?

She looked sharply at him but could read nothing in that remote, stiff expression. He had once more returned to the formal, unapproachable investigator, the man who shoved his emotions inside for fear they would cloud his reason.

"How do I know you don't just have copies of everything?"

His features hardened. "I suppose you can't. Not really. I guess for once you'll just have to trust me."

She wanted to. The urge was overwhelming to throw everything at his feet and simply lean against his strength.

She couldn't. She couldn't go through the pain again. She had lost herself after Wyatt died. The world had become gray and cheerless, all her photos black-and-white and filled with despair.

She was in a good place right now, a place filled with color and light. She was ready to embrace life again.

She couldn't let Elliot break her heart all over again.

"Thank you," she said, doing her best to keep the trembling out of her voice. "For . . . these files and for . . . everything. I'm sorry I doubted you. Whatever you write next, I'm sure it will be wonderful. Good luck with everything."

Though her heart felt as if it would never recover, she spoke the words firmly, with clear dismissal in her tone.

She was saying goodbye.

That was how things had to be. She was broken by her childhood, by losing Wyatt, by all the years of doubt and sadness over Elizabeth. She couldn't give Elliot the love he needed, couldn't be the kind of woman willing to open her heart and embrace all the possibilities with him. She had doubted him on the slimmest of evidence.

He deserved more. So much more.

He studied her intently and she could see the moment he understood everything she had left unspoken. His expression tightened, and for the first time, she could clearly read him.

She had hurt him.

The knowledge burned in her throat.

He looked as if he wanted to argue but he must

have sensed her mind was made up. They could never share more than a few heated kisses and the possibility of what might have been.

"You're welcome. Good night, Megan."

His words had the ring of finality to them as well. He turned and headed for the door, and it took every ounce of strength inside her not to call him back.

SHE SLEPT POORLY, her dreams fitful and tortured. Elizabeth showed up, lovely and troubled and laughing at all the pain she had left behind. Luke was there as well, his features remote and overwhelmed and sad at the same time.

When her alarm went off, she wanted to chuck it out the window so she could stay wrapped under her blanket and shove the world away for the next year or two.

She sat up, blinking away sleep. Her eyes felt achy, gritty, swollen. She hadn't cried herself to sleep. That was what she told herself, anyway. It had only been all the pollen that floated in from sleeping with the windows open to the night sounds.

Right.

The sun wasn't yet up but she forced herself out of bed anyway. She had been gone for two days and could only imagine the work that awaited her at the inn's front office.

Cyrus gave a long-suffering whine from beside

her bed and she sighed. "I know. You need to go out. I'm sorry. I'm coming."

She shivered as her feet hit the floor. The first thing she saw when she opened the door was the dew clinging to the grass and the delicate branches of the trees, as if all of nature wore sparkling diadems.

The second was more of an absence, really. Something that should have been there but wasn't. Elliot's vehicle was gone.

She frowned. Where was he, so early? The sun was barely cresting the Redemptions to the east. Had his sleep been restless, too?

It didn't matter. What he did or didn't do was not her business. She had made that clear to him the night before.

Her cell phone rang just as she was stepping out of the shower. Her brother, she saw when she checked the caller ID.

She had to reveal what they had found. Oh, she didn't want to. How could she tell him it appeared his wife had left him and their babies of her own free will? Megan had always believed it, but now they had solid proof.

She cleared her throat before answering the call but her voice still sounded ragged. "Good morning."

"Morning. Just checking to see if you made it back to town okay."

"Yes. We rolled in late last night."

"We?"

For obvious reasons, she hadn't told him she was going to Colorado with Elliot. Now she didn't see how she could avoid it. In order for her to discuss the interview with Peg McGeary, she would have to tell him the process by which the interview came about in the first place.

She drew in a deep breath, hoping her relationship with her brother would survive what Luke would certainly see as a betrayal.

"Yes. Cyrus came with me." She paused. "So did Elliot Bailey."

As she might have expected, a long, tense silence met her disclosure. "Is that right?" Luke finally said.

She winced at the distant coldness in his voice. She should have told him before she and Elliot left Haven Point. She should at least have mentioned it when she impulsively had changed her mind and called him from the road to tell him about Harry Lange's shocking offer.

Harry Lange.

She hadn't even had a moment to think about selling the inn and what it might mean for her future.

She pushed the thought away. Right now she needed to focus on Luke and how she could tell her brother about the progress she and Elliot had made toward solving the mystery of his wife's disappearance.

This wasn't the sort of thing she could discuss over the phone, she suddenly realized. She had to tell him in person. It seemed the right thing to do, when you were about to tell a man it appeared his wife voluntarily left him behind to face years of whispers and accusations.

"It's a long story," she said, a master of understatement. "I need to talk to you."

"If you want to talk about Elliot Bailey, I'm afraid I'm not interested."

"It's about Elizabeth. Are you home? May I come over now?"

"I'm just heading over to the job site. I was checking to be sure you were safe and see if you need to talk more about Lange's offer."

"Do you have ten minutes to drop by on your way? I can make you breakfast."

She could call the front office and let them know she would be late that morning. Surely she had a few things in the refrigerator and could whip up an omelet for him.

"Will Bailey be there?" he asked, his voice stern and condemning.

"No! It's not—We're not—" Her words faltered. She and Elliot were nothing. She had made sure of that the night before. "I don't know where he is. His car is gone from next door."

"I can be there in ten. I only have a few minutes. I've got subcontractors showing up early this morning."

"Perfect. I'll put on the coffee."

She finished braiding her hair the moment his pickup pulled up in front of her house. When she saw her brother climb out alone, without Cassie or Bridger, she felt a sudden intense longing to see her niece and nephew. She hadn't seen them in days and all at once she missed them desperately.

"I've got toast and your omelet is nearly done," she said when she opened the door to him.

"You didn't have to fix me breakfast," her brother said gruffly.

"I wanted to. I'm sure you didn't have time to eat this morning in the chaos of sending the kids off to school."

"I had a cup of coffee and planned to grab a breakfast sandwich on my way to the site."

"This is better."

She set the omelet down at the table, grabbed a piece of toast for herself and sat down across from him.

"How are Cass and Bridge? Next week is the last week of school, isn't it? Are they excited about summer?"

Luke shrugged, not looking at her as he started working on the omelet. "I suppose. We've almost got the schedule figured out. Mrs. Roberts can only watch them half the day since she has her grandchildren in the afternoons. We'll make do with summer camps and I'll take them with me on the site. Cassie thinks she's old enough to stay home alone with Bridge, but that's not happening."

"I'll help wherever you need me. They can always come here."

Day care had been a constant battle for Luke the last seven years, probably his biggest stress and expense.

She was angry all over again at her sister-in-law for the chaos she had left behind.

"What's this about?" Luke finally said after he was nearly done with his omelet. "What did you need to talk to me about? And why the hell didn't you tell me Elliot Bailey went with you to Colorado? Are you two a thing now?"

She had never kept secrets from Luke. Throughout their tumultuous childhood, he had been her rock and her best friend. She couldn't start now.

The half slice of toast she had nibbled seemed to congeal in her stomach. "He wanted to follow up on a possible lead in Elizabeth's case."

Dark eyes murky with betrayal, he shoved back his chair and stood up. "And you drove him? The man thinks I killed my wife and you merrily gave him a ride so he could prove it?"

"I wanted him to find evidence that would prove you had nothing to do with Elizabeth's disappearance. Luke, that's exactly what he did!"

Luke stared at her for a long moment, then slowly lowered himself back to the kitchen chair. "You . . . what?"

"We found out what happened. Or at least where she went that night."

"What do you mean? What did you learn?"

She had to tell him, no matter how difficult. She swallowed hard. "Luke. Elizabeth left on her own. We found—" She corrected herself. "*Elliot* found a trucker who says she found a woman matching Elizabeth's description in a truck-stop restroom outside of Boise. She was crying and in despair. The trucker, Peg McGeary, says she gave the woman a ride as far as Pendleton, Oregon, but doesn't know what happened after that."

"Pendleton."

The word sounded raw, strangled, as if Luke couldn't quite make his vocal cords cooperate.

"Yes. She's certain of it. Do you know what this means? It means you didn't have anything to do with her disappearance! She was alive when she left Haven Point and Elliot says there are too many witnesses who saw you here that night and again first thing in the morning for you to have played a part. From the time the trucker dropped her off and she might have had the chance to contact you, you wouldn't have had time to follow her there and . . ." Her voice faltered. She couldn't say the rest.

"To follow her there and kill her." He said the words flatly, with no emotion, but his eyes looked anguished and her heart ached for him.

She wanted to touch him in comfort but somehow sensed he wouldn't welcome any gesture from her right now.

"Don't you see? This clears you. Elliot says so. He says as far as he's concerned, Elizabeth chose to leave on her own and there's no law against that."

Luke gazed down at his plate then up at her, his expression haunted. "So that's it. I'm just supposed to say, thanks for confirming I didn't kill my wife, which I've been saying all along for the last seven freaking years. I was just a lousy husband, terrible enough that she walked away from her children rather than stay married to me."

He didn't deserve this. After all they had endured when they were young and the ugliness of their home life—all the times he had protected her and comforted her and sacrificed for her—Luke deserved a happy ending. She ached that she couldn't give him that.

"I'm sorry," she whispered. "So, so sorry."

"I need to go. I'm late." Luke stood up. "Thanks for breakfast."

"Luke."

"I can't talk about this right now. I'll see you later."

He spun around and headed for the door, and she watched him leave, wondering why everything she tried to do turned out so horribly wrong.

SHE DIDN'T WANT to be here.

Two days later, Megan walked into her friend McKenzie Kilpatrick's living room, wishing she had been able to come up with a good excuse to avoid this gathering of the Haven Point Helping Hands.

She could have pleaded illness or trouble at the inn, but that would have been cowardly. She was one of the co-organizers of this effort, a combined potluck and service project to make little knitted hats for babies in the newborn ICU in Shelter Springs.

This was an important project, one she cared about. More than that, she sensed she needed to be here. She missed her friends and could only benefit by surrounding herself with their strength and compassion and enthusiasm for life.

"You look like hell."

Yeah. So much for their compassion. She glanced over at Wyn Emmett, seated across the table from her. "Do I?"

"What's wrong, honey?" Eliza Caine asked, always concerned for others.

"Are you nervous about your photography thing?" Linda Fremont asked. "I sure would be, if I were you. All those people there to judge me? No thanks."

Right. She had the showing in a handful of days to worry about as well. Familiar panic started to well up, until she met Julia Winston's gaze. Her friend rolled her eyes surreptitiously at Linda's typical negativity and Megan's panic receded a little.

"That is certainly stressful," she agreed.

"But exciting, too," Julia said firmly, squeezing her hand. "I can't wait to see the show. It's going to be amazing."

The town librarian quickly changed the subject to the summer reading program she was starting up and Megan sat back with her knitting, finding comfort in the steady, calming motion.

She hadn't seen her brother in two days. He wasn't returning her calls and she assumed he needed time to process everything. She *had* spoken with Cassie, who told her Luke was in a mood and didn't have much to say to anyone.

She listened to the familiar gossip with half an ear, about who was expecting a baby, whose child had taken a summer job somewhere, who was planning a cruise vacation in a few weeks.

It was nice to be distracted from her own troubles for a time. The buffet table bulged with food but she could only pick a bowl of soup and a little salad. She made her way to the tables McKenzie had set up and was trying to force herself to eat a bite of salad when she overheard Charlene Bailey at the next table over, talking to Barbara Serrano.

"I don't know what to do with that oldest son of mine. Do you know he was shot last month and I'm only now hearing about it?"

Elliot finally had told his mother about his injury. It was about time! Had he told her everything, or only bits and pieces?

"You're kidding!" Barbara exclaimed. "That's crazy! Shot? Why wouldn't he tell you?"

Megan tried to listen in to the conversation without making her interest obvious.

"I suppose he didn't want to worry me. Doesn't he know I already spend every moment of the day worrying for all my children?"

She could only imagine what it would be like from Charlene's standpoint, with nearly all of her children involved in law enforcement in some capacity or other—at least until Wyn had left police work to become a social worker. Now Wyn was *married* to a police officer, though.

"Elliot was always such a serious boy. He never gave you a moment of trouble, did he?"

"I can't believe I'm saying this but sometimes I wish he had. He's *too* serious all the time, if you want the truth."

Megan chewed the inside of her lip to keep from protesting. Did Charlene even know her son? The kind man who could help a would-be thief, simply because she had asked and because he saw a need? Or who risked his life and his career to save innocent girls embroiled in the sex trade?

Elliot Bailey did his best to play by the rules, to be the man his parents always expected of him, but inside he had a rebellious spirit he tried hard to conceal.

"Maybe that's what makes him such a good writer, able to wring out emotion from his readers," Barbara went on. "Those books of his are gripping—thought-provoking and well-written and compelling. Once I start one, I can't put it down. You must be so proud of him."

"I am. He's a good man. The most like his father of any of our children."

Even from a table over, Megan could hear Charlene's heavy sigh. "I only wish he would find someone, like his siblings all have. I don't know how that's supposed to happen when he works all the time. He tells me he's happy, that he's married to his work, but he seems so lonely sometimes."

Barbara said something in response that Megan couldn't hear.

"He has so much love inside him," Charlene went on, "if only he could let down his guard enough to offer it to the right woman. If you want the truth, I suspect he's given his heart to someone already."

"Is he dating someone?"

Charlene shook her head. "Not that he's told me. It's just a mother's instinct. I think he's had his heart broken at some point, probably by some foolish woman too shortsighted to know what she was giving up. Like I said, he's the most like his father of our children. Once Elliot gives his heart to a woman, that's it. It's over."

Megan's heart ached at her own stupidity. She loved Elliot. Why couldn't she find the courage to take this chance with him?

She couldn't bear another moment of this conversation about Elliot. She had to get out of here. She set her fork down, but somehow in her awkwardness, she managed to knock her soup bowl, and a healthy portion of Barbara's delicious minestrone splashed out. Both of the older women looked over with concerned features.

"Are you all right, my dear?" Barbara asked.

No. She wasn't all right. She was stupid and frightened and had thrown away something beautiful and right. "Only clumsy," she mumbled. "I don't know what's wrong with me today. Excuse me. I'll clean this up."

A few moments later, Wynona, McKenzie and Julia came into the kitchen, their features concerned.

"All right. What's going on?" Julia asked.

Megan forced a smile. "Nothing. Why do you ask?"

"Maybe because you've been standing at the sink for five minutes trying to get that dishcloth wet," Wyn said. "It's not necessary anyway. We've already cleaned up the spill."

"Oh." She looked down at the dishcloth in her hand, her throat thick with ridiculous emotions.

"Did you burn yourself on the soup?" Wyn asked.

"No. It's just . . ." To her deep and abiding horror, she burst into tears. "I'm sorry. I'm sorry."

Through her tears, she saw the other three women exchange worried looks. "Don't apologize for crying," McKenzie said. "It's delicious soup and I would cry, too, if I spilled even one precious drop."

The ridiculousness of that response surprised a laugh out of her. "It's not the soup. It's . . ." Her voice trailed off. She didn't know how to answer. Everything was so blasted complicated.

"Let me guess. Elliot," Wynona said simply.

Megan caught her breath. "Why would you—? I don't—We're not—" She could complete none of those sentences.

"Oh, honey." Wynona gave her a sad smile filled with so much knowledge and compassion that tears spilled out again.

Julia looked confused. "I don't get it. What does Elliot have to do with anything?"

"Only that he's been in love with our Megan for years. And I suspect she returns his feelings but is afraid to admit it to anyone, especially herself."

McKenzie looked shocked. "Elliot? Mr. Roboto?"

"He's not a robot," Megan snapped. "He's dedicated and caring. He's funny and kind and compassionate. He risked his life and his job to save people who needed help and was shot in the process. He's completely wonderful." She heard her own words and realized there was no point hiding it from anyone, especially herself.

"And I'm in love with him."

Wyn laughed a little and hugged her. "I suspected as much. I've thought so for a few years now."

"A few years? That's impossible. He's only been back in town a few *weeks*. Before that, we didn't have much to do with each other."

"Okay, maybe I wasn't sure if you were in love with him, but I could always tell there was *something* between the two of you, just simmering beneath the surface. You both tried too hard to pretend otherwise when you were together."

Had it been so obvious to his family? She could feel her face heat. "I'm sure that's not true."

"Ask Katrina. We've had a bet going for years on how long it would take the two of you to get together. I'm losing, by the way. I had no idea Elliot could move at the speed of zero when it came to matters of the heart. Katrina knew otherwise."

"It doesn't . . . bother you? I mean, I was dating Wyatt when he died. Doesn't it seem strange to you, the idea of Elliot and I, uh, *together?*"

Not that they were—or ever would be—together. She had made certain of that. Her heart ached again.

Wynona hugged her. "I don't find it strange at all. It's perfect. You and Elliot mesh, somehow, in a way I never quite saw with Wyatt. He was my twin and I loved him dearly and miss him every single day, but even when you were dating him, I couldn't make the pieces fit somehow. As hard as I tried, I couldn't see the two of you together long-term. I don't have the same problem seeing you and Elliot together."

"We're not together. At all. You should know that. We . . . fought."

Wynona looked concerned. "Oh. I was hoping you might know where he is."

The implications of that took a moment to sink in. When they did, she straightened. "Where he is? What do you mean?"

"Mom's been frantic, though she's trying not to show it. He took off a few days ago. He's not answering calls or texts. We thought maybe he had gone back to work, but they called the house looking for him. Did you know he had been shot?"

"Shot?" Julia and McKenzie both exclaimed at the same time.

Megan didn't answer but her silence was apparently all the confirmation Wyn needed. "Of course you knew." She shook her head. "He told you but didn't say a word to his family. We didn't know a thing until his commanding officer or special agent in charge or whatever he was talked to Marshall and told him everything."

"Everything?"

Wyn gave her a closer look. "You know. He told you, didn't he?"

"What happened?" Julia asked. "How was he shot?"

"The guy who called, an Agent Burrows, told Marsh that Elliot had been suspended and was under review for staging an unauthorized rescue where a suspect was killed. Do you know that much?"

"Yes."

"It was a sex-trafficking ring, apparently," Wyn explained to the other two women. "Elliot caught wind of it and insisted on rescuing a dozen young girls who were about to be moved around the country."

"In the process, he jeopardized another investigation," Megan explained.

"Elliot did that?" McKenzie sounded astonished. "Our Elliot?"

Her Elliot. He had always been her Elliot.

"After a shoot-out with the suspect, Elliot was injured and the other man was killed," Wyn said. "But we found out last night, apparently one of the girls he rescued is the granddaughter of a high-ranking diplomat in a province in China. He's not in trouble. They want to give him a commendation—but they have to find him first."

"I don't know where he is. He hasn't checked out but I haven't seen his vehicle outside his cabin since we returned from Colorado earlier this week."

Wyn stared. "He went to Colorado with you? Man, that guy knows how to keep secrets. So do you, for that matter."

She did. Mostly she was good at keeping secrets from herself. She was in love with Elliot Bailey and she couldn't pretend otherwise. Not anymore. She loved him and somehow she had to find the courage and strength to trust him and herself.

Chapter Nineteen

"ARE YOU READY to open the doors?" Mary Ella asked with a warm, bracing smile.

No. She would never be ready. Megan wanted to bar the entrance to the Lange Gallery with any large piece of furniture she could drag in front of the doors and then stand in front to bar the way with her own body, just to be safe.

She didn't want to do this. What if everyone hated her work? What if they thought she was terrible? A talentless poser?

This had been a mistake from the beginning. She should have told this kindly woman thanks but no thanks when Mary Ella first expressed interest in her photography.

She drew in a panicked breath and had to fight for composure.

A large male hand came to rest on her shoulder. "Easy," her brother said, his voice calm and his eyes filled with understanding. Somehow she sensed he knew exactly what was running through her head. "You're going to be great, sis."

His words soothed her. His very presence calmed her more. Things between them had been strained for the last week, since she told him about her trip here to Hope's Crossing with Elliot and about what they had uncovered. To her vast relief, that tension hadn't kept him away from her show opening—or Bridger or Cassie, for that matter. They were all there, dressed up and smiling, which touched her beyond words.

"Thank you," she said, her voice a little tremulous. "And thank you for making the trip in the first place. It means the world to me."

"It was kind of Aidan and Jamie Caine to fly everyone here. The kids loved their first airplane ride."

Her heart swelled when she thought of all the friends and loved ones from Haven Point who had taken time away from their busy lives to support her gallery opening here in Hope's Crossing.

"I hope everyone doesn't feel like this is just a big waste of their time and effort."

"Shut up," her brother ordered. "Right now."

She blinked at his stern tone.

"I'm serious," Luke said. "It makes me sick to hear you put yourself down like this. Stop it now. I know where it comes from. So do you. Are you still giving him that much power in your life, tonight of all nights?"

She swallowed, struck by his words.

"You listen to me," Luke went on. "We shared an ass for a father, a man who had no business reproducing. But we're not him—and we're not all the things he spent our childhoods trying to drill into our heads. *Loser. Stupid. Lazy.* Those are his words and they should have died with him."

Their father had been cruel to both of them, but so much harder on Luke. Megan's mother had tried to protect her stepson but hadn't always been successful.

"You are a beautiful, brilliant, talented photographer. If you won't say it yourself, I'll say it for you. You're kind, compassionate and loving. You have created something amazing here, captured images no one else on earth but you could see. You should just throw your shoulders back, tell those negative voices in your head to shut the hell up and celebrate yourself along with the rest of us who are here to do exactly that tonight."

His words touched her to the core and tears burned her eyes. They were the very words she needed to hear.

"I'm proud of you, Megan," he went on. "Your mother and Gran would have been, too. Tonight, think of what *they* would have said if they were here to see this. Not him."

"You're right. You're so right. Thank you."

"Anytime."

Luke hugged her again and the unease that had prickled between them all week seemed to puff away. She sensed they had crossed some sort of threshold. Perhaps he would one day forgive her for not telling him about her trip with Elliot.

Perhaps he might even be grateful for what they had found.

Her heart twisted, as it did whenever she thought about the man she loved. She missed him desperately. His family still hadn't heard anything from him, according to Wyn, and they were all starting to worry.

She couldn't do anything about that right now. She could only focus on this moment and the wonder of seeing a dream come true.

"All right. It's time," Mary Ella called out, then unlocked the door.

AN HOUR LATER, Megan felt as if she were in a dream. It was surreal and completely unbelievable to see people respond so positively to her work, to art she had created through her brain and her vision, along with her camera and her post-processing computer skills.

She was doing her best not to let the accolades go to her head, but it was tough. She was taking a much needed breather and grabbing another glass of water from the open bar when Harry Lange approached her. "I told you the show would be a smash," he said in that gruff, no-nonsense voice. "My Mary Ella has a sharp eye for talent."

Megan sipped at her water, her throat parched from answering questions about her prints. "I'm so grateful for all the work she has put into the show. She's been amazing."

"She's already planning your next exhibit. You'd better get to shooting."

"I don't intend to stop anytime soon." Photography was in her blood. She couldn't stop now, even if she wanted to.

He gave her a meaningful look. "If things go the way I'd like, you'll soon have more time on your hands, which would be good for all of us."

His not-so-subtle reminder of the offer on the table to purchase the Inn at Haven Point made her catch her breath. For a week, she had been trying not to think about that and the decisions she would have to make soon.

Some of her angst must have shown on her face because Harry gave a short laugh. "I'm sorry I brought it up. Don't tell Mary Ella. I was on strict orders not to mention my offer for your inn tonight or else. And trust me, you don't want to know what *or else* might mean in this case. Forget I said anything. You don't have to worry about that now. Just enjoy your night."

He slipped away, but before she could take a breath, Charlene and Mike Bailey filled his place.

Charlene grabbed her free hand, her pleasantly plump features warm with approval. "Oh, honey. What a wonderful gift you have. I always knew I loved the photographs you shared with us, but it's different when you're only looking at one or two at a time. The opportunity to see so many of your images together at once shows just how amazing you are."

"Beautiful job," Mike Bailey said, giving her a paternal sort of smile that made those emotions flood through her again. She had always loved Elliot's quiet, kind uncle, who had finally married his brother's widow only the year before.

For the first time, she realized the striking similarities between her and Charlene. Both of them had found room in their hearts to love very different Bailey brothers.

Charlene and Mike seemed happy together. Was it possible she and Elliot could find the same joy?

"This one is my favorite, of all of them," Mike said, gesturing to a large print of Lake Haven. It was photographed from Silver Beach, an early summer morning with geese flying in to land among the steam curling off the water.

She remembered that morning vividly—the magical feeling that she was the only one awake there by the lakeshore as the sun came up above the Redemptions, with the air so fresh and sweet she could almost taste it.

"I do love that one," Charlene said. "But how do you pick a favorite? I love that one. And that one. And that one."

Megan followed her pointing finger. The first image was one she had taken over the winter, of old Hiram Ward, who had to be eighty, shoveling the driveway of Dorothy Clemmons, who was pushing ninety. His withered form was bent with concentration over the snow shovel while Dorothy stood on the porch wrapped in a colorful quilt and holding out a mug of cocoa for him.

The second image showed the toy boat parade in Haven Point, a huge part of the town's annual celebration. A trio of children stood on the lakeshore, their little boats gleaming in the sunlight in front of them and their faces tense with concentration.

A third was a shot at dusk on Halloween, with costumed children hurrying down a leaf-strewn street, bags bulging with candy and the lake painted a pale lavender in the twilight.

Warmth seeped through her as she looked at the beauty her work portrayed. It wasn't the photographs themselves; it was the life they captured.

Her life. A full, rich, satisfying life filled with dear friends she loved, with neighbors helping neighbors, with a community that managed to thrive amid hardship.

She loved her life.

All this time, she had been thinking she couldn't wait to escape Haven Point, had imagined that her dreams would be found elsewhere. She thought she would truly be happy if only she could achieve the excitement and adventure of photographing exotic places. Tribal ceremonies, undiscovered lands, wild creatures.

She was so wrong. This. *This* was her destiny.

She looked around this gallery at people talking, laughing, admiring her prints. Roughly a third of them were from her very hometown, hundreds of miles away. Friends, family, loved ones who had made the effort, traveled great distances and taken time away from their hectic lives, solely to support her.

Eppie and Hazel were there, with Eppie's husband, Ron.

Barbara Serrano had left the restaurant to make the journey.

McKenzie and Ben Kilpatrick, Devin and Cole Barrett, Aidan and Eliza, Jamie and Julia.

Even cranky Linda Fremont had come with her daughter Samantha.

She loved them all, each and every one.

In that instant, she knew she couldn't sell the inn. Haven Point was her home and the inn was her legacy.

If Harry Lange's company took over running it, she was sure they would do an excellent job, but she didn't want to sell to him. At least not right now.

There was, however, no reason she couldn't turn more responsibility over to the manager she had hired. Darin Watson was young but he was doing an excellent job. She only needed to give him more responsibility.

Why couldn't she have the best of all options?

She could explore the world through her lens but return home to the people and places she loved in Idaho.

If only she could figure out a way to have Elliot in that world, then it would truly be everything she could ever imagine.

Her gaze danced toward the door, half hoping he might come to see her show, but it remained stubbornly closed.

She had closed the metaphorical door between them. She couldn't blame him for not being willing to push it open and walk through.

ELLIOT STOOD OUTSIDE the Lange Gallery in Hope's Crossing, fingering the slip of paper in the pocket of his blazer and wondering if he should go in.

Through the windows, he could see the place was brightly lit and packed with people.

To his shock, everywhere he looked inside, he saw faces he recognized. His sisters were both there with their husbands and he thought he even saw his mother and uncle. Many of the Haven Point Helping Hands had shown up.

How wonderful for Megan, to have that community support from her friends and neighbors. She deserved all of it and more.

He touched that piece of paper again. This wasn't the appropriate time. He should have handled this privately.

He had been a coward, though. This seemed easier, coming to the one place where he knew he could find her. He wasn't eager to meet in private with her. His heart was too raw, too exposed.

Maybe she could find a few moments for him the next day, before she flew back to Haven Point. He should have called her and tried to meet tomorrow or something, while she was still in town after her big night.

He still could, he decided. That would be a far better option than facing her here.

He turned to go but a powerful compulsion guided him toward the gallery door again. He couldn't leave. As difficult as it would be to face her, he wanted to be here, to share this moment of triumph with her in whatever tiny way he could.

He would go in and say hello, maybe sign a guestbook or something, then leave, he told himself.

Before he could talk himself out of it, he pushed the doors open and entered the gallery. The place was indeed crowded. A string quartet played something soft and sophisticated in the corner while all around him, he heard the sound of murmured laughter and tinkling glasses.

He couldn't see her at first. Then suddenly there she was, surrounded by admirers. He felt a hard, sharp ache in his chest, so intense, it took everything he had not to press his fist to it.

He missed her. He missed her laughter and the

sweetness she brought to his world. He missed the taste of her and watching her while she slept and talking to her about things he'd never discussed with anyone else.

He missed everything about her.

She hadn't seen him and he thought it was probably better that way. He shouldn't have come. Better to go now, before she noticed him. He turned away but he wasn't quick enough. His mother spotted him and headed over with single-minded focus.

"Elliot Bailey! Where have you been?"

He thought of the strange journey of the preceding week and touched that paper in his pocket again. "Long story," he said, his voice gravelly.

He waited for her to bombard him with questions, as she usually would, but Charlene only wrinkled her brow as she studied him. What did she see on his features that made that look of compassion flit across her eyes?

"Never mind. You're here now. You can tell me later. For now, you should grab some champagne and enjoy the evening and these magnificent photographs from our Megan."

His chest gave that sharp ache again. He only wished she was their Megan.

His Megan.

"Don't think you're off the hook, young man. Not tonight, but at some point, I want to know where you've been and why you didn't tell us you had been shot. Your uncle and I are very angry with you."

Her lip trembled when she spoke. Despite her firm words, he knew the emotion stemmed from concern rather than anger.

He kissed her cheek, guilt weighing on him. "I'm sorry, Mom. I was trying to protect you. I didn't want you to worry. Someday, I might learn you're tough enough and don't need protecting."

"I survived giving birth and raising five children, didn't I?"

"That you did."

Another of her friends came up to talk to her then, and as Elliot shifted his attention, his gaze landed on Luke Hamilton.

The paper in his pocket suddenly seemed heavier than a dozen bricks.

Of course.

Megan wasn't the one who needed the information on that paper. Luke had far more right to it.

He looked around the packed gallery. Perhaps he *should* do this another day. But they were both here now. He wasn't sure when he would be back in Haven Point and this needed to be done in person. Besides, hadn't Luke waited long enough to find out the truth?

His heart pounded as he approached the man who had once been his best friend.

The closer he moved, the more tense Luke became. When Elliot reached him, the other man inclined his head stiffly.

"Bailey," he said in greeting, with no warmth whatsoever.

"Hey."

His mind was suddenly flooded with a hundred memories—riding their bikes around the lake, fishing at his dad's secret spot, hiking up the hills behind their house on snowshoes with their snowboards strapped to their backs so they could ride the slope back down.

He hadn't always been a stuffy stick-in-the-mud. Once he had liked shooting basketballs and playing video games and watching movies about superheroes.

He fingered the paper, then pulled it out and handed it over.

Luke took it automatically, staring at it in confusion. "What's this?"

"I found her."

Blood seeped from the other man's features and he leaned against the nearby wall.

"You . . . what?"

"Elizabeth is alive and living on the Oregon Coast. She's had plastic surgery and doesn't look the same but it's undoubtedly her. She's going by another name. Sonia Davis."

Luke stared at him as if he couldn't understand how Elliot could play such a cruel joke on him.

He should have waited for a better time, but he didn't know when that might have been. There was no good time for this kind of information.

"I don't believe you."

Flat-out denial hadn't ever occurred to him. He glanced at the crowd, then back at the other man. "Believe me or not. Your choice."

Luke narrowed his gaze. "If she's had plastic surgery and she's using another name, how could you possibly know it's her?"

"Do you know that the human ear is almost as identifiable as a fingerprint? Her facial features might appear different but her ears are the same. I managed to take a picture of her without her seeing and had an expert I know at Quantico compare it to a known photograph of Elizabeth. They match on every point. It's her."

The other man looked as if he would be sick. "Why did she—? All this time—"

He didn't have those answers. He had only discovered where she was, not why she wasn't in Haven Point with her family.

He looked at Megan's niece and nephew, currently posing in front of one of her prints that featured both of them a few years younger, playing in the snow and looking bright and happy and completely well-adjusted. That guilt he'd felt earlier returned a hundredfold.

"Luke. I'm sorry. I should have stood by you, as Megan did all this time."

She was amazing—loyal and loving and tender-hearted.

"I've been told I can be a robot, cold and unfeeling. I'm trying to do better. I don't deserve it, but I hope someday you might be able to forgive me for not trusting in my friend."

"She's alive. All this time. I thought for sure someone else had—I was so angry the police turned immediately toward me and wouldn't consider other options. I never imagined this."

Luke swallowed, gazing down at the paper like it would come alive at any moment and rip out his throat. "What am I supposed to do now?"

The question mirrored what Megan had asked him several days earlier when he had turned over his files on the case.

Elliot thought of the legwork he had done since then, interviewing dozens of people, following clue after clue, chasing dead end after dead end until he finally found the one snippet of information that led him to a beach town in Oregon and a beautiful Victorian house on the coast and the woman living there under an assumed name.

"Do whatever you think is best for you and your kids. Go after her or go on with your own life. It's your choice."

The other man still looked dumbstruck, as if Elliot had just dropped a live grenade into his lap, which was nothing less than the truth.

He reached a hand out and squeezed his friend's shoulder, knowing that one small act of compassion could do nothing to ameliorate seven years of mistrust.

"I shouldn't have done this here. I'm sorry. It's Megan's night and I didn't want to ruin it for her."

"Why did you?" Luke looked more curious than condemning.

"I saw you there and it seemed right. I figured seven years was long enough not to know."

The other man acknowledged that with a nod. "I'm glad you told me. Even tonight," he said after a moment, his gaze still fixed blindly on the piece of paper in his hand.

Elliot turned to go and in that moment his gaze met Megan's. She looked stunning in a soft silvery cocktail dress that seemed to shimmer and catch the light with every movement, but the expression in her eyes was anything but welcoming. She was frowning between him and her brother, as if Elliot were the last man on earth she wanted at her gallery opening.

His heart aching, he headed for the door. He meant what he said. He didn't want to ruin the night for her. He would leave, before he made things worse.

"WILL YOU PLEASE excuse me?"

She gave a polite smile and turned away, not at

all sure of the words just spoken by the elderly man who had been talking to her about the composition of a photograph she'd taken during the Lights on the Lake Festival the previous Christmas.

She could only hope she hadn't offended someone who might be interested in buying one of her works, but right now her brother needed her.

The moment Elliot left, Luke had sagged onto one of the padded benches set around the gallery and was staring at something in his hands.

"What's wrong? What did Elliot say to you?" she demanded.

Her brother looked at her as if he barely knew who she was. After a moment, he handed her a piece of paper with a name and address in Cannon Beach, Oregon.

"What's this?"

"Elliot found Elizabeth. She's had plastic surgery and is living under an assumed name at this address on the Oregon Coast."

"Oregon."

Troubled or not, why had her sister-in-law walked away from a husband who loved her and two amazing children? Who had she been afraid of? Megan knew it wasn't her brother but now she wondered if there were other secrets she'd never known about her sister-in-law.

Her heart ached with worry for her brother and

what he must be going through. She had always suspected Elizabeth had walked away from a life that wasn't living up to her expectations. It was one thing to suspect it, another to know with surety.

"Are you . . . okay?"

"I'm numb, to be honest. It's going to take some time to process it."

She hugged him, heart aching for the road ahead of him and his children. "What do you need from me?"

"Nothing right now. We don't need to worry about this now. Enjoy your night."

This was what Elliot had been doing for the last week, why no one had been able to contact him. This. He had been looking for Elizabeth. He was a bloodhound, a bulldog, as his family said. He had put those skills to work, relentlessly trying to find her sister-in-law.

For Luke, for Cassie, for Bridger.

For her.

Her heart gave a hard sharp ache inside her chest. She loved him beyond words.

Did she have the strength to take this chance?

She had to. She loved him too much. She couldn't let the possibility of life-changing happiness simply walk out the door.

Showing her photographs to the world had been an act of great courage, something she hadn't been certain she could find the strength to do. It would take far more courage for her to grab hold of this chance with Elliot.

This was a risk she had to take. As with any great risk, the reward would be greater, too.

"Will you excuse me?" she said to Luke.

Her brother looked first at her and then toward the door where Elliot had disappeared. His eyes flashed with the concern of an older brother watching over his sister and then his expression turned to one of resignation.

"You're going after him."

"Yes. I have to. I'm in love with him."

Luke gave a little groan. "I don't want to hear about it. He better treat you right. That's all."

"He will," she promised. Somehow she was certain of it.

She flew out of the gallery, leaving behind everything she had worked her entire life to earn. Only for a moment, she told herself. Elliot was worth that sacrifice and more.

She caught up with him four storefronts down from the gallery, in front of the bookstore and coffee shop she had seen the week before.

Did he notice the window display featuring his new book? He would be blushing in mortification if he did.

She loved that about him, that he could create gripping, intense books that earned him acclaim everywhere, yet still be embarrassed at the praise that justifiably came his way.

They could help each other in that department. She would celebrate his skill as an author while he was very good at appreciating her photography.

"Elliot. Wait," she finally called. In these high heels, she would never catch up with him.

He turned around, shock flaring in his gaze. "What are you doing out here, Meg? You need to go back inside. This is your big night."

"You came."

The emotion of earlier returned a hundredfold and she felt tears begin to trickle out, despite her efforts to hold them back.

"Your show was amazing. Everything I imagined and more. I didn't get a chance to take a look through the whole exhibit, but the pieces I did see were spectacular. Well done."

She wanted to clutch his words to her chest and hold them there. "Thank you. Thank you for making the effort to be here and for what you just did for Luke. You found her. He told me."

"I didn't solve any mystery. We still don't know what happened to her after Pendleton or what she's been doing all this time. That's a riddle Luke will have to solve, if he wants."

Would her brother go after Elizabeth? She didn't know the answer to that. Right now that didn't matter. Luke would figure it out.

"That's what you've been doing the last week, isn't it? You've been searching for her."

"Luke and his children deserve some answers. So do you."

Oh, she loved him. He could be reserved sometimes and focused on his work, but he was a good man. A tender, kind, compassionate man who would always watch out for her and do all he could to give her what she needed.

"Thank you," she whispered. "We might never know the whole story but at least Luke now knows how to open the book."

"You're welcome."

She had to tell him. She couldn't let this awkwardness remain between them. "Elliot, I—"

"Go back inside, Meg. This is your night. I shouldn't have come. All I did was distract you."

She tried to find the courage to tell him she loved him but the words wouldn't come. "Did you know the FBI is looking for you?" she asked instead.

He gave a rueful half smile. "That's the rumor."

"Do you know why? You're not being punished further for the shoot-out. In fact, you're to earn a commendation. You rescued the granddaughter of an important man."

"I heard. I was finally in contact with the higher-ups in the FBI. Apparently everything's all good now. I'm no longer the Bureau's fall guy."

"You sound bitter."

"Not bitter. Maybe a little cynical. I don't see

why the identity of any of the girls matters. I didn't know one of them was the granddaughter of some bigwig when I rescued her and the others. I didn't care. My decision would have been the same, no matter whether they were all Chinese peasants or granddaughters of Chairman Mao."

He did the right thing for the right reasons. That would always be Elliot's motivation.

She stepped forward and touched his cheek. "To me, you're a hero. You've always been a hero."

He gazed down at her, eyes suddenly blazing. How could she *ever* have been so blind as to think him stoic, unemotional?

"Megan."

That low ragged voice breathing her name seemed to sear through her. She heard everything he hadn't said, tenderness, warmth, and a vast, deep love.

Joy began to seep through her, sweet and healing and beautiful.

"Elliot. I'm sorry I pushed you away. I was wrong. I was afraid."

"Of me?"

She shook her head swiftly. "Never. I was afraid of myself. I've spent a lifetime questioning my own judgment, probably a holdover from my past. But I was wrong to ever question this."

He blinked, looking stunned and wary at the

same time but with a slow, dawning joy that seemed to send every last insecurity trickling away on the cool mountain air, replaced by the courage she found in knowing Elliot was the perfect man for her.

"I love you, Elliot Bailey," she murmured.

He stared down at her, that same fierce happiness in his eyes. Then he shifted his gaze back down the streets of Hope's Crossing to the gallery where most of her friends and family were here to celebrate with her.

"You're telling me this *now,* in the middle of your gallery opening?"

The happiness inside her bubbled out into a laugh. "Crazy timing, I know. But that doesn't change the fact that it's true. I'm in love with you. Wyn pointed out to me that I have been for a long time."

Before the words were even out, he was pulling her to him with a groan. His mouth found hers and everything inside her seemed to sigh. This was where she belonged. Right here, in his arms.

He kissed her with heat and wonder, wrapping his arms around her as if he didn't intend to ever let her go.

After a long, delicious moment, he lifted his head. "I don't even want to ask how Wyn possibly knew how you felt before I did."

"Before *I* did, too." She smiled against his mouth, unable to contain all the joy inside her.

"I love your family, Elliot. But not as much as I love you."

"I'll never get tired of hearing that." He cupped her face in his hands and kissed her with so much gentle tenderness, her throat welled up with tears.

"I love you. I have loved you forever, Megan. You make me laugh and ache and *feel*. This last week without you has been miserable. The entire time I was in Oregon, I wanted you with me to bring out the beauty around me with your camera. It's a gorgeous area, but I saw none of it because you weren't with me. You bring color and life into my world. I never knew how desperately I needed that until these last few weeks."

She had to kiss him then and it was several more moments before she finally forced herself to pull away.

"Will you come back inside? I want you with me tonight. That's the only thing that could make this night more perfect."

"You won't be able to get rid of me now," he vowed.

She didn't want to. As they walked together down the streets of Hope's Crossing, hand in hand toward the gallery where a few of her dreams had come true, Megan caught a hazy glimpse of the future.

She could see the two of them at her little cottage on Silver Beach. He would be working on his books and doing some cold-case investigative work on the side, simply because he was the sort of man who needed to find answers. She would be running the inn and taking pictures and loving every moment of her life beside the man she loved.

She couldn't tell if that tiny glimpse was a vision or wishful thinking, but she supposed it didn't really matter.

However the future worked out for her and Elliot, it would be perfect. They would face it together.

Epilogue

IF LATE SPRING was her favorite time of year in Haven Point, late summer ran a close and competitive second.

As August trickled into September, Megan stood beside the lakeshore savoring the long shadows of the evening and the warm, pine-scented air.

She wasn't ready for summer to end—especially this summer. It had been a magical one, filled with more joy than she could ever have imagined.

She and Elliot had packed hundreds of memories into the summer—visits with him in Denver, long weekends at her cottage on Silver Beach, hiking trips into the mountains around them.

And this.

Family and friends.

She filled her viewfinder with images of Mike Bailey wearing a brightly colored birthday hat, his sturdy, weathered features beaming at the children racing around the yard of his and Charlene's house along the lakeshore while a trio of dogs scampered along in joy.

The yard was packed with people, including children of various ages playing a heated game of soccer accompanied by much shrieking, barking and chaos. Right now her niece, Cassie, had control of the ball, her chin tucked as she focused on sneaking past Marshall's son Christopher, six years older. Then she went in for a goal, to the delight of everyone.

She smiled and cheered along with everyone else, thrilled to see Cassie and Bridger fitting in so well with the Baileys.

Elliot's family had made a concerted effort to include Luke and the children in their family gatherings over the summer. After a little initial reluctance, Luke had come around and brought them to more events.

"Way to go, Cass. That's it," he called now.

Megan shifted her camera to the sidelines of the makeshift soccer field, where her brother sat with Marshall, Elliot and Cade Emmett.

All were handsome men but her gaze immediately went to Elliot. He was smiling at something Cade said and everything inside her seemed to sigh, as it always did when she saw his too-serious features in a lighter moment.

Oh, she loved him. Sometimes it washed over her like a soft predawn rainstorm. Other times it was a torrent of emotion she couldn't hold back.

She lifted her camera stealthily. Somehow she never could manage to take a picture of him without his knowledge. He always seemed to know. It had become a bit of a game between them, with her trying to surreptitiously shoot him and him invariably catching her at it and giving her a half-amused, tolerant look.

This time was no different. As she tried to click the shutter silently, he raised an eyebrow, a small, secret smile playing around his mouth.

She loved that mouth, too, and the delicious things he could do with it . . .

"What are you doing over here in the corner?"

Megan flushed as Elliot's mother plopped into the chair beside her. She could only be grateful the other woman couldn't read minds.

Megan held up her camera. "Um. Capturing the moment."

Charlene looked a little guilty. "I hope you know that when I asked you to take pictures at Mike's birthday party tonight, I didn't mean for you to spend the entire evening in the corner with your camera in your hands."

"I haven't been," she assured her. "I've only been here a few moments. I can't resist, with the light so perfect right now. We don't have many more summer nights left this year, do we?"

"Isn't it glorious? They're that much more precious because they're so rare."

The fading sunlight turned the other woman's plump, rather average face into a serene work of art that Megan couldn't help trying to capture, though she didn't have the ideal lens on her camera body for a shot at this closer range.

"It really is," she said.

"I'm so glad you and Luke and the children could join us to celebrate Mike's birthday."

"Thank you for inviting us. We wouldn't miss it."

"You're part of the family, like it or not," Charlene said, eyes crinkling with her smile.

Megan did like it. She loved being part of the Bailey clan, in any capacity.

She had worried a little about how Elliot's sisters and mother would react once their relationship status became public—especially considering she had dated Wyatt first—but her concerns were unfounded. His family had embraced her, literally and figuratively—and that welcome quite clearly included Luke.

She felt extraordinarily fortunate to have been loved by two such very different men.

She and his mother sat in companionable silence for a few moments, watching the soccer match and the laughing children. After a moment, Marshall got up to demonstrate a move to his stepdaughter, Chloe, and that seemed to be the signal for all the adult men to join in, too—even Elliot, who showed some seriously impressive footwork to steal the ball away from his brother and head down the field with it.

"I suppose his shoulder is okay now for him to be out there playing soccer," Charlene said.

She could personally attest that Elliot was in

top physical form right now. Again she felt that blush steal over her features.

"He should be fine."

Elliot laughed then, a sound that never failed to ripple down her spine as if he'd pressed his mouth along each vertebra. In the fading sunlight, he looked gorgeous—lean and hard and dangerous, even as his smile seemed to catch the fading sunlight.

Charlene, always free with hugs and advice, suddenly sniffled and gave Megan a tight hug.

"Oh, I do love you so," Charlene said. "I don't know what magic you have wrought over the last few months with my son, but I can't thank you enough for it."

"I haven't done anything," she protested.

"Yes, you have. More than you know. You've given me back my son. The one who laughs at silly jokes and brings me flowers just because and can loosen his tie and join a pickup game of soccer when the mood arises."

Charlene rested her cheek against Megan's for a moment then pulled away. "He needed someone to remind him life is about more than work and duty and responsibility," Charlene said. "He's become too serious over the years. I don't think it was on purpose, mind you. He has always been driven, maybe because of the things he has seen at the FBI or the dark things he writes about in his books. These last few months, he's happier than

I've ever seen him. He's a lucky man to have you."

"We're both lucky," Megan said softly.

"Hearing you say that makes me happier than I can ever tell you."

She couldn't tell his mother yet about the question Elliot had asked her, the one she had answered in the affirmative. By this time next summer, they would be married, but they weren't ready to share their plans with the world yet.

She loved having this little secret between them, the boundless possibilities the future held.

After a few more moments, Charlene stood up reluctantly. "I suppose I'd better put the food out before the children decide they have to fish for their dinner."

"I'll help you as soon as I put my gear away."

His mother opened her mouth as if to argue but finally shrugged. "I'll let you help, simply because that's what family does."

She was just about to return her lens to its padded slot in the camera bag when she happened to catch sight of Luke out of the corner of her gaze. He was standing on the edge of the makeshift soccer field talking to Dani Capelli, the new veterinarian who had come to town a few weeks earlier and was living just a few houses away from Charlene.

The woman was pretty in a dark, intense way—though Megan couldn't help feeling a little pang of sympathy for her. She seemed a bit overwhelmed by the noise and the crowd and chaos.

Though they were too far away for Megan to hear what they were saying, she saw Luke point to something on the dog's head and watched Dani bend down to examine the spot.

Somehow Megan had the impression the new vet was more comfortable with the dog than with the humans at the party, though she couldn't have said why she had that impression. A moment later, Dani's younger daughter approached her mother with a question and the two of them walked away, leaving Luke once more alone.

Though he had made an effort to do more things with the children, he still always seemed that way. On the fringe.

Heart aching, she finished putting away her camera gear then carried her bag to him. "How are you holding up?"

He glanced down at her, and for a moment, she saw something raw and stark flash across his expression before he quickly concealed it. "Fine. It's a fun party. Good for the kids to get out and socialize, I guess, even though I have plenty of other things I should be doing."

"I saw you talking to the new veterinarian a minute ago. She seems nice. Dani, right?"

Luke frowned. "Yeah. That's right. I'm doing a little work on the house she's renting from Doc Morales. It needs a new toilet and sink."

"She's got cute kids, too. We ought to invite

them to dinner one night. You know, welcome her to town. I can cook at your place if you want."

Her casual tone obviously didn't fool her brother for a moment. His mouth tightened. "Are you matchmaking, Meggie?"

She refused to feel guilty. "Is it a crime to want my brother to be happy?"

"Don't."

The word was short, succinct, final—and left her aching with sadness for him.

"Why not? She's pretty."

"And I'm married."

To a woman who had abandoned him and their children.

"You can't spend the rest of your life like this, with more questions than answers," she finally said.

He was quiet for a long moment, his features remote. Then he sighed. "I know."

As he walked away with Wyn's dog in his arms, Megan wondered—not for the first time—why he didn't go to Oregon and confront Elizabeth once and for all.

Maybe he was afraid of the answers he might find.

"It's a birthday party. You're supposed to be having fun, not sitting here frowning."

Elliot appeared out of nowhere, his sleeves rolled up and his hair only a little messy from the soccer moves.

"I'm having fun," she insisted. "Just a little frustrated right now."

"Let me guess. Luke."

She made a rueful face. "How did you know?"

"I'm a trained investigator. It's what I do."

He pulled her into his arms and she settled there, inhaling the scent of him. He kissed her forehead. "Give the guy a break, okay? He has the information. When he's ready, he'll do something with it."

That had been Elliot's position from the beginning. He insisted Luke would know when the time was right to find the remaining puzzle pieces to the mystery of his wife's disappearance.

"You're right. I know."

If not for Elliot, Luke wouldn't have what little information he did. She knew now the complicated steps and tireless work Elliot had undertaken to find Elizabeth.

Megan still wasn't completely certain the waif-like woman in the photograph he had shown them was actually Elizabeth, though she could see certain similarities in eye color, cheek structure and forehead.

Elliot had laid out his case in great detail and with unerring logic. He was certain, and so was Luke.

Megan couldn't help it if some tiny sliver of doubt remained in her heart, despite their confidence. Somehow she still couldn't wrap her head around the idea that any woman could simply walk away from her children and spend years living in apparent isolation.

She wouldn't worry about that right now, Megan decided. Elliot was right. When Luke was ready, he would find those answers.

She refused to ruin this perfect but fleeting summer evening by brooding about something out of her control.

She wrapped her arms around him, savoring his heat and strength and wishing he didn't have to fly back to Denver first thing the next morning.

"So I had a phone call earlier."

His voice had a curious, offhand tone to it that made her lift her head. "Is it a lead on the case you're working?"

"Not exactly."

His eyes glittered in the fading light with an emotion she couldn't quite read.

"Remember I told you I had that buddy at the Boise field office who went through Quantico with me? I've been putting out some feelers about relocating. Turns out, they're looking for someone with my particular skill set."

Boise. Two hours away instead of nine! "Are you serious?"

"I never joke about the Federal Bureau of Investigation, ma'am," he said in a deadpan voice that made her laugh.

"Are you considering it?"

"That may depend on the things we talked about this morning."

Their future together, creating a family here in this community they both loved.

Despite his doubts in May after he had been shot, his future in jeopardy, Megan had realized over the summer that Elliot wasn't ready to leave his career at the FBI yet.

He was a Bailey. Protecting and serving was in his blood.

Maybe someday he would be able to walk away from a career in law enforcement and write full-time. Not yet.

That dedication to duty was one of the many reasons she loved him.

"They're looking for someone to start this fall. I was thinking I could commute from here," he said. "You don't by any chance know of any cottages for rent in the area?"

She smiled, her heart overflowing with all the possibilities.

"It so happens I do know of one. It's small but comfortable, on a beautiful beach along the lakeshore. I should warn you, the landlady is a handful. She's pretty demanding."

He grinned down at her, her tough, dangerous FBI agent, and her heart seemed to soar along with a trio of geese taking off from the lake.

"I think I'm up to the challenge."

She was sure of it, she thought as he kissed her.

Books are produced in the United States using U.S.-based materials

Books are printed using a revolutionary new process called THINKtech™ that lowers energy usage by 70% and increases overall quality

Books are durable and flexible because of Smyth-sewing

Paper is sourced using environmentally responsible foresting methods and the paper is acid-free

Center Point Large Print
600 Brooks Road / PO Box 1
Thorndike, ME 04986-0001 USA

(207) 568-3717

US & Canada:
1 800 929-9108
www.centerpointlargeprint.com